THE BLACK FLAME

'Melissa bargained with me not to cane you but I'm no longer sure my acceptance of that arrangement was such a good idea. Before I ask a favour from you, I think we need to deal with your atonement.'

She stared at him, turning her back to the mirror and forgetting all about the sensation of being watched. 'No,' she stammered hurriedly. 'I've said I'm sorry and I mean it. I'll be good now.'

He climbed out of his chair and retrieved his cane from the carpetbag. 'I couldn't agree more with either of those sentiments. You look sorry, and you will be good, and I know that's true because I'm going to make it so.'

THE BLACK FLAME

Lisette Ashton

This book is a work of fiction.
In real life, make sure you practise safe sex.

First published in 2001 by
Nexus
Thames Wharf Studios
Rainville Road
London W6 9HA

www.nexus-books.co.uk

Typeset by TW Typesetting, Plymouth, Devon

Printed and bound by
Clays Ltd, St Ives PLC

ISBN 0 352 33668 4

Prologue

Verity screamed when she saw the horned one. He towered seven foot tall, his yellow eyes gleaming in the candlelight and his erection long and thick – and there was nothing about him that wasn't truly terrifying. If she hadn't been tied to the corners of the pentagram, naked and vulnerable, Verity would have fled from the field. Because her hands and wrists were bound, spreading her open and ready for him, all she could do was stare up and continue to scream.

'Silence, probationer.' The warning came from Dinah, the mother goddess. She held a long, black candle in one hand and a taper in the other. Her voice was stern enough to make Verity's screams trail off to a sob. 'We need silence for the ceremony, so we may all concentrate on this spell.'

Verity sniffed back her tears and tried to nod agreement. She was secured inside the pentagram and her long, mousy tresses had been tied to the point above her head. Nodding made it feel as though her hair was being pulled from the roots. Resisting the urge to groan, she switched her gaze between the horned one and the mother goddess as they both glowered down at her.

Four more of the coven chanted as they danced around her spread-eagled body. There were two men and two women – third-degree priests and priestesses – and all in the same sky-clad condition. Ignoring their nudity, Verity searched each passing face for a reassuring smile or a flicker of sympathy. Those that didn't glare back at her, studied her lewdly. Brilliant stars peppered the midnight sky and stared down on her as coldly as the blind eye of the full moon.

'The time is nigh,' Dinah told them. 'Beltane is upon us and tonight the magical forces are strong enough for the task we ask of them.' She guided the taper towards the wick of the black candle and paused until the flame had caught.

'We could have waited for Samhain,' the horned one growled. He was trying to whisper but his voice was naturally deep and gravelly. His words carried easily above the guttural chants of the coven. 'Samhain is only six months away and we could have waited.'

'I know when Samhain is and I can't wait that long,' Dinah told her consort. 'My decision has been made.' Her tone was weary and bordered on impatience. Even Verity could hear she was tired of the argument. 'This is the ideal time. Beltane is perfect for this ceremony. No more arguments, my symbolic husband. Let's just begin.'

The words chilled Verity more than the damp grass beneath her flesh. The black candle was bearing a huge flame, maintaining strong life in spite of the night's spring breeze. Hardly aware she was doing it, she tested her wrists and ankles against their bindings. Although she doubted there was any possibility of breaking free and fleeing the coven, a part of her insisted that she try.

The chanting became more sonorous, ringing in her ears as the priests and priestesses continued to circle. Dinah, holding the candle with both hands, stepped closer to Verity and shrugged the cloak from her

2

shoulders. She stood naked, displaying her nudity to anyone who cared to look. Her breasts and broad hips were silvered by beams of moonlight and her full lips had widened into a smile.

Staring up at her, Verity wondered what this ceremony would entail. She was a probationer and had been since the end of April the previous year. Tonight, on the sabbat of Beltane, a year and a day after she had become involved with the coven, she was to be invested as a neophyte. It was her first proper step to initiation and because of that she tried to dismiss those fears that made her want to escape from the company of her fellow witches.

Dinah's chest heaved up and down as she stood over Verity. She stared towards the moon, whispering words of thanks for the bounteous season that had just ended, then voicing her hopes for the one that was about to begin. The candle was clutched against her chest, its wavering beam catching highlights of gold in her hair. Her naked body, in spite of its aesthetic perfection, seemed somehow frightening from Verity's perspective and she wished she didn't have to look at her. Dinah's breasts looked unnaturally swollen, tipped by nipples that were thick with excitement. Her broad hips sloped sensuously down, drawing Verity's eye to Dinah's golden pubic mound. She looked too large and too imposing but Verity's gaze was drawn to the mother goddess as powerfully as the moths were drawn to the light of her candle.

'Fear not,' Dinah whispered, smiling at Verity. 'Beltane is a celebration of the good things in life. Any suffering that you do endure will not go unrewarded.'

Her words gave none of the reassurance they were meant to offer. Verity struggled to free her wrists, knowing there was no hope for release.

3

Dinah's smile remained patient. She lowered herself to her knees and her bare thighs stroked Verity's hips. The scrub of her pubic mound tickled Verity's abdomen and she was unsettled by the implication of nearness that came with the sensation. She was painfully aware of her own nakedness, embarrassed that her breasts were exposed for the rest of the coven to see and that, between her open legs, her sex was on show to all of those gathered. But this intimacy, the feeling of Dinah's pubic hairs stroking over her stomach, was almost more than Verity could tolerate.

'You want to become a neophyte, don't you?' Dinah whispered the words into her ear. Her phrasing was almost playful, as though she was trying to coax Verity into co-operating.

Considering her helpless position, and knowing she would remain securely bound regardless of her response, Verity wondered why the mother goddess was tormenting her with such a teasing tone.

'You *do* want to become a neophyte, don't you?'

Pained by her own greedy need for that title, Verity nodded. The threat of tears stung the corners of her eyes and she blinked them away. Dinah leaned closer and Verity was unsettled to feel the weight of the woman's breast against her own. The pressure of a nipple, hard and obviously excited, rubbed over the stiffening bud on her orb. The friction was only subtle but it evoked a response that felt more magical than any of those ceremonies Verity had witnessed.

'The ceremony of Beltane won't disappoint you,' Dinah assured her.

Her warm breath sparked a ripple of gooseflesh through Verity's body. The fears she had been harbouring began to scatter and a calm overwhelmed her.

4

'There might be some discomfort,' Dinah allowed. 'But this ceremony is designed to reward any pain with threefold pleasure.'

With arousal taking precedence over her fears, Verity found the words more calming than logic told her they should have been. She smiled shyly into the mother goddess's face and was pleased to be met by her grin.

'You like the sound of that, don't you?'

Having already learned her lesson about nodding, Verity whispered a simple yes. The night's tension was mutating into anticipation and her body was thrilled by the transformation. Another shiver of arousal stole through her and she tried to dismiss the sensation, sure it was inappropriate for a probationer to harbour such feelings.

'Should I show you how the rule of three works for this ceremony?'

Before Verity could decide whether she wanted an example, Dinah was moving. She rested on her haunches, then tilted the candle sharply.

Verity watched a sliver of molten wax fall from beneath the flame. She tried to scream in protest but before she could make a sound she was daubed by the burning liquid. She held her breath, not daring to take in air for fear that it would augment her suffering. Her breast was aflame with intense heat and her nipple was a shriek of delicious agony. Every muscle in her body pulled taut against her bindings. As the pain began to ebb away, her breath resumed in ragged bursts.

'That was the pain,' Dinah whispered. 'But the pleasure is threefold.' To illustrate, she moved her mouth over Verity's breast and pursed her lips. She blew lightly, cooling the flesh before scratching the solidified wax away.

Furiously aware of every sensation, Verity writhed on the wet grass and tried to pull herself free.

Dinah drew her tongue over her lips, moving her face closer to the throbbing teat. She placed her mouth around the exposed breast and Verity was treated to the exquisite balm of the mother goddess's tongue. Her nipple was sucked and licked, inspiring pleasures that she had never encountered. In the candlelight, spread out in the pentagram beneath the leering smiles of the priests and priestesses, the perversity of what was happening no longer troubled her. The euphoric sensations shivering through her were the only things that existed and, because they were so magnificent, Verity was happy to endure them.

'Would you say that was threefold reward?' Dinah had moved her lips from the nipple and she asked the question with a throaty chuckle.

'Threefold at least,' Verity agreed. Her own voice was thick with the same arousal as she could hear in Dinah's.

'Can I show you that it's not a unique phenomenon?'

Verity frowned, trying to understand exactly what the mother goddess was asking. Her meaning became clear when Verity saw the candle being tilted over her other breast. She watched the sparkling trail of black wax trickle down to her unmolested nipple, then writhed valiantly in an attempt to stave off the searing sensations.

'The rule of three,' Dinah reminded her. The words sounded as though they were coming through a tunnel, with Verity at one end and Dinah, far away and distant, at the other. 'Threefold pleasure in return for pain.' She moved her head down to Verity's stinging nipple and blew the wax rigid before scratching it away.

The pressure of her tongue was as debilitating as it had been before. Shocked by her own response to this delicious torment, Verity still fought against her restraints, but now it was only so she could thrust her breast more firmly against Dinah's mouth.

Almost reluctantly, Dinah drew away. She held the candle near her cheek, its steady orange glow turning her features macabre. Rose-gold glimmers danced from the horns of the figure behind her. They reminded Verity that he was watching intently. Her unease heightened when Dinah began to wriggle her body lower. The scratch of pubic curls tickled slowly down her stomach and sparked infuriating sensations. For one heady instant she thought she felt the kiss of the woman's pussy lips against her bare torso. Then Dinah was moving over her pubic mound, and squatting between her legs.

'The rule of three demands that all things should happen in that number,' Dinah told her quietly.

Verity blinked, unable to grasp what this meant. Illumination flooded over her when she saw that Dinah was preparing to tilt the candle for a third time. With the combination of darkness and her bound position, it was difficult to gauge distances but Verity felt certain the wax was going to scald her pussy. She attempted to struggle, to gasp a refusal, and tried to make her protest as insistent as her bondage would allow.

Dinah ignored her and tilted the candle. Black wax flooded from beneath the flame, scorching against the sensitive lips of Verity's sex.

Her scream rang shrilly in the night, louder than the deepest chants of the coven. A volcano of heat bubbled against her sex and the sensation was so severe she wondered if consciousness would escape her before her body could learn to cope with it. Part of her wanted the release from this torture that fainting would bring but another part insisted she fight to stay alert. Memories of the threefold pleasure were still fresh enough to seem appealing. The idea of receiving three times the pleasure between her legs was enough to make her want to tolerate the pain.

Dinah placed the candle on the grass and lowered her head between Verity's legs.

Verity bit back an expectant sigh, silently anticipating the pleasure her body was about to enjoy. She had already convinced herself this wasn't a sexual encounter between her and another woman. It wasn't perversity of any description in her mind. It was simply the preparation she needed before being included in the casting of tonight's spell. Any personal pleasure she gained was merely a fortuitous by-product. After this, she would be able to wear the robes of a neophyte, and Dinah would be satisfied that the Beltane ceremony had been conducted with a worthy subject. With those reassuring thoughts ringing in her mind, she tried to relax against the carpet of grass and resigned herself to suffering whatever Dinah had planned.

The heat against her cleft remained long after the wax had solidified. Its sting became less intense and, while the burning warmth lingered there, the pain was quickly replaced by a more enjoyable sensation. This time, rather than scratch the wax away, Dinah carefully peeled it from Verity's pussy lips. She performed the chore slowly, making the agonising pleasure long and drawn out.

'Three times the pleasure,' Dinah promised her. Without another word she lowered her head.

Verity felt the pressure of a tongue sliding at her hole and was rocked by her own response. Her sex lips had never felt so aware or so in tune with the sensations they were receiving.

Dinah continued to tongue her cleft, sparking joy through Verity's heat. A release of orgasmic proportions was building and she wondered frantically if it would be permissible to climax while being tied inside a pentagram. Having heard tales of the orgiastic ceremonies that neophytes, practitioners and priests sometimes performed, she decided it wouldn't be sacrilegious and began to relax.

Dismissing her worries, Verity drew a deep breath and savoured the slippery feel of the lips at her hole. Dinah's kisses became more intimate, lapping at the flesh and occasionally burrowing inside her. Her clitoris was teased and she was shaken by the bolt of raw bliss erupting from her sex. It would take only one more touch – a final thrust of the woman's tongue against her wetness – and Verity knew she would be screaming with the pleasure of release.

Dinah moved her mouth away and reached for the candle.

Stung by a wave of disappointment, Verity stared at her with disbelief.

'It's time for the ceremony to begin,' Dinah intoned solemnly. 'Beltane is the longest festival of our calendar but it doesn't last for all time. While the festival's powers are strong, we will be asking a lot from it tonight.'

'This could wait until Samhain,' the horned one reminded her.

Dinah ignored him. She held the candle between her breasts, and stood in the centre of the pentagram with one leg on either side of Verity's body. When she spoke, she was directing her words towards the moon, making them clear enough for everyone to hear. 'Our thoughts must be focused on tonight's spell,' Dinah proclaimed. 'The coven requires a new leader, someone strong enough to take my place. The festival of Beltane will help to guide us so we may make the proper choice.'

Dinah turned to smile at her symbolic husband. She extended a hand, welcoming the horned one to join her inside the pentagram. He took two tentative steps, placing himself between Verity's legs. His erection remained hard and he stroked himself absently as he prepared for what was to come.

'The candle will show us the way,' Dinah declared loudly.

The priests and priestesses turned her words into a chant. *'The candle will show us the way . . . The candle will show us the way . . .'*

Verity mumbled the words to herself, experience within the coven giving her no qualms that this would happen. It sounded facile to say that she believed in magic but she had witnessed enough convincing evidence in the coven to know it did exist. While those outside her religion would have ridiculed her ideas, the witches with whom she worshipped accepted Verity's belief as nothing more than an awareness of truth.

Dinah was smiling fondly at the horned one. 'Are you ready to let your infidelity choose my replacement?' she asked softly.

He held her hand, his features unreadable. 'I'm not ready, and I don't want to choose a replacement for you.' His voice contained a petulance that Verity thought unbecoming for a deity. 'But I'm not the leader of this coven, therefore I don't have any say in things, do I?'

'None of us has a say in these things,' Dinah whispered. 'We are all autumn leaves in the winter winds of the spirits.'

'Then wait until autumn,' he pressed. 'Wait until Samhain and maybe I can get a transfer and . . .'

'Stop whining, Steve,' Dinah warned him. 'This is a sacred ceremony. My decision has been made and you will act accordingly.'

Her words cut through his argument. He pushed his shoulders back, straightening his goat's-head mask before glowering down at Verity.

Of course, she had known it was Steve all along, Verity told herself. He had performed the role of the horned one in all those ceremonies she had been allowed to attend during her first year of indoctrination. When he wasn't celebrating his religion with the rest of the witches, he was the gruff-voiced manager of the local sports hall, famed for an Olympic victory in the archery event. His physique suited someone in that occupation, being solid and muscular without an inch of spare fat on his frame. Dressed as the horned one, with ceremonial ermine flowing over his shoulders and the goat's-head mask concealing his face, he was the symbolic husband of the mother goddess, not the epitome of the devil that the ignorant mistook him for. He was the representation of man's hunting spirit, second-in-command of the coven beneath Dinah's matriarchal rule. And, Verity thought, he was also one of the horniest-looking guys involved with their celebration of witchcraft.

Verity stared dreamily up at him, anticipating the thrill of having his powerful body press down against hers. She didn't consider herself promiscuous and knew that this union of the flesh wasn't a sexual act, but simply another facet of the ceremony. However, the idea of having Steve was something she had occasionally dared to fantasise about and she licked her lips as she studied the solid erection he was wielding.

'*The candle will show us the way . . . The candle will show us the way . . .*'

11

The voices around her became louder. Deep baritones and mumbling sopranos filled the air with a mystical reverence. Dinah released Steve's hand and stepped back so she stood over Verity's head. Staring directly up, Verity could see the folds of skin creasing the woman's sex. With the candle still at her breast, the cleft was held in shifting shadows, but Verity felt sure she could see wet labia pouting down at her.

'The candle will show us the way,' Dinah repeated.

As one, she and Steve began to lower themselves. Verity glanced towards the horned one as he knelt between her legs, then she turned away. She didn't want to stare into the glassy, yellow eyes of the goat's-head mask while Steve was making love to her. Still feeling nervous and vulnerable, she looked for reassurance in Dinah's kindly smile.

But Verity's view of the woman's face was obscured as Dinah's thighs closed around Verity's head when she knelt. The only visible parts of her body were the glistening lips of her pussy. The labia had peeled apart and the opening of her sex stared wetly down.

Between Verity's legs, the weight of Steve's erection pressed against her cleft. The sensation promised to give release to those unsatisfied urges that had built when Dinah kissed her. Verity braced herself for his entry, anticipating the rush of pleasure that would come from his thrusting. In the same moment she realised Dinah had nudged herself lower. The lips of the woman's pussy hovered enticingly above Verity's mouth, begging to be kissed. Wondering if this was expected of her, or simply a tempting accident, Verity contemplated the sight and tried to resist the urge to use her tongue.

Steve bucked his hips forward and plunged into her.

The thrust was enough to make Verity catch her breath. His length filled her tight confines, triggering paroxysms of pleasure through the whole of her sex. Her wetness was copious, brought on from the teasing of Dinah's tongue, and his entry came in a smooth, velvety rush. Above the chanting of the priests, she could hear her sex lips slurping greedily on him. In the flat acoustics of the night, the sound was almost deafening.

'With this act of betrayal, you break the sacred vows of our marriage,' Dinah declared.

Steve made no response. His hardness continued to thrust into Verity's warmth, frightening her with the pleasure he was giving. Supporting himself on one hand, he reached forward and traced his fingertips around her breast. As his nails scratched over one stiff bud, Verity bristled with arousal. She had been close to achieving her climax before – and had almost been crushed with disappointment when Dinah stopped kissing at her pussy – but now the promise of that nearly savoured orgasm returned.

Dinah lowered her pussy lips towards Verity's face. The scent of musky excitement brushed her nose, and the shadows of Dinah's sex shrouded her face. With no hesitation at all, Verity ran her tongue against the dewy sex lips.

Dinah gasped, faltering slightly on her haunches as pleasure vied for control of the muscles in her legs. 'With this act of involvement, I forgive your transgression,' she intoned. Her voice had lost the powerful delivery it possessed before but she spoke with sufficient clarity for Verity to hear what was being said.

Steve's laboured breathing was augmented inside his mask. His fingertips teased her other nipple and he rekindled the painful pleasure that the nub had already suffered. His shaft plunged steadily in and out, but she sensed there was a gradual quickening in his pace and she was delighted it matched the advancing pulse of her own need. With more pressing matters weighing on her mind, the thought was little more than a distant observation. Determined to savour the taste of Dinah's cleft, Verity pushed her tongue boldly against the mother goddess. Her efforts were rewarded by a faraway sigh of pleasure and the squirming of the sex lips against her face. The pressure of Dinah's clitoris rested on Verity's chin and she felt the nub of flesh pulse excitedly. Surprised by her own greedy need, Verity continued to lap the intoxicating taste from Dinah's hole. The forbidden flavour, along with the intimacy of the moment, was almost enough to make her forget that she was lying naked in a midnight field.

Dinah shifted again. She lowered herself to her knees, giving Verity a brief glimpse of what was happening above her. Steve's goat's-head mask continued to glower menacingly down, but the image no longer filled her with a chilling dread. She glanced awkwardly back, needing to see if Dinah was wearing the satisfied smile that had been prevalent in her voice.

The mother goddess continued to hold the candle between her breasts. Her obvious enjoyment was clear in the grin that split her face. She glanced down at Verity and gave a reassuring wink before shifting positions again. Once more, her pussy lips hovered over Verity's mouth, and then she was writhing down on to the probationer's face.

Verity was smothered by the pressure of wet labia covering her mouth and nostrils. Valiantly, she tried fighting against the kiss, using her tongue to quicken the climactic moment that would undoubtedly allow her to breathe again.

14

'With this act of involvement, I forgive you,' Dinah intoned.

'You said that once,' Steve reminded her.

Dinah made an irritable noise and Verity wondered whether she had been responsible for the mother goddess's lapse in concentration. The idea hinted at a disrespect for the forces they were worshipping but Verity still felt warmed by the notion. She was glad to think she had given enough pleasure to distract Dinah and she worked her tongue more purposefully against the sodden cleft, determined to keep up the momentum.

'With our mutual pleasure, we cast our spell and ask for guidance.'

The chanting of the priests and priestesses became louder. '*The candle will show us the way . . . The candle will show us the way . . .*' Their tone was far more boisterous than Verity thought appropriate for a midnight celebration of any sabbat but she shunned the fear of discovery, knowing the coven had always been blessed with a divine good fortune when it came to maintaining their secrecy.

But those thoughts were as distant as all the others her mind entertained, paling in significance beneath the waves of enjoyment that now stole over her. Steve's thrusts became quicker and she could detect a change in his stiffness that told her he was on the brink of ejaculation. Every vigorous entry sparked another bolt of joy from her pussy lips and she found herself able to ignore the discomfort of her bound arms and legs.

And yet, in spite of her own euphoric response, and Steve's obvious enjoyment, it was clear that Dinah was extracting the most pleasure from their union. When she spoke, her tone was inflected with ragged arousal, and shrill groans of joy interspersed her

15

words. The pulse of her clitoris beat more firmly and the flow of her excitement grew more profound. Verity found she was no longer savouring the fragrant wetness that had been there before. Dinah's response was inspiring such a copious flood of musk that Verity had to swallow mouthfuls so her tongue could return to its chore. She happily accepted the warm rush of liquid, aware that sticky dribbles were wetting her cheeks and chin. The belief that she was responsible for the mother goddess's arousal gave Verity a satisfying thrill. She worked her tongue harder against Dinah's clitoris and squeezed her inner muscles around Steve's shaft.

He groaned. The fingers that had been teasing her nipple squeezed but it seemed as though every action performed was now governed by the rule of three. As soon as he released his fingers the burst of pain mellowed to a wave of release. Giddying sensations rippled through the orb and carried eruptions of bliss to every pore in her body. The moment of her longed-for climax grew nearer and Verity squeezed her muscles tight, hoping to return all the marvellous sensations she was receiving.

Dinah collapsed away from her, one hand still clutching the candle between her breasts as the other reached down to the lips of her sex.

Verity glanced awkwardly back, not surprised to see the mother goddess penetrating her own wetness.

Steve was riding faster. His length plunged as deep as her sex would allow before he eventually relented and drew back. Every full thrust banged the head of his erection against the neck of her womb and Verity knew she was hovering on the brink of another climax. She groaned, unable to mute the sound as the eruption built inside. Still unwilling to stare at the goat's-head mask, scared that the sight would spoil her arousal, Verity strained her neck to watch Dinah.

16

Dinah sat in the point of the pentagram where Verity's hair was secured. With an expression of grim determination she was wanking furiously. The candle remained clutched between her breasts, its flame lapping dangerously close to her bare flesh. Dinah seemed unmindful of the danger she was courting, more intent on squirming her knuckles deeper between her pussy lips. Her eyes were squeezed shut as the orgasm finally took command of her body.

Verity watched a spray of musk spatter from Dinah's sex and the sight was enough to trigger her own orgasm. She tugged her arms against her bindings, wanting to embrace Steve and thank him as her body endured the full throes of joy. Her inner muscles trembled with the quickening of her release and she felt the first pulse of his ejaculation.

Dinah's groan became a wail. Her orgasm seemed to grow as the pleasure took its hold.

Still savouring the fading remnants of her own climax, Verity blinked at her mentor through a misty haze. Steve continued to pulse inside her, his wet explosion giving a completeness to her satisfaction. His flailing shaft rode in and out but the intensity of her response was now ebbing away.

'Yes! Yes! Yes!' Dinah shrieked the words into the night, following them with guttural incantations that Verity assumed were memorised lines from *The Book of Shadows*. The mother goddess had slipped three fingers inside herself. Her elation was visible in the strained muscles on her neck and the purple hue of her cheeks. It was a thrilling sight and Verity was disappointed that her gaze refused to focus on this. Instead, having noticed some peculiarity about the candlelight, Verity found herself concentrating on the flame.

For one moment – an incredulous, crazy moment – Verity thought she saw a change in the candle's

17

light. Rather than a pale, orange glow, the colour grew more intense. The wick darkened, then the upturned teardrop of the flame followed suit. Giving nothing but the most eerie light Verity had ever seen, the candle began to burn with a black flame.

'The candle will show us the way . . . The candle will show us the way . . .'

The chant was now a monotonous echo, unnerving her with its sudden relevance.

Oblivious to the phenomenon she held in her hand, Dinah continued to rub hard at her sex. The black flame flickered darker than it had burned before and Verity thought she saw a wavering line of smoke trail from its tip.

Dinah shrieked as her body attained another pinnacle of release. She collapsed heavily on to the grass, her body thrashing maniacally as climax after climax tore its way through her. Remaining in the uppermost point of the pentagram, she caught Verity's bound hair but the discomfort was barely acknowledged by the probationer.

Verity's attention was focused on the candle. She watched as fingers of sooty smoke trailed between Dinah's bare breasts. The peculiar colour of the flame changed abruptly and Verity was left wondering if it had really been black. It burned yellow now and, seeming aware that it no longer had a role to perform in this spell, Dinah carelessly cast it aside. Thick layers of smoke and black wax daubed her bare chest but Verity was allowed to glimpse these stains only for an instant. As the orgasm treated Dinah to a final barrage of pleasure, she clawed at her breasts. A smile of grateful release twisted her features and she cried happily into the night.

'It's worked,' Steve gasped.

Verity felt his flaccid length fall from her pussy, aware it was followed by a dribble of his copious seed. She tested a thankful smile on him but the goat's-head mask wasn't directed at her. He was staring avidly at Dinah's breasts and Verity glanced awkwardly behind herself to see what had caught his interest.

Dinah was staring down at her chest. Her palms were soot-blackened and turned into crippled fists. Her face was a mixture of surprise and elation. Between her breasts, looking as though it had been finger-painted by a clumsy, unartistic hand, lay a cross standing on top of a triangle.

'What does it mean?' Steve asked.

Verity blinked her gratitude at him, having wanted to ask the same thing herself.

When she returned his gaze, Dinah's smile possessed the reassurance of a devout believer. 'It means that our spell has worked,' she decided boldly. 'This is where we will find our new leader.'

Verity stared doubtfully at the sooty drawing, not sure how it could fit into any magical plan. She wanted to ask how it had happened, and why it had happened, but a knowledge of her inferior position in the scheme of things held her silent.

'What's it meant to be?' Steve insisted. 'I still don't get it. I don't think the spell has worked.'

'It's worked, Steve,' Dinah said impatiently. She was still studying herself but now Verity could see that the mother goddess was also frowning, as though she was struggling to interpret the message that had been given to her.

'It's the church,' Verity said suddenly. She didn't know where the knowledge had come from, or how she had dared to find the voice to break her silence. It simply seemed imperative that, once she knew, she had to tell them. 'We'll find our leader in the church,' she said, knowing that she was speaking the truth. 'She'll be there when we arrive.'

As Steve shifted himself away, Verity thought she detected a change in his attitude towards her. He had seemed intent on pleasure as they enjoyed the climax for the spell but now she could sense an aura of annoyance emanating from him, and she suspected it was directed at her.

Dinah lifted herself from her haunches, standing on unsteady legs above Verity's head. Her sex was still sodden with pussy honey but Verity barely noticed. Her mind was whirling with ideas of what might lie ahead in the night.

'We have work to do, and Beltane is already growing old,' Dinah declared. 'My replacement has been chosen and now we must find her and welcome her.'

The priests and priestesses broke their circle to release Verity's wrists and ankles.

'Congratulations, neophyte,' Dinah told her. She knelt beside Verity's head and began unfastening her secured tresses.

The only thing that Verity noticed was the woman's use of the word 'neophyte'. In her excitement she had forgotten that was the reason why she had agreed to be the focus for the ceremony. Now, the thrill of her climax and the inexplicable knowledge of their new leader's whereabouts seemed trivial and unimportant. 'Neophyte,' she repeated happily.

Dinah nodded and placed a kiss against her cheek. 'You performed well,' she whispered. 'You should be proud.'

Verity was, and once her hair had been untied she said so. 'That was an invigorating experience.'

Dinah's smile was careful. 'Let's hope you still think that when we've finished with the festival of Beltane.'

Verity frowned uncertainly. 'I thought we just *had* finished with it.'

Dinah shook her head. 'The festival of Beltane is peculiar in our calendar because it lasts for two days. We all have a lot to do before Beltane is ended, and you will be an integral part of every aspect.'

Verity considered this and then smiled slyly into the mother goddess's face. 'Will it be like we just did?'

Dinah shook her head but her smile wasn't unkind. 'It won't be "like we just did". From this point on, you'll find things just get better and better.'

One

Melissa sat on one end of the settee, her sister on the other. She glanced unhappily around the austere furniture of Dr Grady's study, wondering why she felt so uncomfortable. Admittedly, it wasn't the most welcoming environment. The cabinets and sideboards were dark and imposing and the solemn decor seemed imbued with religious sobriety. While she suspected that her reasons for being there could have been causing her unease, Melissa thought there was more to her nervousness than that. She wasn't usually one for believing in hunches or instincts but this evening she felt certain she was being watched. Each wall was decorated with a crucifix and she supposed it could have been the presence of those martyred figures that gave her the impression of being under scrutiny, but Melissa didn't think that was the case. A part of her wanted to associate the idea of being watched with the huge mirror that stared back at her from above the fireplace, but she couldn't accept that such a strong notion was caused by something so simple. She didn't even think the feeling was down to Jasmin's sideways glances, although her sister was casting enough of those to make Melissa feel as if she were under a microscope. However, when Dr Grady returned to the room, Melissa dismissed the niggling of her intuition and concentrated on the reason for being there.

'Ladies,' he began, bowing curtly at each of them. 'Thank you for coming here at this late hour. It's a pleasure to finally meet you both. I only wish the circumstances were more felicitous.'

From the corner of her eye, Melissa watched Jasmin cast her another nervous glance.

Exercising a polite smile for their host, she empathised with her sister's unease. Dr Grady was tall and he seemed as solemn and forbidding as the surroundings of his study. It occurred to her that he looked too young to be the Dr Grady that their father had sent them to see. This man seemed almost attractive in a sinister, dangerous kind of way. He was dressed in a black shirt, black trousers and black jacket, all cut with a style subtle enough to reveal that he had a muscular physique beneath. His swarthy good looks, jet-black hair and expressive brown eyes gave him the appearance of a male model, but Melissa knew this was the right Dr Grady, having reasoned there could be only one person holding such a name and credentials in her home village. The idea was confirmed when she watched him fasten the clerical dog collar around his neck.

'University life must have been very exciting,' he started. His tone was almost affable, as though he was trying to break down the formal chill that stood between them. 'Parties, drink, young men and temptation. I imagine you had quite a time while you were there.'

'It was a blast,' Jasmin told him.

Dr Grady frowned. Melissa had thought he was frowning when he came in but, as his features twisted, she realised solemnity was part of his natural disposition. The menacing scowl he now wore looked far more threatening than the one he had used before. He stood with his back to the blazing coal fire and the crackle of the yellow flames seemed to bristle like his worsening mood. 'A blast,' he repeated dourly. 'And did you think your expulsion was "a blast" as well?' He was staring straight at Jasmin and his ferocious glare looked unsettling. 'Did you think it was "a blast" when Principal Dean called you into his office and handed you your expulsion papers for handing in too little coursework?'

'I think Jasmin and I indulged in too many excesses to finish anything on time,' Melissa said, trying to supply the answer that her sister was too scared to give.

He flashed his gaze at her but his scowl softened. He considered her words, nodding sagely as though he was contemplating a mildly contentious argument. 'There are those who would agree with that,' he said. 'Your father, Major Atkinson, seemed to believe you'd indulged in too many excesses, which is why he had you sent here on your return, rather than allowing you to go straight home.'

Jasmin sniffed but Melissa didn't bother looking at her. Even though her sister sounded close to tears, and Melissa desperately wanted to comfort her, she couldn't break her gaze from Dr Grady's mesmeric stare.

'And, while we're on the subject, how many excesses did you indulge in?' Dr Grady asked quietly. 'How many parties? How many drinks? How many young men offered you temptation?'

'Too many,' Melissa replied carefully. 'But I think we'd both begun to realise that we were on a downward spiral. I'm sure that if Principal Dean hadn't expelled us we would have curbed our wayward habits anyway. The pressure of all those improper pleasures was wearing us both out.' She didn't mean a word of it, but she thought that was what he wanted to hear. She watched his features, wondering if he was going to play the role of a charitable preacher and bless them with his forgiveness. Considering his scowl, Melissa thought it unlikely, but she couldn't see any other hope.

'I'd like to believe you,' he told her. 'It would gladden my heart to think the young people of today were genuinely seeking atonement for their numerous sins. But I suspect you're lying to me.'

'No,' Melissa said quickly.

'Not at all,' Jasmin told him.

'I suspect you are saying what you think I want to hear, in order that I'll give you my blessing and let you return home.'

'That's not how it is.'

'It's really not like that.'

'But I don't believe you,' Dr Grady concluded. He spoke as though they hadn't interrupted him. 'You say you were on the verge of abandoning those carnal pleasures but I don't believe you. Look at the way the pair of you are dressed. I have it on good authority that you dressed the same way while at university. You look like harlots from Beelzebub's own brothel. Am I really supposed to believe your claims of piety when you come here dressed like that?'

Melissa glanced down at her clothes and wondered how he could say such hurtful things. Side splits on short skirts were still popular, even if they weren't the ultimate in vogue. The cropped top was tight, but that was only so it hung properly and showed off her pierced bellybutton. Admittedly, it did display the full contours of her breasts – and revealed to anyone with a passing interest that she wasn't wearing a bra – but it was nowhere near as immodest as Dr Grady was implying. She glanced at Jasmin and for the first time that day noticed that her sister was wearing a similar outfit. Good legs were a hereditary trait and common to the women in their family. The split on Jasmin's skirt was exhibiting a splendid length of upper thigh. Knowing they also bore a facial similarity, Melissa thought it would have been like looking at a mirror image of herself if Jasmin hadn't been a brunette.

She combed nervous fingers through her own blonde tresses and stared at Dr Grady indignantly. 'We don't look like harlots from anyone's brothel. This is what everyone's wearing nowadays.'

'The empire of Sodom and Gomorrah grows broader,' Dr Grady sighed wistfully. 'You *look* like harlots. You might as well both be sitting there naked.'

Jasmin started to cry.

Melissa fixed her gaze on Dr Grady's cold frown. 'We came to see you because our father instructed us,' she started. 'And, as we're both obedient daughters, it was only natural to do as he asked.'

'I'm glad to see there is some hope for salvation within you.'

'However, neither Jasmin nor I are going to put up with your rudeness for a moment longer.' She stood up and reached out a hand for her sniffling sister. 'Come on, Jas,' she said kindly. 'We don't have to take this shit off anyone.'

'You'll sit down, harlot,' Dr Grady said menacingly. 'You'll sit down until I say you can leave.'

'Stop calling me a harlot,' Melissa warned him. 'I don't like that.'

'The truth hurts?'

He was standing close, intimidating her with his nearness. She could smell a cologne on his body, something reminiscent of incense, and beneath that there was the scent of his excitement. The fragrance chilled her but she struggled to keep her fears hidden.

'I wouldn't know what a harlot looks like,' she told him defiantly. 'It seems like you're the expert.'

He raised his hand and for an instant she felt sure he was going to strike her. His cheeks had flushed to a furious crimson and he held his open palm high in the air. The image was frightening and Melissa knew she wasn't alone in her fears because she heard Jasmin gasp in shock. The moment passed and, rather than strike her, Dr Grady lowered his hand and glowered.

Melissa knew now was the time to act if she wanted to have any hope of getting out of the place. 'We're leaving,' she said simply. 'We don't have to stay here and listen to your insults. Come on, Jas.'

'Are you really leaving?' His tone was dripping with sarcasm. 'And may I ask where you think you are going?'

'If it's any of your business, we're going home.'

He nodded, a cruel smile surfacing on his thin lips. 'You think you'll be allowed back there, do you?'

Jasmin stared at him fearfully.

Melissa caught a disquieting undercurrent in his words. 'Of course we'll be allowed back into our home,' she snapped irritably. 'What a ridiculous thing to suggest.'

'Major Atkinson told me you wouldn't be allowed back without my approval. He wanted my opinion as to whether or not you were truly sorry for what you'd done. He said you wouldn't be allowed back in the family home unless I thought you were properly repentant.'

Melissa studied his face, wondering if this was true. Her father had been outraged when he heard about the expulsion and this clause didn't sound wholly unlike him. Not wanting to submit to her fears, she said, 'I don't believe you.'

Dr Grady pointed at the telephone. 'Call him and he'll confirm it for you,' he offered. 'It will save us all time in the long run.'

'We could leave anyway,' Jasmin said defiantly.

Dr Grady nodded. 'Of course you could,' he agreed affably. 'You wouldn't be allowed home and, now that you've been expelled, Principal Dean assures me your room at the university will have been relet. But I don't doubt you'll find a bed for the night in one way or another.' Casting a meaningful glance at her exposed thigh, he sniffed disdainfully and added, 'I'd be very surprised if you didn't find a bed for the night.'

Jasmin's face crumpled and she hid her eyes before Melissa could watch the tears drag black lines through her mascara.

'This is ridiculous,' Melissa hissed. She tried to glare at Dr Grady, wishing that he didn't intimidate her. 'It's not even as though you're a proper priest. You only pretend that you are.'

Dr Grady smiled the rebuke away. 'It's true that I'm only a simple lay preacher,' he started quietly. 'And perhaps I haven't enjoyed a recognised ordination, but Major Atkinson has always put great stock in my opinion.' His grin turned cold as he added, 'From your point of view, that's all that matters right now.'

If it was a battle of wills Melissa could see she was losing. She glared at Dr Grady, hating him for being in control and making her feel like a naughty child. The temptation to walk out was still strong but she knew it would be a foolish thing to do. If she and Jasmin couldn't return home they would have nowhere to go and that prospect was more frightening

28

than staying and listening to Dr Grady's sermon on their sins. If she'd had only her own predicament to think of, Melissa would have left anyway. However, because she felt a genuine need to watch out for her younger and less worldly sister, Melissa realised she had to try to find some way of getting them back into the sanctuary of the family home. Enduring an evening with Dr Grady and his insults seemed like the only way to get to that destination, and she sighed wearily when she saw she had no other recourse. 'What do we have to do?'

He smiled at her from beneath a raised eyebrow. 'Are you coming around to my way of thinking?'

'We don't have any option, do we? What do we have to do?'

He sat down, encouraging her to do the same.

Melissa placed herself back on the edge of the settee and watched him warily. While she was ready to listen to what he had to say, she still didn't trust him.

'Atonement is never easy,' Dr Grady began carefully. 'Any one of us can say we are sorry for our sins but true atonement comes from learning the meaning of that word.'

Melissa glanced at Jasmin but she found no encouragement or support there. Jasmin was wiping her eyes and blinking miserably as she stared at the floor.

'You both seem like intelligent young ladies, so I'm sure it won't take you long to learn this lesson.' He smiled cheerfully at Melissa and said, 'If you learn quickly, you might even show your gratitude by doing me a small favour.'

'What favour?'

He shook his head and waved the question away with his hand. 'All in good time. All in good time. We have to help you seek forgiveness first.' He eased himself out of his chair and walked towards the book cabinet behind the doorway. Melissa hadn't noticed it before but she now saw there was a schoolmaster's cane sitting on the top shelf. She watched Dr Grady lift it down, then test its elasticity by bending it between both hands. His smile grew broader until he snatched the cane back and sliced it whiplike through the air. As the harsh cry of the cane echoed through the room, his features transformed. Any trace of good humour that may have been there evaporated at once.

Jasmin glanced up and Melissa guessed her sister had the chance to catch a glimpse of his malevolent grin before she hid her eyes and returned to her crying.

'What the hell do you think you're going to do with that?'

'I resided at a very strict school when I was your age,' he began wistfully.

'I don't care about your school,' she said hotly. 'I asked you a question. What the hell do you think you're going to do with that?'

'I didn't particularly care for the discipline at the time,' he continued, speaking as though she hadn't broken in. 'Not only did it hurt and humiliate, I always thought it was completely unjustified. I never believed that any of my sins could have been so severe that I merited such a vicious form of castigation.'

'You're not using that on us,' Melissa told him.

'But looking back on those days, I see that they benefited me greatly.' He fixed her with a meaningful smile. 'They taught me how to feel sorry, even on those occasions when I thought there was no need for my atonement. It was a valuable lesson and I think it's one that I should share with you now.'

'Hit me with that and I'll . . .' She heard her voice trailing off, not sure what she would do by way of retaliation. Given the control that Dr Grady had over her and Jasmin, she didn't think there was anything she could do. 'You'd just better not hit me with that,' she finished weakly.

He continued to smile. 'Which frightens you the more? The prospect of being punished? Or the fear that you might genuinely regret your sins?'

'I'm not going to have you cane my hand with that thing,' Melissa told him indignantly. 'It's demeaning.'

'Did I say I was going to use it on your hand?'

She blushed, sickened by the meaning behind his sentence. 'You're not serious.'

He stepped closer, still holding the cane. His gaze was fixed on hers and in his cruel smile Melissa saw there was no hope of escaping the punishment he had planned. 'I'm perfectly serious,' he assured her. 'You're going to learn all about repentance and forgiveness and this is the only way I can think to teach you those lessons.'

'You're not smacking my arse,' she told him. 'I won't allow it.'

'You don't have a say in it,' he returned coldly. 'I'm going to teach you to be sorry for what you've done, and you'll either suffer that or I'll cast you out on the streets.'

It was a melodramatic way of phrasing things but Melissa didn't think it was an understatement. She considered glaring at him, then stopped herself, sure that such defiance would worsen his anger.

'Of course,' he began quietly, 'there is a way that you could lessen the punishment that I'm going to mete out.'

She studied him suspiciously.

He moved closer and lowered his voice so that Jasmin couldn't hear. 'I don't need to punish both of you,' he explained. 'Volunteer to take the cane yourself and I'll only punish you, not your sister.'

'That's meant to be a tempting offer, is it?'

He shook his head as though he was disappointed with her. 'I think you've succumbed to enough temptation already,' he told her. 'It's not meant to be a tempting offer. You're here to atone for your sins. Suffer this penalty for the sake of your sister and you'll be taking your first step on the pathway to forgiveness.'

Melissa was disturbed to find herself contemplating the idea. She didn't want to have her backside caned by this sinister bully but, if it meant they would be allowed home afterwards, she was prepared to tolerate the indignity. The idea of helping Jasmin avoid the same fate appealed to her because it meant she would be fulfilling those duties that came from being the elder sister. 'Cane me, and you promise you won't cane Jasmin,' she whispered.

'That's what I said.'

She considered saying no for a final time, then refused the idea. She cast a deciding glance in her sister's direction and saw that Jasmin was still snuffling into her handkerchief. 'All right,' Melissa agreed.

'I'm glad to see you have the seeds of redemption inside you.' He took a step away and said, 'Bend over, exactly where you stand, and let's see if we can thrash those demons out of you.'

Jasmin turned her face up. Melissa watched her startled expression take in the scene with one horrified glance before she opened her mouth to voice her protestations. 'You're not really letting him do that to you, are you?'

'It's cool, Jas,' Melissa told her. She placed a finger over her lips, willing her sister to stay silent and not make things worse. Exactly how things *could* be any worse was an idea she didn't want to contemplate, but she tried to exercise a reassuring grin for Jasmin's benefit. The expression stretched her lips and she felt sure it looked sickeningly false. 'It's cool, Jas,' Melissa repeated. Hoping she was speaking the truth, she added, 'I know what I'm doing.'

'I want you to watch this, harlot,' Dr Grady growled.

Without looking back, Melissa knew he was talking to Jasmin. She thought about asking him to stop using that insult, then decided there would be no benefit in stirring that same argument again.

'See how severe punishment can be for the sinners of this world,' Dr Grady told her. 'Then, perhaps, you might think twice before surrendering yourself to temptation again.'

'Does Jasmin have to watch this?' Melissa asked.

'I think that's imperative,' Dr Grady told her. She could hear the smile in his voice and briefly wondered what sort of sick mentality could glean pleasure from this style of humiliation. 'Bend over, touching your toes, and prepare to suffer for the enjoyment of your excesses.'

Every instinct in her body was telling her she was wrong for doing as he asked. Melissa knew she should have been storming past him, dragging Jasmin back to the family home and discussing the whole episode with their father. But her fear of the reception they would meet held her beneath Dr Grady's commands. She lowered herself, thrusting her backside out for him as she struggled to reach her toes without bending her knees.

'I barely have to lift your skirt to see my target,' he grumbled. 'What on earth possesses you young women to dress like such slatterns?'

33

Melissa knew it was a rhetorical question and she didn't rise to the challenge by defending herself. She felt him brush the short hem of her skirt away from her bottom and realised he would see the thong she wore. It was a favourite piece of underwear that had allowed her to cheerfully moon at the university's rugby team while retaining a small degree of modesty. Now, she realised the thong was probably the most inappropriate item she could have had on this evening.

'A harlot's knickers,' he breathed.

There was excitement in his tone and now more than before it worried her. She had heard a lot of emotions in his voice during their brief visit to his study – mainly anger, disgust and contempt – but this time she was sure that his words were carried by lust.

'It would be easy to blame society for your current problems,' he mused. 'We live in a world where garments like this are considered acceptable. Either the media or peer pressure could accept the blame for forcing you to wear them. But you and I both know that would just be using a scapegoat.'

She wished he would stop ranting and get the chastisement over and done with. The position was shameful and degrading and she doubted the physical punishment could hurt any worse than the mental torment she was already suffering.

His hand caressed her. His fingertips stroked over the orbs of her backside, inspiring a shiver. Melissa was sickened by her body's lecherous response to him.

'Wanton harlot,' he growled.

As he snatched his hand away she heard the whistle of the cane bearing down on her. Jasmin shrieked and Melissa heard her own startled cry explode from somewhere beneath that sound. Her backside was stung by an electric barb that burned across both cheeks. As soon as the ferocity of the blow began to wane, it left a dull, aching thud in its wake.

'Stop that,' Jasmin broke in. 'You can't do that to her.'

'Stay silent, harlot.'

Jasmin did as she was told.

Glancing at her, Melissa saw that her sister was sitting on the edge of the settee looking torn between the choices of obeying the instruction and trying to intervene. Melissa turned her gaze away before their eyes could meet.

'Ask for my forgiveness,' Dr Grady demanded.

Melissa spat the words between clenched teeth. 'Please forgive me.'

He raised the cane and it landed hard. She squealed as it cut against her flesh. The force of the impact was so severe it almost toppled her.

'Confess your sins and seek repentance,' Dr Grady told her.

'I don't know what my sins are,' Melissa whispered meekly. It was humiliating to hear her own voice so close to tears. 'I don't know what you want me to say.'

The cane struck again and another burning flare shot through her backside.

'Have you been a drunkard?'

It wasn't how Melissa would have phrased it, but she supposed that, if getting blasted now and again was a sin, then it was one that she had committed. 'Yes,' she cried. 'I've been a drunkard.'

Three stripes assailed her cheeks. The force of each subsequent blow increased by the tiniest measure. The first was cruel and punishing, the second harsher, and the third crippling. They landed in such quick succession she didn't have time to snatch the breath necessary to prepare herself for each of them.

'Absolution,' Dr Grady gasped tersely. 'Your sin of drunkenness is now forgiven.' He paused for a moment and Melissa could hear him struggling to catch breath. 'Now, confess your other sins,' he demanded.

She blushed, able to see what confession he wanted and unwilling to voice it. Although the threat of tears stung the corners of her eyes, she dared to glance at Jasmin. Their eyes met briefly and something intuitive passed between them. In that instant Melissa knew her sister was recalling the night they had shared one of the rugby team, pleasuring themselves on his young, muscular body.

He had been the boyfriend of an acquaintance who was away from the university, enjoying some exotic holiday with parents. Melissa had taken pity on his lonely status and invited him to share a drink with her and Jasmin. As they all grew tipsy on cheap wine the sisters had teased him with vulgar jokes about rugby players' balls. The conversation had grown more lurid and, before she realised it was happening, Melissa had been unfastening his pants while Jasmin let him suck at her breasts. From there, the evening had degenerated into an orgiastic mass of their writhing bodies.

It had been a marvellous night for exploration and discovery and the three of them had enjoyed themselves immensely. Melissa had sucked the boyfriend to climax, and watched Jasmin do the same while he tongued her hole. They had both ridden him, revelling in his climaxes and treating each explosion as an excuse to try to rekindle his interest. She supposed that it had been a revelation for all three of them, sure that her younger sister hadn't known such an ambitious lover and certain that she herself had never met such a capable man. Throughout the night he had used her mouth, her sex and her anus, and given Jasmin the same pleasurable benefit. They were still fucking when morning finally broke and had continued until exhaustion finally got the better of them.

That had happened more than a month ago, and since then the sisters had joked about the occasion, fondly remembering the orgasms he had taken them to as the three of them rolled naked together. This was the first time that the memory had filled her with a sense of shame and Melissa could feel her blush glowing crimson.

'Confess your other sins,' Dr Grady demanded.

The cane whistled and the cheeks of her arse were treated to an explosion of raw pain. Melissa bit back her cry this time and hissed, 'I've had sex.'

He paused, the sound of his rasping breath growling hungrily in the silence. 'Say that again,' he insisted. 'I want to hear you say that with shame in your voice. Say it again.'

Mortified, Melissa swallowed and struggled to repeat her confession. 'I've had sex,' she told him quietly. 'I've had sex.'

'Harlot,' he growled. 'Base, licentious harlot.'

She braced herself for another blow but this time it didn't fall. She glanced behind her shoulder and saw he was staring at Jasmin.

'Go into my kitchen and wait for me there.'

'I'm not leaving you alone,' Jasmin said defensively.

'You'll do as I say.'

'Do as he says,' Melissa encouraged. It was hard to make her tone sound normal but she struggled to manage it so Jasmin would obey Dr Grady's instruction. She didn't really want to be left alone with him but if it meant her punishment would come to a swifter conclusion then she was anxious to do whatever was necessary.

Casting a wary look between the pair of them, Jasmin seemed set to refuse. Melissa implored her with a silent plea and, not hiding her reluctance, Jasmin nodded unhappy agreement. With her shoulders slouching defeatedly, she disappeared from the study.

Dr Grady waited until they were alone before speaking again. Even then, his voice was lowered to a guttural whisper. 'You've indulged yourself in pleasures of the flesh,' he observed. 'And yet still you refuse to accept the title of harlot. They didn't teach you much in that university, did they?'

'Not everyone who has sex is a harlot,' Melissa insisted. 'I wasn't doing anything wrong.'

'You were sinning, and sinning is always wrong. You need to repent your ways and beg for forgiveness.' Without warning he sliced the cane against her three times. He delivered the blows as before, striking with rapid succession. The force left her weak at the knees and she tried to snatch breath for her helpless screams of protest.

'Are you going to beg for forgiveness?'

She paused before replying, determined that he wouldn't hear the nearness of tears in her voice. 'If that's what you want to hear, then yes. I beg for forgiveness.'

The cane slapped sharply against her, leaving a blazing line of heat across her backside.

'I want to hear you sound properly repentant,' he told her. 'Perhaps your position isn't humiliating enough to teach that lesson yet.'

She didn't understand what he meant at first, sure that her position couldn't be any more humiliating. His intentions became clearer when his leg brushed the top of her thigh. He had stepped closer and his fingertips stroked the ravaged cheeks of her backside.

His hands moved up and she realised his caress was aiming for the waistband of her thong.

'I suppose this is my own foolishness that I should blame,' he muttered. 'How can I expect you to feel properly repentant when you're still wearing a harlot's knickers?'

Blushing furiously, Melissa could think of nothing to say in her own defence. She stayed perfectly still as he eased his thumbs beneath the fabric of her panties and began to draw the garment away. His caresses reminded her of those sly students she had met who plied her with drink before cajoling her into bed. She remembered those incidents as drunken affairs, instigated by wily youths who had remained purposefully sober while she slipped into a state of tipsy compliance. None of those encounters had been truly memorable but she couldn't honestly call one of them unpleasant.

The thong was peeled slowly away from her labia.

His thumbs slid against the cheeks of her arse, then tickled at the top of her thighs as he pulled the garment further down. He continued to touch her legs as he moved the flimsy fabric to her ankles. Without looking back she knew he had to be bending to pull the thong so low and she wondered how close his face was to her cleft. His warm breath whispered against her upper thighs and she was stung by the moment's shameful intimacy.

'Beelzebub certainly has a hold over you,' Dr Grady grumbled. 'You look more ready to have sex than suffer beneath my cane.'

She drew a shocked breath, intending to tell him that wasn't true. Her chest felt tight with a band of anticipation and she decided against voicing the sentiment, not sure it would be entirely honest.

'Your womanliness gapes at me like the foulest temptress.' He was still squatting behind her, the breath from his every word causing a warm breeze to tease her pubic curls. His voice had lowered to a whisper and Melissa tried to shut out thoughts of what he might do to her now she was displayed so obviously. As though he was responding to her unspoken question, he raised a finger and stroked it against the lips of her pussy.

She was shocked by the sensation. After suffering the weight of his cane her body felt inordinately sensitive. The touch of his finger was more pleasurable than she would have thought possible. A thrill coursed through her and she cursed each bristle of enjoyment for arriving at such an inappropriate time. She dared to glance back at him but he didn't meet her gaze. His brown eyes stared intently between the cheeks of her arse and Melissa was able to watch as he drew his tongue across his lips. She could see he was savouring the sight and the thought filled her with conflicting emotions. She had discovered at university that it was always pleasant to be admired – even lecherously admired – but Dr Grady's interest seemed unsettlingly perverse. Her own libidinous response seemed even more unacceptable.

As she watched, he raised his hand back to her cleft. His finger drew lightly against the folds of her labia and, because she was so acutely aware of what was happening down there, she knew that her pussy lips had parted for him. The sensation was sickeningly pleasurable. A shiver of anticipation fluttered down her spine and she bit back the groan that her lungs needed to release.

'You respond like a harlot as well,' he observed. 'The demons are deep within you.'

His finger remained at her sex, a constant reminder of her inferior position beneath him. She could have tried to stop him – turned on him with a look of outrage and then taken Jasmin and run for home – but she knew that the plan wouldn't work. This humiliating intimacy had occurred only while they were alone and, as Dr Grady had already pointed out, their father put a lot of stock in the lay preacher's opinion. Major Atkinson had been employing him in the village's general practice for the past ten years and visits home from boarding school and university hadn't been complete without some mention of the lay preacher's brilliance. If she asked her father to take sides in accusations and denials between herself and this well-respected pillar of society, Melissa knew that he would choose against her. Things might have been different if she and Jasmin hadn't been expelled from university but, even if that had been the situation, Melissa would still have had her doubts.

'I wonder how deep inside you those demons are,' Dr Grady mused.

The weight of his finger grew firmer. The tip had been nuzzling between her labia and now she realised he was attempting to penetrate her. The experience was bitterly shameful, more so, she thought, because it was tinged with a pleasurable friction. She hadn't expected her body to be so welcoming and was surprised by the easy way he managed to glide the digit inside. She wondered if the caning had sparked her wetness, then quickly shut that thought from her mind. She tried to shut everything from her mind but, as his broad finger pushed deeper, she found her denial was impossible.

'Do you think I could touch one of your demons?' he asked. 'I imagine that most of them reside somewhere close to here. I imagine they are here to tempt the unsuspecting and force you to follow the basest of urges.'

She could barely hear his words, much less under-stand them. He could have been chanting Latin for all that Melissa could comprehend. His finger had burrowed deep inside her sex and he was trying to wriggle it deeper. Patiently, almost as though he knew it was the caress that she wanted, he stroked against the inner wall of her vagina. Sparks of raw delight erupted between her legs and she was shocked by the ecstasy he managed to inflict. Her stomach lurched uneasily and, as she drew a shuddering breath, Melissa realised he was fuelling a furious need inside her.

'But Beelzebub sends temptation to us all,' Dr Grady whispered.

He slid the finger from her and Melissa almost sobbed as she realised he was putting an end to the pleasure. His hand moved away from her cleft, leaving her feeling empty and unsatisfied.

'He even manages to tempt me with the promise of carnal bliss that you display,' Dr Grady said quietly. 'But, unlike you, I am not a weak vessel. Unlike you, I am not going to succumb to temptation.'

She heard the whistle of the cane in the micro-second before it hit her. The explosion of pain was ferocious but it did nothing to curb the appetite he had awakened. Her pussy lips were brushed by the pressure of the cane's descent and her body became charged by an overwhelming need to climax. As the second blow landed she realised the blistering pain was threatening to transport her beyond the realms of satisfaction.

'You're a shameless harlot, and I'm not going to be able to teach you anything, am I?' he spat angrily.

He hurled the cane down for a final time and Melissa was smacked by the pleasure of release. The eruption of her climax pulsed through her, sending tremors of joy to every nerve ending. She released a jagged sigh, thankful the sound could be mistaken for suffering rather than delight.

'You're beyond the hope that simple chastisement can offer,' he growled. 'How fortunate for you that I have other plans that can make use of your sin.'

She remained where she was, still unable to understand what he was saying. The final eddies of her pleasure were fading and the grim reality of the surrounding room began to bleach the memories of the climax she had just achieved.

'Stand up,' he barked. 'Cover yourself and hide your temptation from me.'

She heard the words clearly enough and brushed down the skirt as she levered herself upright. Her thong was pooled at her ankles and she wondered if she should bend to put it back on, or simply step out of the garment. The idea of going knickerless beneath the skirt was more daring than she would normally entertain, but she was frightened to ask which course he wanted her to take.

Glancing at him, Melissa noticed he was holding a hand over his groin. Like his shirt and jacket, the trousers were black, but she was able to discern the shape of his erection. The knowledge that his excitement had come during her punishment should have been disturbing but, instead, Melissa found the idea warming.

He caught the line of her gaze and his frown deepened. He raised the cane, as though he was going to use it simply to beat her, then lowered it to point at her feet. 'Throw your harlot's knickers on the fire.'

She knew he was pointing at the thong and the idea of refusing only briefly occurred to her. Her arguments about how it completed a set, and had cost a small fortune from a London boutique, wouldn't work against him. If this was one part of the price she had to pay to convince him of her repentance, then Melissa knew she had to do it. She stepped away from the thong and stooped to pick it from the floor. Throwing the garment on the fire, she watched the flames lick around the delicate fabric, then take hold and turn it black.

'You're making your first steps on the pathway to absolution,' he growled. 'You will now follow my instructions and possibly earn forgiveness before morning light.'

'What do you want me to do?'

A smile surfaced on his lips. Melissa recognised it as the same cruel leer that she had seen before. 'Behind this house is an abandoned church,' he told her. 'I've been meaning to find funds to restore it to its proper glory, but unfortunately such work is very expensive.'

She remained silent, waiting for him to make his point. She knew of the abandoned church and had done since she first started exploring the village as a little girl between terms from boarding school.

'Go in there, and spend the evening praying for forgiveness,' Dr Grady told her. 'Perhaps you might find some hope of redemption in the sanctuary of that holy place.'

She didn't move, defiantly holding his gaze. 'I'll take Jasmin with me.'

He shook his head and his smile became more malevolent. 'You'll go there on your own, and you'll wait until I come to excuse you.'

'What if someone finds me there?' she asked. 'I know the church isn't your property. I could get into worse trouble than I'm already in if I'm charged with trespassing.'

He laughed softly. 'I strongly suspect someone will find you there, but don't trouble yourself with that worry now. Whoever you see there, whatever they ask of you, you will simply tell them that is where you are meant to be. Even if your sister turns up, you won't speak to her until the morning comes. Am I making myself clear?'

He wasn't making himself clear but Melissa nodded anyway. He was telling her to sit in the church and pray and that much she could comprehend. But, for some mad reason, he seemed to think the place would be filled with people and they would all be asking her who she was and why she was there. The idea seemed more insane than anything else she had encountered this evening – and that was saying quite a lot.

'Am I making myself clear?' he repeated.

'Yes,' she replied solemnly. 'You're making yourself crystal clear.'

He nodded and she thought he was going to let her go. Instead, he continued to spell out his demands. 'You won't tell anyone that I sent you. You won't even mention my name. If someone does mention me, you'll pretend that you've never heard of me. And, should I happen to have need to arrive there, you'll treat me as though we've never met before. Do you understand?'

Melissa didn't understand, and she didn't know what she was agreeing to, but she could see there was no alternative. He had already told her that she would either do his bidding or find herself homeless and, in Melissa's mind, that didn't qualify as a choice. Sullenly, she nodded.

'Very good,' he said stiffly. He glanced at his watch and his frown deepened. 'Now go, harlot. You've already wasted too much time trying to lure me with your temptation. Go now. And hurry all the way there.'

She thought of defying him, and insisting that he let her take Jasmin. The idea of leaving her younger sister alone with Dr Grady felt like betrayal, but Melissa saw she had no choice.

He seemed to read her fears from her frown and his grin was infuriatingly placating. He glanced towards the door where Jasmin had disappeared and smiled his reassurance. 'You needn't worry about your sister. She'll be perfectly safe in my care.'

Melissa thought the words would have been more comforting if he hadn't been holding the cane as he spoke. Not dwelling on this thought, she turned her back on him and left the house for the abandoned church.

It was only when she stepped into the darkness of the night that she realised the feeling of being watched had finally stopped troubling her.

TWO

Slowly, the screen fluttered back to life. There was a
hiss of grey snow and the image rolled twice before
settling to black-and-white stability. The speakers
blared with a final angry crackle, faded to silence,
then picked up the end of a conversation.

'. . . needn't worry about your sister. She'll be
perfectly safe in my care.'

On screen, Melissa gave Dr Grady an untrusting
glance. With obvious reluctance she turned her back
on him and then walked out of the room. Dr Grady
remained motionless until she had left. He barely
flinched when the door was closed with a thunderous
slam.

Jo Valentine turned to face Sam and Todd, not
bothering to disguise her anger. 'Have you two been
taking incompetence lessons?'

Todd looked away.

Sam glanced coyly back at the monitor, adjusting
her spectacles. It showed Dr Grady with his back to
the CCTV lens. Their camera was hidden behind the
mirror above his fireplace giving a fish-eye view of the
entire room. Through the crackly speakers, all three
of them heard him call for Jasmin.

'What the hell were you two up to?' Jo demanded.
'Or should the answer to that be obvious?'

Sam continued staring at the monitor. 'I thought you weren't talking to me.'

Jo chewed her lower lip, not wanting to get into the petty argument about who wasn't talking to whom. She wished theirs was still an active BDSM relationship, rather than the subversive normality that their living arrangement had become. Jo had always found that there was a lot of fulfilment to be had from spanking Sam's bare backside and she believed that to do it now would be doubly satisfying. She backtracked quickly over what she had said and glared at Todd as she purposefully ignored her partner. 'What the hell did you think you were doing?' she repeated.

'I'm sorry,' Todd mumbled.

'Tell her it can't be helped that your end fell out,' Sam encouraged. She glanced at Todd, made eye contact, and their attempts at humility vanished. Holding each other for support, the pair giggled helplessly beneath Jo's irate gaze.

Jo snorted with impatience. She knew Sam was referring to the end of the CCTV's connector cable and she was aware the play on words had been used entirely for Todd's benefit. Sam and Todd had been flirting with each other throughout the whole of this clandestine operation and Jo felt more than a little peeved that they weren't taking the case seriously. She always tried to approach her work with the utmost professionalism and the couple's constant levity was galling. It was in her nature to try to do her best for each client and she only wished Sam and Todd would show the same conscientious effort. Rather than putting their energies into this surveillance operation the pair were cavorting like hormonally unbalanced teenagers.

After Todd had set up the CCTV equipment to record events in Dr Grady's house, Sam had asked him if he liked 'watching'. Once Sam had finished adjusting the monitor's reception controls, Todd had complimented her on the way she 'handled knobs'. Sam had asked if his equipment would be able to manage the whole night for her and the banter had gone on and on and on and on. They had gone from innuendo to innuendo, never seeming to tire of making the same repetitive comments as they assailed one another with lecherous glances and lewd winks.

But it wasn't the lack of professionalism that bothered Jo the most. To date, Todd was the first employee of the Flowers & Valentine Detective Agency that Sam hadn't slept with and, for the moment, Jo was wanting to keep it that way. Those employees whom Sam slept with had a depressingly short shelf life. They started off as the greatest find in the world, being marvellous in bed and diligent at their job. Once Sam had grown bored with them, Jo found her office became a hostile environment. Invariably, it stayed a hostile environment until she or Sam concocted a valid reason to relieve the employee of their position without running the risk of a tribunal. The entire cycle happened with such monotonous regularity that Jo considered signing on new staff with a three-week contract.

And, while a short shelf life was something of a blessing with most of the misfits that Sam employed, Jo wanted to retain Todd's services. He was something of an electronics wizard, more than competent with a computer keyboard, and wholly without scruples when it came to the surveillance work they put on his shoulders. His skills were a genuine asset to the agency and Jo wanted to learn a lot from him before he eventually left. She also had other, more personal, plans for Todd but it was those schemes that had resulted in her and Sam being locked in the week-long battle of wills that still prevented them from talking to each other.

Todd, constantly grinning and looking boyishly corruptible, shifted position in his chair. Jo saw he was sporting a bulge in the front of his combat pants. Sam seemed to have noticed this too and she slid closer to him. Admittedly, in the claustrophobic interior of the surveillance van, it would have been difficult for her to sit away from him, but Sam seemed intent on getting as near to Todd as was physically possible. The shape of her nipples jutted through the front of her T-shirt and, with forced casualness, she rubbed her leg against his thigh.

Watching them, Jo tried not to give in to the rush of arousal that wanted to sweep through her body. They were both attractive and she could have happily given herself to either of them. If she had been prepared to make an apology and a single, bold suggestion, Jo knew that the three of them could have . . .

She shook her head, not daring to complete the idea.

'It's back in now,' Todd told Jo. 'And I'm not going to let it fall out a second time.' He spoiled the delivery of his line by spluttering giggles through the last three words.

'Why don't you tell her you had difficulty finding the hole but I rammed it inside for you?' Sam suggested. She managed the sentence with enough naïveté to be convincing, but her grin grew broad and mischievous.

In an attempt to quell her annoyance, Jo turned her gaze back to the monitor. She felt sure the cable had become disconnected when Sam reached across Todd's lap on the pretence of grabbing a can of Coca-Cola. Her red-haired partner had made a deliberate point of rubbing her chest over his stomach and, although Jo hadn't been watching intently, she felt sure Sam had also teased a sly hand against his crotch. Todd had stiffened, and his leg had shot out as though he was startled. After that, his foot had disappeared briefly among the jumble of wires that trailed from the backs of the receivers and electrical boxes. When he dragged his leg back the picture had disappeared from the monitor and the van had been made unbearable by the deafening hiss of static. For the last twenty minutes he and Sam had been struggling to connect the right cables to make the sound and picture return.

'You're not the first man to have problems with his equipment while working with the two of us,' Sam told him. 'Perhaps Jo's thinking that, if we're not hard on you, you won't be hard on us.'

'It should give you satisfaction for the rest of the night, now,' Todd returned.

'Forgive me for interrupting this witty repartee,' Jo growled. 'But, while the cable wasn't connected, does that mean we didn't get our pictures?'

Todd's smile vanished and he turned momentarily serious. 'The last twenty minutes of tape will have just recorded static,' he said grimly. 'We can only hope that something good happens in the next couple of hours.'

'That's what I was hoping, too,' Sam told him. The pair pressed closer together, chuckling intimately.

Jo rolled her eyes. 'You're like a bloody *Carry On* film without the subtlety and finesse,' she said icily. 'I am so pissed off with the pair of you I could spit. What do you think are our chances of catching Dr Grady doing something worth watching twice in one night?'

Sam shrugged off her good mood and frowned. 'The other girl's still there,' she said defensively. 'And we don't even know that he did something worth watching with that first one.'

Jo shook her head. 'He'd reached for the cane when the CCTV blinked off. When it came back on you could tell from the way she was walking that something had happened to her.' She thought of saying it was the same way that Sam shuffled after receiving a good caning, then remembered she shouldn't even be talking to Sam. They hadn't spoken properly since the argument and Jo was determined that she wasn't going to be the weak one who gave in this time.

She also suspected the pair would use anything she said to elaborate on their flirting. The air was already charged with sexual tension and Jo was loath to fuel the atmosphere by revealing intimate aspects of the relationship that she enjoyed with Sam. That sort of comment would only force the dialogue on to another lurid course and distract them from the goal of making a quick success with this assignment.

'I'm going to follow her,' Jo decided.

'Are you sure that's wise?' Todd asked.

'You're not going to remind Jo that she'll be leaving you and me alone here if she does that, are you?' Sam asked. She directed the question at Todd but Jo knew the words were meant for her. 'Who knows what we might get up to if we're left unsupervised?' Sam pressed. She traced a fingernail down the chest of Todd's T-shirt, then drew the hand away as she graced him with a teasing smile. 'Who knows what we might get up to if we're left alone?'

'I'm going to follow her,' Jo repeated. She nodded at the monitor and asked, 'Can I trust you two to change the tapes in the VCR and keep an eye on events here?'

'I should be able to handle anything that pops up in your absence,' Sam said. She didn't meet Jo's gaze as she replied. Her hand had fallen into Todd's lap and she was casually rubbing back and forth. Todd was struggling to keep his features locked in an inscrutable mask but the corners of his lips twitched involuntarily upwards.

'I'm serious here,' Jo warned them both. 'I'm going to follow her and see if she can tell us what happened when the CCTV went off. I want you two to keep your eye on the monitor and keep your hands off one another.'

'Does this mean that you've stopped "not talking" to me?'

'No,' Jo snapped. 'I'm still not talking to you. I'm just reminding you to do your job and keep your clothes on. I can always find you a new chastity belt if that's what's needed to make you remember the no-fraternisation rule.'

Sam responded indignantly. 'I'm not the one who broke that rule,' she said hotly. 'I'd been abiding by that rule when I caught you and –'

Jo threw open the van door and stepped out into the night.

Her sudden exit caused Sam to stop abruptly.

Jo hadn't bothered collecting her mobile phone from inside the surveillance van but she couldn't find the courage to go back and retrieve it. She knew that if she stayed in the van for another moment they would end up going through the argument again and that was the last thing she wanted. Standing alone in the night's cool air, she listened in case Sam called an apology after her.

From behind the van door, she heard Todd ask, 'Did you really use to wear a chastity belt?'

'Jo made me wear it constantly,' Sam confided. 'But it started to chafe, just there, where you've got your finger.'

'Is that why you stopped wearing it?'

'No. It accidentally got cut to small pieces one night when I was at a party.'

'Did it chafe you bad?'

'I think it's healed so that I look quite pretty down there again,' Sam admitted. Her voice was coquettish and playful. 'Should I show you?'

Jo slammed her fist against the van door, not wanting to hear any more. She didn't know if they would follow her instructions and she was beyond caring. As long as they remembered to change the tapes in the VCR, she would be able to study the footage later. She told herself that even Sam and Todd couldn't screw up such a simple task, then tried to convince herself that she believed the thought.

It was imperative to make some swift headway with the investigation.

Their client wanted usable information on Dr Grady and he was willing to pay well if it could be delivered quickly enough. Normally Jo wouldn't have accepted such a case – not unless she had been really desperate – but on this occasion she found herself instinctively trusting the customer. He had explained his worries about Dr Grady, saying that he didn't trust the man and describing him as 'a manipulative piece of shite'. However, he had insisted they shouldn't contrive any situation, simply wanting the Flowers and Valentine Detective Agency to record and monitor Dr Grady's behaviour until some usable event occurred. This was the first night of the investigation and Jo had thought they were already on the verge of finding something that would help him. She strongly suspected that if Sam and Todd hadn't been playing silly buggers they would already have the footage their client needed.

Rather than dwell on the nuisance of a missed opportunity, she glanced around the moonlit streets, trying to make some positive action. The van was parked close to Dr Grady's house because Todd had said the reception equipment would work effectively only over a limited range. He had actually been speaking to Sam and his exact words were, 'You'll get the most benefits from my equipment if you're sitting right on top of it,' but Jo had understood what he meant.

Because the late-night streets were deserted, Jo was able to see Melissa easily enough. The blonde had started towards the abandoned church behind Dr Grady's house and Jo wondered why anyone would want to go to such a creepy place after midnight. She watched Melissa take the pathway through the gravestones and stealthily followed. The night was clear and clement and Jo was surprised to find the walk wasn't the chilling escapade that should have been evoked by a walk in a moonlit graveyard.

The blonde climbed the steps and entered the church through its front doorway.

Walking quietly behind her, Jo counted to ten, then followed.

The building was as desolate on the inside as its derelict exterior. All religious artefacts had been removed or vandalised and the little that remained made the building look like a slightly modernised ruin. Jo was annoyed to discover that Melissa was nowhere in sight and she wondered where the girl could have disappeared to inside an empty church. A quick glance along the pews told her that she wasn't hiding there, and seeing an open doorway to the vestry made Jo think there could be only one hiding place left. She was on the verge of taking that path, walking through the nave to the back of the church, when a noise at the doorway startled her. She could hear running feet, a group of people by the sound of it, and it seemed as though they were about to enter the building.

Jo realised she was standing in front of a cupboard and quickly stepped into the discretion it offered. It was as gloomy as she had expected it would be and she tried to position herself so she could still see what was happening inside the church. There was a loose floorboard inside and she almost stepped on it before sitting. Used to working in such secretive environments, Jo felt its weight yield, threatening to give her away with a protesting groan. She moved her foot from it carefully and made a mental note not to forget that it was there. The door had been cracked from the effects of age and neglect and there was enough of a gap for her to peep at the crowd of intruders who ran into the church.

When she saw them, Jo struggled not to cry out with surprise.

'Where is she? You said she'd be here. Where is she?'

Jo wondered if this was the tail end of some bizarre fancy-dress party. It was a poor explanation that she knew couldn't be true because it implied most of the guests lacked imagination. Five of them had dressed as monks, one had come as a billy goat and the other was a naked woman with soot smeared on her breasts.

'She is here. I can feel a presence, can't you?'

'The only thing I feel is cheated.'

The blonde with the sooty breasts stiffened at this. She turned to the man with the goat's-head mask and grabbed the lapels of his robe. Without a word she dragged him away from the rest of the group. 'Search the place,' she barked. Her command instantaneously dispersed the five. 'Steve and I are going to have a little chat.'

Jo listened more intently. The couple were nearing her cupboard and she held her breath, hoping they didn't discover her.

'A little chat,' Steve grunted. 'That's not long overdue, is it?'

'You're not behaving like a true believer, Steve. In fact you're making things really fucking awkward this evening.'

'Then why don't we call this off until Samhain?' he insisted. 'Would it kill you to wait that long and see how –'

'I don't have the time to wait until Samhain,' she replied tiredly. 'My transfer happens in less than a week.'

They talked as they neared Jo, their tones lowered to conspiratorial whispers. Jo guessed her location seemed like the most discreet area of the church and she supposed it was understandable that they should choose to have a private conversation in such a hiding place. She only hoped they didn't decide to use *her* hiding place to give them that little bit more discretion.

'Why are you accepting this transfer so glibly, Dinah? Why don't you just say you don't want it and make *him* go.'

'This argument is becoming repetitive. You know *he'd* never go *there*. The health centre's based in an inner-city development zone. He calls the place Beelzebub's sewer pit.'

Amending her first thought, Jo realised Steve wasn't *dressed* as a goat – that was only the mask he wore. The robe hung loosely over his naked body and as he walked she was treated to the occasional glimpse of the physique he hid beneath. It was an invigorating sight, almost as arousing as the delights of Dinah's nudity. The woman carried her naked body with an arrogant assurance that made her seem all the more exciting and powerful. Unaware she was doing it, Jo licked her lips as she studied them.

'What if I could *make* him take the transfer?'

'Don't be silly, Steve. You couldn't do that. No one can make him do anything he doesn't want. You know what he's like.'

'But what if I could? What if I could force his hand in some way? Or –'

She embraced him, a placating gesture that silenced his argument. 'I'd take any opportunity available to stay with you, Steve,' she said kindly. 'But we both know it's not going to present itself.'

'If it's because you don't want to be with me, you should just say so.'

'That wouldn't be true.'

They were standing directly in front of the cupboard. Jo could see them clearly through the gap in the door and pressed herself back, fearful they would see her. It was a foolish way to be thinking but her closeness to the couple heightened her unease.

'You know I want to be with you,' Dinah went on. 'It just seems that circumstances are working against us.'

'Prove that you want to be with me.'

'Do what?'

'Prove it. Show me that you want to be with me.'

'This is ridiculous, Steve. We haven't got the time or the –'

'We'll make time.'

'The others are –'

'The others are still looking for our new leader. We'll have plenty of time before they return.'

Jo could see that Dinah was torn between obeying her own instincts and Steve's demands. She watched the flicker of hesitation sparkle in the woman's eyes, then dwindle as her smile grew broader. Avariciously,

Dinah studied Steve as though she was seeing him for the first time. Her gaze appraised his body and she tilted her head to one side. 'Perhaps I should,' she ventured. Her hand had disappeared inside his cloak and Jo watched the woman's forearm move up and down. 'This length of yours had to make do with Verity earlier, didn't it? Perhaps you need to be reminded of how a real woman feels.'

'I didn't notice you complaining about Verity,' he grunted. His mouth hovered over hers and he lunged forward to kiss. They stood in tableau for an instant, their lips working together as Dinah continued to move her wrist up and down. Steve reached for the woman's breast and cupped her orb in one large hand. His thumb rubbed over the jutting bud of her nipple and Dinah responded with a shiver.

'Verity has talents that surprised me,' Dinah told him between kisses. 'She can tongue pussy better than any other neophyte I've ever initiated. It'll be a shame to leave this coven now that I've found someone so gifted.'

Steve didn't appear to be listening. His mouth moved away from hers and he placed his lips over the breast that he held. He suckled against the teat, teasing the stiff flesh between his teeth and using the end of his tongue to titillate. His other hand had slipped down to Dinah's waist and his fingers were aimed for her cleft.

'Perhaps we shouldn't be doing this here,' Dinah whispered.

'It's never troubled you before,' he grunted. 'And you have to admit that most of our special gatherings usually end up here.'

'That's not true.'

'When was the last time we had a special gathering and it *didn't* end up here? It happens so regularly it's almost becoming predictable.'

Dinah looked hurt and Jo could see Steve was annoyed with himself for upsetting her. 'Besides,' he continued carefully, 'it's abandoned, and, since we intend to use this place to welcome and inaugurate our new leader, perhaps we need to solemnise it with some symbolic gesture of our religion.'

Dinah laughed dryly. 'If that's just bullshit to try to get a fuck from me, it was rather good.'

'Thank you,' he grinned. 'Has it worked?'

'Yes.'

She smiled at him, her eyes shining and her need for him apparent in her lecherous gaze. She swept the robe from his shoulders, exposing an athletic figure that was completed by a massive erection.

Jo watched Dinah ease herself from the kisses he was planting against her breast. She could see what the pair were about to do and the idea of watching wasn't wholly unappealing. However, she hadn't visited the church with the intention of being a voyeur and the whereabouts of the missing Melissa still weighed heavily on her mind. The knowledge that she was wasting valuable time was annoying and Jo cursed the stupid turn of events that had led her to be trapped in this situation. A devilish part of her mind hoped the pair would put on a good show to provide some sort of compensation but she dismissed that thought, sure it was unwholesome for a woman in a cupboard to be thinking such a thing.

Dinah moved her mouth over Steve's chest. She sucked on his nipples, treating each one to a brutal kiss that had him gasping. Her hands moved down to his hips and she dragged her fingernails hard against his flesh. Lowering her mouth down his torso, she left small, reddening bite marks in her wake.

Jo's attention to these painful blemishes faded to insignificance when Dinah started to manipulate

Steve's shaft. The blonde drew her tongue against his length and smiled up from her position beneath him.

'I can taste Verity's pussy on you,' she grinned. 'She's a sweet little thing, isn't she?'

'Maybe,' he returned, beaming back down at her. 'But she's no substitute for the real thing.' He placed his hand on the back of Dinah's head and held her still as he thrust forward. His length slid into her open mouth and she closed her lips around him.

Jo struggled not to cry out loud. The pair were behaving so explicitly she was almost shocked by what she was seeing. Of course, she had watched similar encounters before but usually it wasn't from such a secretive viewpoint. Ordinarily, she was able to view scenes like this with the opportunity of participating and, if she had stayed in the van with Sam and Todd – and if she had been stupid enough to allow it to happen, Jo cautioned herself – she felt certain the evening could have produced a similar turn of events.

A memory of her earlier arousal returned and Jo tried to wish it away.

While she had been with Sam and Todd, the knowledge that something might happen between the three of them had been a reassuring promise, even if it hadn't been exactly how she wanted the evening to progress. Regardless of whether or not they got the footage they wanted, Jo knew the three of them could have ended the night with a torrid exploration of troilism. The scene being played out before her didn't look as though it would be any less gratuitous but, because she was meant to be watching discreetly, Jo knew she couldn't participate. Nevertheless, the heat between her legs began to grow more demanding and the need to touch herself preyed on her thoughts like a compulsive habit.

Dinah's chin glistened with a meld of her own saliva and Steve's pre-come. Rather than simply suck on him, she allowed his shaft to fall from her lips so she could work her tongue up and down his length. The sweat from her excitement had washed the sooty smears away and, for the first time, Jo saw Dinah's that breasts were tipped by stiff pink nipples. The woman caressed one nub, shivering with obvious exhilaration as a bolt of pleasure coursed through her. Her other hand was out of sight, although from the angle Jo guessed Dinah was touching her lower ribs. The observation didn't quite work for Jo because Dinah's responses became far more passionate and obvious.

But, regardless of what Dinah was doing with her hidden hand, Jo envied the woman her freedom to touch herself so intimately and she wondered if she dared to caress herself in a similar way. She knew it was wrong to entertain such an idea, reminding herself that she was there to work on an investigation rather than simply watch and wank. But, for all her noble reminders, once the idea had occurred, it remained unshakable.

'Tell me you're not going to miss this,' Steve grunted. 'Tell me you're not going to miss the taste of my cock and I won't believe you.'

Dinah moved her mouth from his shaft. Her lower lip was glossy with their combined wetness and a shimmering string of his pre-come fell to her chin. 'You're a conceited bastard.'

'You are going to miss it, aren't you?'

'Of course I'm going to miss it. The coven and your cock are the only things I'll miss about this village.'

Jo thought the word coven wasn't entirely out of place, having already suspected that the pair were involved in some sort of witchcraft. Far from quelling her growing excitement or unnerving her, the idea heightened her need for satisfaction. She tested a hand inside her jacket and found her nipple was rigid and hyperresponsive. Even through the fabrics of her bra and blouse the touch of her own fingers left Jo shivering. She swallowed down the growl her body wanted to release and stepped closer to the door. It was only as an afterthought that she remembered the loose floorboard and she thanked the good fortune that had allowed her to step past it.

'That's not true, though, is it?' Steve murmured. 'You'll miss more about this village than my cock and the coven. You'll miss your practice and your patients. In fact, I think the only thing that you won't miss is –'

'This isn't the time to be talking about him,' Dinah broke in.

'Of course,' Steve agreed. He grinned down at her and asked, 'Have you got it wet enough for me?'

'It's wet,' Dinah told him. 'But I don't think we have time for that.'

He was still holding the back of her neck and he pulled her away from his shaft. 'We have to make the time,' he insisted. 'If we do find your replacement tonight I'll become the sworn consort of another woman and it would be sacrilegious for you and me to do anything after that.'

'You know that I want to,' Dinah whispered.

Jo pressed closer, sure she would miss something if she wasn't as near to the action as was physically possible. Barely aware she was doing it, she stole a hand to the waistband of her jeans and began to silently tease the zip down.

Steve pulled Dinah from the floor and held her in a tight embrace.

It was obvious that Dinah shared his need for more satisfaction. After allowing him to hold her for a moment, she pulled herself out of his arms and

63

reached for his shaft. She rubbed his swollen end between her legs and the couple shivered as they shared a simultaneous thrill. They both grinned broadly as Steve allowed her to tease him, and Dinah drew his end back and forth against her wetness.

'I could bring myself off just by doing this,' Dinah gasped.

'Don't let me stop you,' he grunted. 'Just don't expect things to finish with that if I haven't come.'

They both turned with the approach of footsteps but Jo saw that neither of them was attempting to disguise what they were doing. One of the cowled subordinates, a young girl with long, mousy hair, approached the couple. She passed a faltering glance between their faces and looked to be studiously trying to ignore their intimacy. Jo thought her attempts at discretion failed miserably. Her cheeks flushed crimson and her gaze kept dropping to the joining of flesh between Steve's cock and Dinah's pussy lips.

'What is it, Verity?' Dinah asked quietly.

'We haven't been able to find her.'

'Then go and look some more,' Steve growled.

Verity glanced at Dinah.

Jo could see she was waiting for the woman's dismissal rather than simply obeying the man in the goat's-head mask, and that single, questioning expression said who really controlled the coven.

'She should have been here when we arrived,' Verity complained. 'That was the sign I got during the ceremony.'

'I'm sure we'll find her,' Dinah said. 'Carry on searching, Verity. You've done well.'

'She could have stayed,' Steve said, once Verity was out of earshot. 'If she's as good with her tongue as you said, she could have stayed and made our last bout of togetherness truly memorable.'

'I'll leave you to make it truly memorable without anyone else's help,' Dinah told him. 'And, if you don't, I might even cast a nasty spell on you.'

The threat made him laugh. He tugged her from his embrace and turned her around so she was facing a pew. His actions were swift, revealing an urgency that his controlled voice and arrogant disposition had managed to conceal. With a brisk shove, he bent her double, exposing her backside and the wetness of her gaping cleft.

Jo managed to steal a glimpse of Dinah's sex before Steve stepped in front of the view. The woman was dripping with excitement and Jo envied the satisfaction she looked set to endure. Even when the sight was hidden by Steve standing behind her, the image lingered in her mind's eye. She could easily picture his shaft preparing to thrust inside Dinah's wetness and that mental image fired a licentious charge. Her zip was already lowered and Jo stole a hand through the opening.

'You want me to make it memorable,' Steve said. His hands had fallen to her hips and the ends of his fingers buried dimples into her flesh. 'I think I can cope with that instruction.'

He bucked forward and Dinah screamed. Her shrill cry echoed around the flat acoustics of the church, surprising a handful of nesting birds that had been lurking in the rafters. Their startled calls shrieked in sympathy with Dinah's gratified moans.

Watching the couple, Jo was afforded the perfect view of Steve's backside pounding away. He had his legs on either side of Dinah's and his vigorous rhythm dictated a tempo that was simultaneously frantic and controlled. The sight augmented her excitement and she moved her fingers beneath the waistband of her pants. The pulse between her legs was pounding and her growing need insisted she do this to herself. Delving through the forest of her pubic curls, Jo finally touched her sex lips.

Dinah was crying out, each gasp being forced from her by the thrust of Steve's entry. He made his own satisfied grunts but seemed more intent on inflicting pleasure rather than succumbing to it. When he bent forward, Jo pressed closer to the door of her hiding place and watched his hands encircle Dinah's torso. She didn't need to see to know that he was playing with her exposed breasts and the idea heightened her greedy need for orgasm.

Keeping one hand inside her jeans, Jo used the other to touch her own breast again. The delicious sensation was intoxicating. She pressed tighter against the wetness between her legs and shivered as euphoric tremors rippled through her body. Her rational mind insisted she was crazy for touching herself like this but it was easy to ignore that nagging voice as she gave herself over to the hedonistic thrill.

'Not this position,' Dinah gasped.

Steve paused. He had just slid into her and held himself rigid with his entire length filling her pussy. 'You want us to stop?'

'I don't want to come in this position,' Dinah hissed. She was half turning to face him. Her cheeks were flushed crimson and her eyes shone with a sparkle of genuine adoration. 'If this is to be our last time together, I want to be in your arms when I come. I want you to be kissing me when I feel your cock pulse inside me.'

Jo was struck by a sudden pang of shame. Although the pair had seemed unmindful of what they were doing when Verity approached, Jo now realised they were enjoying a peculiarly private liaison. Perhaps there was a streak of exhibitionism in both of them but she doubted it would have extended to the words that Dinah had just murmured. The knowledge that she was sharing their intimacy made Jo feel guilty. However, the negative emotion did little to spoil her need to see more.

Steve slid his length from Dinah and turned her around. He positioned her so her buttocks were perched on the back of the pew, then placed himself between her legs. She grabbed his hips, sliding her hands to his backside.

Jo's fingers began to work furiously inside her jeans. Her clitoris was pulsing and she trapped it between her index and middle fingers. It was an awkward position for masturbation but she was desperate to feel the orgasm and easily able to overlook a little discomfort. She contemplated trying to tease a finger inside her own wetness, then decided that wouldn't be worth the trouble. The throbbing bud between her legs was where she needed to be stimulated and she focused her thoughts on that notion. Pressing her face against the cupboard door, she squinted at the pair and watched them enjoying each other.

Dinah clutched Steve's buttocks but it was difficult to say whether she was embracing him or simply holding on. He rode into her with a metronomic rhythm, curling one hand behind her back and using the other to hold between her shoulder blades. Dinah raised a slender leg and curled it around his back, keeping the other planted on the floor for stability. Steve pounded into her again and again, his vigorous thrusts forcing her to release tiny squeals. When he lowered his head to kiss her, Jo expected these sounds to stop but, instead, they continued and grew breathless with passion. He placed his lips against her neck and chin before daring to meet her mouth.

Jo caught the ball of her clitoris firmly between her fingers and squeezed it tightly. The onset of orgasm was so close she could almost taste its heady flavour. Her other hand remained at her breast and she tweaked the tip of her nipple with a punishing force.

'I'm coming,' Dinah shrieked. 'I'm coming! I'm coming.' She raised her other leg and wrapped it around his back. Because she kept her buttocks on the back of the pew he was able to continue thrusting into her. The cries of his own approaching climax were a mere whisper beneath Dinah's elated shrieks but Jo could see he was close.

The pair leaned into a passionate embrace and their mouths melded.

Jo pressed hard against herself, knowing that if she didn't come now the moment would be robbed from her for ever. A bolt of raw satisfaction ground through her body and, while it wasn't the drawn-out climax she had craved, it was enough to temporarily satiate her appetite. She had almost convinced herself of this thought when her fingers squeezed again, inspiring a second, more fulfilling rush.

Steve's body stiffened as he exploded inside Dinah. The cheeks of his arse looked to have been carved from granite as he held himself rigid. The only movements he made were the tiniest of involuntarily ripples as his cock pulsed inside her.

Dinah didn't make the screams Jo had expected. She held herself tightly against him and seemed to extract her pleasure with a sullen inevitability. Her fingers clawed against his backside and she rocked her hips hard against him. But, throughout the brunt of her orgasm, she remained silent and pressed wordless kisses against his chin.

Knowing it would be madness to continue touching herself, Jo slid her hand from her jeans and wiped her sticky fingers dry against her hip. She saw how close she had come to nudging the door open and was amazed by her own daring. Trying not to think of the embarrassment that would have come from discovery, she took a tentative step backwards. The notion that she had been on the verge of revealing her hiding place was distinctly unsettling. Without realising she was doing it, she placed her foot on the loose floorboard and heard its deafening creak echo through the church.

'What the hell was that?'

Jo glanced through the crack and saw that the pair were staring at her hiding place. She closed her eyes, mentally kicking herself for being so clumsy.

'Was it a rat?' Steve asked.

'If that was a rat it sounded like a fucking big one.'

Jo cursed herself. She could see them studying the cupboard and with paranoia rising it looked as though they were able to stare through her spyhole and look right at her.

'It came from in there,' Steve said, pointing. 'Do you want me to take a look?'

'It could be our new leader,' Dinah ventured.

Jo stepped back, trying to think of a way of extricating herself from whatever interrogation she was about to endure. She straightened her clothes, hoping that in the darkness she could find some way of disguising what she had just been doing.

'You think our new leader would be hiding inside a cupboard in an abandoned church?' Steve's tone was condescending. 'What sort of a misfit do you think is going to lead our coven?'

He stepped closer to the booth and Jo held her breath, expecting to be discovered at any instant. She turned over a dozen lines in her mind, quickly trying to formulate an excuse that would explain her improbable presence there. Unaware that she was doing it, she squeezed her eyes tightly shut to concentrate.

'Bloody hell! There is someone here,' Steve cried.

Jo opened her eyes, expecting to find herself staring at the goat's-head mask. Instead, the door to her booth remained closed and the activity seemed to be going on outside her range of vision. She moved her face towards the gap, determined to find out exactly what was happening. This time, she was careful to avoid the loose floorboard.

'Step outside,' Dinah commanded. 'You're here for a reason, aren't you?'

As Jo watched, Melissa stepped out of an adjacent cupboard. She blinked warily around the church and Jo could see that the girl was uncomfortable beneath their questioning expressions. Those members who had been searching through the church were now gathered around her, studying her expectantly. The crowd of seven looked intimidating, even though Jo could see they were trying to make her feel welcome.

'The candle has shown us the way,' Verity whispered quietly. 'The candle has shown us the way.'

The rest of the group took up her words, converting them into a chant. *'The candle has shown us the way . . . The candle has shown us the way . . .'*

Jo wasn't sure what that meant and she didn't want to dwell on it. She took a wary step backwards, unnerved by the mystical tone of the chanting group. At the last moment, she realised her foot had found the loose floorboard again and it creaked noisily. Glancing fearfully through the crack in the door, she saw that the coven members were staring suspiciously at her own hiding place.

'Is there someone else in there with you?' Steve asked.

'No,' Melissa told him.

Jo saw him glance behind her, as though he suspected she was lying. Seeming satisfied that she had been alone in her own cupboard, he marched to the booth where Jo was hiding and tore the door open. He released a startled cry when their eyes met.

'What is it, Steve?'

He shook his head. 'You won't believe this.'

Dinah appeared by his side and the pair studied Jo with worrying frowns.

'Another one,' Dinah muttered.

'Where does that leave us?' Steve asked.

Dinah encouraged Jo to step out, her smile surprisingly welcoming. 'That leaves us with the dilemma of deciding which of these ladies is the rightful new leader of our coven.'

'And how the hell are we supposed to do that?' Steve asked.

Dinah's smile was tinged with the subtlest inflection of cruelty. 'I've got a few ideas,' she told him carefully. 'I've got a few ideas and, while a couple of them might be a little uncomfortable, they should soon sort out the pretender from the rightful one.'

The glint in her eyes unsettled Jo and there was something about the way she spoke that made her think she was in for a rough time. Remembering that Sam and Todd were oblivious to her having visited the church, and that her mobile phone was still sitting in the surveillance van, Jo realised there was no hope of being rescued. As she stepped into the view of the entire coven, that thought more than anything else frightened her.

Three

Jasmin glanced unhappily around the study. 'Where's Melissa?'

Dr Grady was bent over a table in the corner of the room. He had his back to her and seemed engrossed in a chore involving a crucifix and an orange bottle and a paint brush. Jasmin stepped closer to see what he was doing but, even when she was peering over his shoulder, she still couldn't understand what she was seeing. It looked as if he was painting the contents of the bottle over one side of the head of the cross. The work was meticulous and involved but she thought it was pointless. The addition added nothing except for a pungent fragrance of liniment.

'What are you doing?' she asked.

'This doesn't concern you yet,' he said, without looking up. 'You'll find out about this in plenty of time.' Not hurrying, Dr Grady finished his chore, then deposited the crucifix into a sturdy carpetbag.

Watching attentively, Jasmin saw that the bag already contained a leather bound bible, a silver chalice and the cane he had used to stripe Melissa's backside.

'You didn't answer my question,' Jasmin remembered. 'Where's Melissa? What have you done with my sister?'

'I haven't done anything with her,' he said, clearing away the bottle and paintbrush he had been using. 'Your sister is running a small, private errand for me,'

'At this time of night? Where?'

'It's a *private* errand,' Dr Grady repeated carefully. 'The *where* is not your business, although I'll be asking something similar of you shortly. First of all we have to sort out the atonement for your sins. If you'll make yourself comfortable perhaps we can discuss it.'

Jasmin studied him doubtfully. He was trying to smile for her but after the events she had already seen this evening she couldn't bring herself to trust him. She flicked another suspicious glance around the room, then sat sulkily on the settee. 'What's this favour you want?'

He settled himself in the adjacent chair. 'We'll come to that in good time. Before we begin, tell me what's upsetting you. You look uncomfortable, as though there's something weighing on your mind. What's wrong?'

She turned her eyes to the crackling flames in the fireplace. It looked as though the fire was burning its way through the remnants of some sort of fabric and she tried to imagine what could have been thrown there to smoulder in such a way. The blackened shape was a triangle and she wondered why it should remind her of the front panel of a pair of panties.

'I asked what's wrong with you,' Dr Grady repeated. 'Are you going to give me an answer?'

She flashed her eyes at him again, then cast her gaze around the entire room. She took in the mirror over the fireplace and the crucifixes hanging from the walls. She allowed her gaze to take in all of the antiquated decor before meeting his solemn frown. 'I just don't like being here,' she explained. 'I want to go home.'

'Sinners seldom enjoy being in this room,' he replied piously. 'And you should be able to go home soon enough. There shouldn't be any problems if you and your sister do exactly as I tell you. Do you want to hear about the favour I was going to ask?'

Jasmin considered him sceptically, then lowered her gaze. 'What did you do to her? When I wasn't in here I mean? Did you cane her really bad? Did you make her cry?'

From the corner of her eye she saw him blush. His cheeks were tinged by high spots of colour and he looked away. 'I concluded her punishment.'

'And is that why you've brought me in here now? Are you going to conclude my punishment?'

He laughed and placed his hand on her leg. Jasmin supposed the touch was meant to reassure her or offer some comfort. Instead the weight of his fingers unnerved her. If Dr Grady hadn't been so intimidating she knew she would have brushed his hand away or slid her leg out of his reach. Because the man frightened her so greatly, Jasmin allowed his fingers to stay on her upper thigh.

'I realise that you and your sister aren't the worst sinners in the world,' he began. 'You and Melissa have fallen by the wayside in some respects but there are plenty in the world who are far worse than the pair of you. This village is a hotbed of sin and vice but compared with other parts of the country – the hateful inner cities, for example – it's a veritable convent. There are dozens around here who ought to suffer with more than the spanking that Melissa received, but circumstances seldom put them beneath my cane.' His frown deepened and, while his voice turned wistful, there was a note of steel carrying his words. 'If I was allowed the chance to punish some of those pagans, they would really have something to fear. If I was allowed the chance to punish some of those heathens and . . .' He broke off without concluding the sentiment. Dismissing the distraction with a wave of his hand, he tested an uncomfortable smile and said, 'But all that is by the by. My punishment for Melissa was simply intended to guide her back towards the path of the righteous.' He glanced at Jasmin and added, 'Because she's such a strong influence on you, I'm sure that you'll follow her lead towards a better way of life without needing to suffer the cane.' As though he was trying to encourage her to see his way of thinking, Dr Grady squeezed her leg.

She wanted to shiver with revulsion and it was all Jasmin could do to hold herself still. 'Does that mean you're not going to cane me?'

He shook his head, beginning to look exasperated. He gave her thigh a final caress before snatching his fingers away. 'If that's what's making you uneasy, I'll assuage your fears now. I'm not going to cane you. Does that satisfy you?'

It should have done but Jasmin felt compelled to answer honestly. She was thankful he had moved his hand away but she still felt intimidated by him and there was also an additional worry preying on her thoughts. 'No. It doesn't entirely satisfy me. I still don't feel comfortable. May I go back to the kitchen?'

'What's wrong with our talking in here?'

She shrugged and, before she could stop it, the gesture turned into the shiver she had been trying to suppress. 'This room gives me the creeps,' she replied. 'I feel like I'm being watched.'

Dr Grady sniffed away the suggestion. 'You have an overactive imagination. That's possibly one of the things that's led you into so much trouble.'

'No. I mean it,' Jasmin insisted. Now that he was no longer touching her she felt more able to confide in him. 'Can't you feel it?' she asked. 'I don't know how to describe it properly, but it feels like someone's spying on us.'

'You're being ridiculous.'

'I'm not,' she cried indignantly. 'Melissa and I have always had a touch of the mystics. We're inordinately sensitive.' She glared at him, trying to impress him with the sincerity of her conviction. It was obvious he wasn't going to be won over by anything she said but Jasmin felt a need to show him that there were grounds for her belief. 'We're being watched,' she insisted. 'I know that we are.'

'The idea's beginning to irritate me now,' he warned her. 'May we get back to your atonement and the favour I was going to ask?'

Jasmin missed his threatening tone. She was studying every corner of the room, trying to decide where the source of her unease was emanating from. 'We were known for our sensitivity at the uni,' she told him. 'A couple of guys said we were like a pair of witches in the making.' She giggled as her mind allowed her another memory of the same two guys, then she flushed when she realised how inappropriate the thought was in the presence of the lay preacher.

'I'd thank you not to talk about witchcraft in the sanctity of this room,' Dr Grady said firmly. He spoke with enough menace for Jasmin not to miss the warning this time. 'I find that brand of paganism particularly repugnant and I refuse to have it mentioned in this house.'

Jasmin muttered an apology, surprised she had offended him with such an innocent remark.

'I'd also thank you to stop staring at the walls of my house as though they have eyes,' he finished quietly. 'It's becoming tiresome.'

'But we *are* being watched,' Jasmin told him. She felt certain she was right, sure that it could be the only explanation for the disquiet that niggled at the back of her thoughts. Determined to prove herself correct, she stood up and walked to the fireplace, where the sensation felt at its strongest. She didn't know why but for some reason she felt sure that if she moved the mirror away from the wall she would see a face, or some sort of camera lens staring back at her. Without thinking, she stood on tiptoe and reached for the sides of the mirror to see if it was loose.

'You shameless harlot,' Dr Grady growled. 'How dare you?'

Jasmin glanced down at herself, startled by his outburst. She was standing on tiptoe and bending forward so as to reach over the fire without standing in the hearth. The posture had forced the hem of her skirt to rise and display the lower moons of her backside. From his position in the chair next to the settee she realised Dr Grady was afforded a direct view of the cleft between her legs.

She had dressed quickly that morning and not bothered to put on a pair of panties. It wasn't the first day she had gone without underwear and there had been plenty of times at university when she had done it for the sheer devilment of being so brazen. Melissa often went without panties and Jasmin knew this because she had seen her cheekily moon at the rugby team before some of their big matches. Although her sister said she wore a thong to retain some degree of modesty, Jasmin felt sure she knew the real truth of what was happening. And, because she longed to be more like her sophisticated, elder sister, she occasionally dared to copy the habit.

However, this was the first time Jasmin had forgotten about her knickerless status and it was also the first time she had been so painfully embarrassed by it. Blushing apologetically, she stammered the word 'sorry'.

'Your sister wanted to save you from having to endure the wrath of my cane.'

Rather than staring at her face he was studying the cleft between her legs. His smouldering gaze was frightening to watch and Jasmin couldn't decide whether she was more unsettled by his attention or his growing anger. 'Melissa bargained with me not to cane you but I'm no longer sure my acceptance of that arrangement was such a good idea. Before I ask a favour from you, I think we need to deal with your atonement.'

She stared at him, turning her back to the mirror and forgetting all about the sensation of being watched. 'No,' she began hurriedly. 'I've said I'm sorry and I mean it. I'll be good now.'

He climbed out of his chair and retrieved his cane from the carpetbag. 'I couldn't agree more with either of those sentiments. You look sorry, and you will be good, and I know that's true because I'm going to make it so.'

Jasmin stared at the cane fearfully. The idea of enduring that humiliation was so chilling she was struck mute as she tried to find the words to appease him. 'Please not that,' she gasped. 'I'll do anything if I don't have to suffer that.'

He paused and she saw a flicker of something dark in his expression. He licked his lips and his smile was tinged with a lascivious edge. 'I can imagine you made that sort of promise quite frequently while you were at university.'

She frowned, backtracked over what she had just said, then a wave of understanding washed over her. His low opinion of her made Jasmin feel worse than ever. He was glancing at the cane in his hands and she wondered whether she should take the opportunity of his distraction to run past him and escape. She entertained the idea only briefly, knowing there would be no benefit in running away. Melissa still had to return before she could leave and there was also the matter of Dr Grady contacting their father.

'I promised your sister I wouldn't use this,' he remembered. He glanced up at her, his dark eyes glowering menacingly. 'Because I'm a man of my word, I'll try to remain true to that promise but, if none of my other plans work, you can rest assured that the cane will be a final option.' He placed the length of wood by the side of the fireplace and Jasmin frowned at him worriedly.

'What do you intend doing to me?'

'You really are obtuse,' he told her. 'God only knows the sins that Major Atkinson committed to make him deserve sluts like you and your sister for offspring.'

She glared at him, hating the way he managed to say things that made her want to cry. If anyone else had said such unkind things she would have shrugged them off but, because Dr Grady was a lay preacher, Jasmin was worried that he might be speaking the truth.

'A successful man like that,' Dr Grady mused, 'in control of a thriving medical practice here and that second GP's surgery he's just acquired. You would think that someone so accomplished and affluent would be beyond the reach of the Lord's wrath. It's remarkable the way our saviour still manages to find ways of punishing his flock, wouldn't you agree?'

Determined not to give in to the threat of tears this time, Jasmin defiantly held his gaze. 'I don't want to be punished.'

'Of course you don't want to be punished,' he agreed affably. 'No one ever *wants* to be punished. But you do *need* it.'

'You promised my sister you wouldn't punish me,' Jasmin reminded him. She was speaking quickly, painfully aware that her rising tone revealed her nervousness. 'You promised my sister you wouldn't punish me, so you can't do anything to me. You're a lay preacher and you can't break your promise.'

'I promised your sister I wouldn't *cane* you,' Dr Grady told her. 'I never said you would escape punishment.'

Jasmin swallowed and digested this in fearful silence.

'And,' he continued, 'if I feel that you still merit the cane once I've finished with you, it won't matter how many promises I've made to Melissa. I have no qualms about breaking my word where sinners are concerned, and your sister is certainly one of those. Therefore, you'll feel the slice of the cane if I deem it necessary.'

Jasmin tried to back away from him as he stepped closer. She was standing on the edge of the fireplace and the tips of the flames licked at her backside. The heat was almost unbearable but not as unbearable as the idea of simply giving in and allowing Dr Grady to chastise her. 'I don't need punishing,' she told him.

'Get down on your knees and pray for forgiveness,' he growled.

She started to shake her head, then did as he asked. It occurred to her that if making her pray was all the punishment he intended meting out then she could happily endure it. She doubted Dr Grady would really let her off so lightly but the hope flourished with her desperation.

'Turn around,' he barked. 'You were so eager to show me the secrets that lay beneath your skirt before. Turn around and show them to me again.'

It was a sickening command and Jasmin felt loath to comply, but she knew there would be a penalty for refusing. Slowly, she turned around and faced the fire. Because he had asked her to reveal herself, she placed her hands on the hem of her skirt and raised it so she was displaying her bare backside for him. It was a shameful position to be in and the humiliation of the ordeal began to weigh heavily on her mind. 'Please don't cane me,' she whispered.

'I said that I only intend to use the cane as a last resort. The first instruction I just gave was for you to pray. You may start doing that now.'

Numbly, Jasmin tried to recall the words for any prayer her mind could conjure up. It was a futile mental search because she could remember only the first three lines of the Lord's Prayer and she suspected Dr Grady would chastise her for her ignorance if he thought she had forgotten the remainder of that. All the other prayers she had ever learned were gone from her mind and the few sentences she could recall sounded suspiciously like Meatloaf lyrics. Knowing he needed to hear her making some effort, she began to mumble her way through 'All Things Bright and Beautiful'.

'You're an attractive little thing,' he told her. 'And you raise an urge in me that could spoil the meticulous plans I've laid down for this evening. Are you going to apologise for that?'

She wasn't sure she understood what he was talking about but if he wanted an apology Jasmin was more than happy to give him one. She interrupted her mumbled rendition of the hymn's chorus and whispered, 'I'm sorry.'

'It's nearly one o'clock,' he growled. 'I'd wanted you and your sister out of here by this time, so you could both wait in the abandoned church and cause chaos where it's needed most. Because you're both so obtuse you've made me waste a lot of time.'

'I'm sorry,' Jasmin whispered again.

He was walking around her, his slow pace infuriating her with its forced air of calmness. She watched him circle, appearing from her left, taking two thoughtful steps past her face, then disappearing from view at her right.

'You're also firing a need in me,' he told her. 'And, for some of the things I had planned tonight, that could prove to be my downfall.'

'I'm sorry,' she told him again.

'I'm anticipating a visit from my estranged wife before tonight is over. Like you and your sister, she has base appetites and the ability to fuel a blinding need in every man she meets. Do you think I should be meeting someone with that sort of power while I'm suffering from the arousal that you awake in me?'

He circled again and brought himself to a standstill directly in front of her. Beyond her praying hands, Jasmin could see the crotch of his black trousers. The shape of his bulge distorted the fabric. Her heart pounded madly inside her chest and she tried to shut out the thoughts that scurried through her mind.

'I asked a question,' he reminded her. 'Do you think I should be meeting someone with that sort of power while I'm suffering from the arousal that you awake in me?'

'No,' Jasmin whispered.

'You and your sister aren't the only ones who indulge in vices,' he confessed. 'You are both slaves to sins of the flesh and, while I can't condone that, I can sympathise and use it. I have my own weaknesses – while caning your sister's backside I was visited by one of them – so perhaps we're in a position to help each other.' He reached down and brushed a dark curl away from her cheek.

The gesture was almost affectionate and with anyone else – in any other circumstance – Jasmin

82

might have responded eagerly. Instead, because he was still intimidating her, she flinched from his touch.

'Can you see the opportunity for atonement standing before you?' he asked.

He stepped closer and she could see the shape of his erection was clearly defined against the front panel of his trousers. The revelation of his size and nearness was giddying and she wondered whether she should acknowledge his arousal or just pretend not to have seen it.

'Can you see that the opportunity to make up for your sins is almost within your hands?'

With unsettling clarity she understood what he meant. She knew what he was asking and also that there was no other option except to surrender and do his bidding. Slowly, she reached a tentative finger towards the zip on his trousers. As she traced his shape, her pulse began to beat more quickly. His stiffness twitched beneath her touch and she was stung by a sudden shock of arousal. He didn't slap her hand away as she had feared he would and Jasmin daringly reached for the tab on his zip. She eased it slowly down and watched his shaft burst through the opening.

He was thick and hard, the end of his circumcised dome gleaming a dusky purple. The head of his erection was only millimetres from her face and she wondered whether he was expecting the same thing as she suddenly wanted. Trying to encircle his girth with one hand, she rubbed a sweaty palm along his length and heard him sigh.

'An outside observer could view this as exploitation,' he mused thoughtfully. 'You're an impressionable young girl and I'm supposed to be a custodian of your spiritual welfare. Under those circumstances, what I expect of you could be viewed as being wrong.'

83

She glanced up at him and saw he wasn't looking at her. He was staring happily towards a far corner of the room behind her. Jasmin couldn't remember the layout of the room exactly but she thought it seemed possible that his fond smile was fixed on a crucifix. Still gliding her hand along his stiffness, she worked his length until a bead of pre-come was squeezed from its single eye. Unable to resist the impulse, Jasmin darted her tongue against it and lapped the pearl away.

'But I'm not asking you to do anything that you don't want to do, am I?'

'No,' she murmured. She said the word as she drew her tongue against him. Her lips were tracing the shape of the dark blue veins that ran along the length of his shaft.

'And this favour could be a double-edged arrangement,' he went on. He moved his hand back down to her face and began to toy with her hair as she licked him. 'If you satisfy me sufficiently, I can do more than just offer you forgiveness. I can get you reinstated at university.'

Jasmin glanced up at him, wondering whether she had heard correctly. Reinstatement was an option she hadn't considered but, now it was offered, she realised it was the one answer that would solve all her and Melissa's problems. 'Are you sure that's possible?' she asked quickly. 'Principal Dean was quite piss–' She stopped the swearword before it could be fully formed. 'Principal Dean was quite angry when he called Melissa and me into his office.'

Dr Grady guided Jasmin's mouth back to his shaft and didn't answer until her tongue was lapping at him again. 'Principal Dean and I are old friends,' he explained. 'He's done several favours for me in the past. I'm sure that if I told him you'd learned the

84

error of your ways he would find it in his heart to have a change of mind.'

There was something in the way he spoke that made Jasmin feel certain Dr Grady had already discussed her and her sister with Principal Dean. She was wondering whether he was in some way responsible for their expulsion, not sure why the idea seemed so right, only knowing that it felt like a logical explanation. She was about to raise the suspicion and ask him if that was what had happened.

He wound his fingers into her hair and pulled her face on to his length. His shaft filled her mouth, staunching the words she had been about to question him with. 'You will give me relief before my estranged wife arrives,' he explained. 'But because this is supposed to be your atonement I will impose a condition on it.'

His hand held her firmly against his shaft and Jasmin had no choice but to suck. She passed him a questioning glance from her place on the floor but with his length thrust in her mouth she wasn't sure if the wordless gesture was conveyed properly.

'You will satisfy me, but you won't be allowed any pleasure for yourself. If I think you've been gleaning satisfaction I will retrieve my cane and make sure you learn the proper way to atone for a sin. Do I make myself clear?'

She nodded. Her head bounced up and down and his erection came close to falling from her mouth. She steadied it with a gentle hand, pursing her lips around the swollen end. Once the head was properly back inside she pushed her fingers into his trousers and began to tease the pubic curls around his scrotum.

'Suck the need from me,' he insisted.

His voice was rising and she thought his tone showed the strain of a nearing climax.

'Relieve me of those base urges that could spoil my plans.'

She did as he asked. She tickled his scrotum and sucked hard on the end of his shaft. As a passing thought it occurred to her that his arousal must have been severe because his shaft pulsed inside her mouth instantaneously. A warm spray of semen jetted against the back of her throat and she swallowed quickly, still holding his length between her lips.

The taste of his seed was the aphrodisiac she had feared it would be and a growing tingle began to burn between her legs. Surreptitiously, she stole a hand towards her cleft and touched the pulsing nub of her clitoris. Her sex was slippery with excitement and her fingers were a tactile bliss against the dewy folds of her labia. The nub of her arousal was painfully responsive and when she touched it a bolt of pleasure spat from her pussy. Unable to stop herself, Jasmin cried out.

Dr Grady glared down at her. His fierce expression showed none of the gratitude or warmth she expected to see. His hand remained entwined in her brunette tresses and he snatched her head up sharply. The abruptness of the gesture tugged his failing shaft from her open mouth. His obvious displeasure was enough to stop her mounting excitement before she could give in to it.

'Didn't I tell you there was a condition to this arrangement?'

She shook her head, wishing he would speak so she could understand him more clearly. 'I was only –'

'Don't bother to explain,' he growled. 'I know exactly what you were doing. You were going to pleasure yourself. Didn't you hear me say that you wouldn't be allowed any sexual release during this atonement? Didn't you hear me say you'd be punished if I caught you gleaning satisfaction?'

86

She remembered that he had said something like that and, now the meaning was explained to her, she studied him with renewed desperation. 'You won't cane me, will you?'

His smile was cruel. 'I'd enjoy caning you,' he reflected. 'I still have appetites that I want you to satisfy, and caning might be a way of achieving them, but we'll see if you can manage the task without my help.' He shook her head with a brisk movement of his wrist and guided her mouth back to his spent length. 'Make me come again,' he told her, 'and you'll be a step closer to getting out of here.'

She licked at him, then held him in her hands as she tried to coax a stiffness back into his soft flesh. She distrusted and despised him more than she had ever loathed any other individual, but that didn't stop her need to feel his hardness back inside her mouth. Driven by a carnal appetite that surprised her, Jasmin placed her mouth over his erection and licked and sucked greedily.

His breathing had lowered to a dull rasp and she could hear frustration in his tone. 'It's not working this way,' he told her. 'I think I'll have to cane you. That always fires my need.'

She shook her head and looked up at him helplessly. 'I can make it hard again, and I *will* make you come,' she promised. She started to raise herself from her kneeling position and then paused, knowing it would be unwise to make any move without having his permission first. 'Would you sit down?' she asked.

His frown lingered for a moment, then disappeared when he nodded. He walked over to the same chair he had used before caning her sister and Jasmin followed him. She waited until he was settled before straddling herself over the padded arms of the chair. Holding on to the chair's back, she balanced herself so her sex was hovering over his groin.

'What do you intend doing?'

'I'm going to make you hard again.'

'You know I won't tolerate your getting pleasure from this,' he reminded her. 'If I think you're enjoying this, I'll use my cane on you and then you really will learn to repent.'

Already aware of this condition, Jasmin nodded and reached for his shaft. The flesh remained soft to her touch but when she began rubbing his dome against her pussy lips it started to thicken. The pliant length grew rigid and she could see its life being resurrected as he started to become hard.

'You surprise me,' he murmured.

Jasmin wasn't listening. She rubbed the stiffening head against her labia, trying not to think of how needed that friction was. Her sex was aflame with a deep-seated longing and the growing shaft between her legs silently promised to fulfil that need. She rolled his dome along her pussy lips, teasing him with the threat of penetration before rubbing him over the engorged pulse of her clitoris. If he had been a lover from university she would have pulled her top aside and allowed him to suck her breasts as she did this. Her nipples were stung by the same yearning that beat between her legs and she longed to have them caressed. Knowing he would refuse or even punish her for such a suggestion, Jasmin tried to ignore their aching need and concentrated on the task of relieving Dr Grady.

He placed his hands beneath her buttocks and cupped the shape of her backside. His fingers were close to her sex and she tried not to think of how tantalising his caress was. His thumbs stroked the sensitive crease of her groin and she shivered excitedly.

'You aren't receiving pleasure from this, are you?'

She blinked at him through a haze, infuriated by his shrewd gaze and tight-lipped smile. His erection had grown fully in her palm and, as she rolled it against her sex, she could feel it twitch eagerly. The knowledge that he was enjoying so much pleasure and still denying her the same privilege was maddening. Knowing better than to antagonise him, she tried to distance herself from her body's sensations while she shook her head. 'I'm trying not to,' she said earnestly.

He nodded approval and brushed her hands from his shaft. Guiding the erection on his own, he aimed the tip for her pussy lips and began to torment her. While she had been holding him Jasmin had been able to maintain some control over her needs. Now that he was dictating the tempo her sex lips shrieked with renewed demands for satisfaction. She bit back her cry, desperately trying to conceal the arousal he had awoken.

'Do I need to remind you to curb your urges?' he asked. 'Do I need to remind you that there's a caning waiting for you if I think you're enjoying this ordeal?'

He didn't need to remind her of that but she began to think the threat was no longer as intimidating as it had been. Not only was she trying to convince herself it might be a price worth paying, but Jasmin also believed it might be an enjoyable experience.

'Are you resisting your urges?'

'Yes,' she hissed.

'I'm so pleased to hear that.'

There was a smile in his voice and Jasmin watched it stretch across his face as he bucked his hips forward. His shaft plunged inside her, filling the craving that had nestled beyond the lips of her sex. His thick girth spread her wide as he impaled her. Rather than try to resist his entry, she eased her thighs wide apart and allowed her sex to slide fully over him. Her inner muscles enveloped him and she could feel herself being stretched to bursting point.

Dr Grady groaned beneath her. His fingers reached for her breasts and, although she pushed herself forward, he tore his hands away at the last moment. He shook his head from side to side, giving her a knowing look. 'We both want me to do that,' he told her. 'But I'm not sure it would be good for you. Undoubtedly it would satisfy your passion but that's not the point of this exercise, is it?'

Growling with frustration, Jasmin refused to meet his eyes. She raised and lowered herself on to him, not wanting to think of the burgeoning euphoria that his penetration was giving. Gripping tightly on to the back of his chair, she rode him furiously as she tried to shun all thoughts of her own satisfaction from her mind.

His hands were on her hips and she realised he was helping her to keep up the brisk pace she had started. The weight of his palms should have been a sexless caress but, with her body reaching new heights of desperation, Jasmin even found stimulation there. She stifled a frustrated sob and willed herself not to think about the joys that were battering their way through her pussy lips.

He shivered and groaned, not bothering to disguise the nearness of his orgasm. His hands went from her hips and he dragged his length from her sex.

Jasmin wanted to howl with disappointment. She had felt his shaft tingling and knew he was on the verge of coming. While she had been trying to ignore the intimacy, her body had wanted to experience the pulse of his orgasm. At the back of her mind she suspected it would trigger her own climax and she had been hoping he would be too wrapped up in his own pleasure to notice. With the removal of his length, her sex was left feeling open and unfulfilled. Even when he stroked the head against the swollen need of her clitoris, her response was only a shadow of what she knew it could have been.

He orgasmed with his shaft pressed against her sex lips. His thick spray daubed her pussy lips and thighs, spattering her flesh like warm droplets of sweat. The groan of his climax disguised her growl of frustration.

'Tremendous,' he muttered. 'Keep satisfying me like that and I shall have nothing to fear from my estranged wife.'

The words made her want to cry. 'Am I really only doing this so that you don't feel horn–' She stopped herself, suddenly worried that 'horny' might be a swearword that offended him, and trying to think of the right one to replace it. 'Am I really only doing this so that you don't feel aroused when she gets here?'

Dr Grady chuckled. 'Of course not,' he told her softly.

His hand went to the crease of her sex and he scooped up a dollop of his spend from there. When he offered the seed in front of her mouth, Jasmin studied him warily before lapping his fingers clean.

'Of course you're not just doing this for that reason,' he assured her. 'This is also part of your atonement, remember?'

He pushed his fingers back to her pussy and drew another palmful of his load from her sweating flesh. When his fingers were placed back in front of her mouth, Jasmin paused before putting her lips to them. 'And, once I've done this, you'll phone my father and I can go home?' she asked doubtfully. 'Is that our arrangement?'

He waved his hand in front of her mouth, silently telling her that she wouldn't get a response until she was doing exactly as he wanted. She placed her lips over his fingers and began to savour the cooling remnants of his climax.

'You've done well so far,' he assured her. 'As I told you before, I'm going to send you up to the abandoned church after we've finished, so you can cause chaos among the heathens and pagans who will be gathering there.' He glanced at his wristwatch and frowned when he read the time. 'It really is growing later than I had anticipated but, before you go, I want to be certain that I'm truly spent of arousal.'

She toyed with his flaccid shaft, wondering how she was supposed to satisfy him for a third time. Those youths she had enjoyed at university seldom went soft when she was around and she considered the challenge as though it was a complex puzzle. Allowing instinct to guide her, Jasmin placed her mouth over his spent cock and tried to suck him back to hardness.

Firmly, he guided her head away from his erection.

'My arousal began while I was caning your sister,' he confided. 'I think I told you before that I've always found that sort of diversion quite stimulating. Indulge me and then you can go.'

She glared at him fearfully. 'You want to cane me?'

He shook his head. 'I have promised you and your sister that I won't use the cane. I'm sure I can take care of this by just using my bare hands.'

Unhappily, Jasmin turned her backside up for him and prepared herself for the indignity he was promising.

Four

Not for the first time in her life, Jo Valentine didn't know what was going on. She and Melissa stood on either side of the altar, surrounded by the circling priests and priestesses. Their mystical chants droned through Jo's mind, upsetting her train of thought and making her more and more uneasy. Steve, still wearing the goat's-head mask, stood imposingly between them. He held a Y-shaped piece of willow in loose fists and concentrated furiously on it. Dinah paced from Jo to Melissa and back again, glaring at anyone who annoyed her. The mousy girl they called Verity lingered outside the circle, hurriedly performing all the errands she was given.

'This would all be a lot simpler,' Dinah began. Her tone was rich with mounting exasperation. 'This would all be a lot simpler if one of you could tell me that you are the chosen one.'

Jo and Melissa exchanged glances but said nothing.

'What are you doing here?' Dinah directed the question at Melissa, standing close as she asked it. Her bare breasts were almost touching Melissa's cropped top and her naked leg brushed against the young woman's exposed thigh.

'This is where I'm meant to be,' Melissa replied. It was the sixth time she had been asked the question

93

and it was the sixth time she had answered with the same reply.

Dinah shook her head. 'Why do you say that? What does that mean?'

Melissa shrugged. It was the sixth time she had responded with the same vague gesture.

Dinah turned to face Jo. She placed her body close, using her physical presence to intimidate. Jo could feel the weight of the woman's breasts against her own and the pressure of a bare thigh on her leg.

'Why are you here?'

'Where else is a girl supposed to go on a Saturday night after the pubs have chucked out?' It was the sixth time she been asked the question but it wasn't the sixth time she had answered like this. On the first occasion Jo had told Dinah to mind her own business. After that she had tried to counter the woman's intimidating tactics with her own brand of humour. She had said she was waiting for a number 42 bus; she had said an estate agent sent her, saying this was the best time to view the property; and, in a moment of characteristically bad taste, she had also said, 'This is the house of my father.' She hoped Dinah would soon grow weary of asking the question because Jo doubted her repertoire of surreal one-liners would prove inexhaustible.

'Have you divined anything, Steve?' Dinah asked.

Jo followed her gaze and realised the twig he was holding was meant to be some sort of dowsing rod. She had watched documentaries where people used similar devices for detecting water and she wondered what purpose it was meant to serve by being pointed between her and Melissa. Not sure she wanted to know, she glanced towards the church door, where it looked like Verity had done a good job of securing it closed. Unable to stop herself from cataloguing escape routes, she glanced at the doorway to the vestry and wondered if there was a chance of getting out through there. She had yet to explore that corner of the church, but Jo had seen everywhere else. Simple deduction told her that, if there was going to be an emergency exit, the only place left for it would be through the vestry.

'This is madness,' Dinah growled. 'Why can't one of you say that you're the coven's new leader?'

Jo and Melissa glanced at each other but neither replied.

Dinah glared at each of them, then turned on Steve. 'The dowsing isn't working,' she told him. With two brisk steps she was standing in front of him. She slapped the piece of willow out of his hands and it flew towards the pulpit. Behind him, the coven's artefacts had been laid on the altar and she studied the collection as though she would find something there that might be of practical use.

Jo had watched the altar being prepared. Verity had used a besom broom to sweep dust from where they now stood before using a piece of chalk to inscribe a pentagram on the floor. After lighting candles on either side of the altar, Verity had rummaged through the bulky holdall that the coven had brought with them. She selected various items from inside before positioning a chalice, wicker doll and silver dagger between the two flames. Verity had done this while mumbling the droning monologue that the priests and priestesses were currently chanting.

The whole episode had unnerved Jo.

'If we're going to find out which of these women really belongs here, we're going to have to use more practical methods of detection,' Dinah decided. She reached for the dagger and toyed with it absently.

Dazzling shards of candlelight reflected from its polished surface.

'What are you wanting to do?' Steve asked.

Jo listened more intently, unsettled by the way that Dinah was looking at the knife.

'We'll have to check them both,' Dinah told Steve. 'Maybe one of them has the true mark of a witch.'

There was a space beneath the base of the goat's-head mask where Jo could see Steve's jaw. She watched him grin when he heard this suggestion and wondered why he suddenly seemed so enthusiastic.

'Which one do we check first?'

'Her,' Dinah replied, using the dagger to point at Melissa. 'She was the first one we found. She was the first one we saw. We'll test her first.'

Jo breathed a sigh of relief.

Dinah stepped over to Melissa and said, 'You realise we're witches, don't you?'

Melissa nodded.

'Our coven is looking for a new leader and we believe that you, or this other woman, might have been sent here to fulfil that role. There are signs that show a true witch and we want to see if you have them. That doesn't trouble you, does it?'

Meekly, Melissa shook her head. It was clear to Jo that this troubled her a lot but it was also clear that Melissa was too intimidated to say so.

'Why are you doing this to us?' Jo asked.

'Silence,' Steve barked. 'You will only speak when the mother goddess permits you to.'

'I was only asking –'

Dinah turned to glare at her. 'Please be silent,' she started softly. 'I need to concentrate on this if I'm to do it properly.'

Jo nodded and held her tongue. She watched Dinah turn back to Melissa, then push the knife towards the girl's stomach. Rather than try to cut her, Dinah used the blade to lift the edge of Melissa's cropped top. The knife was sharp and sliced easily through the fabric. Before Melissa was able to whisper her first worried sob, the knife had cut up to the neck of her garment. Melissa's breasts spilled free and she released a mortified groan.

There was a moment's silence, as though no one had expected Dinah to do this. It was only when the priests and priestesses began to chant again that Jo realised the shock had swept through them all.

'You're a fine-looking woman,' Dinah told her. She moved her hand to the tattered remnants that still hung on Melissa's frame, then brushed the garment away. Her fingers lingered on the blonde's arm, casually stroking downwards.

Jo watched the pair, unhappy that she was becoming excited by the sight.

Wordlessly, Dinah took her blade and grazed the edge against Melissa's thigh. She pushed the point towards her hip, where it disappeared beneath the hem of her skirt. There was the sound of fabric being torn and Melissa released another shocked cry as her rent skirt fell to the floor.

Steve made a growl of approval and, if Jo hadn't agreed with his whispered verdict, she would have glared at him.

Melissa held herself defiantly in front of Dinah, allowing the mother goddess to study her naked body. 'You really are a fine-looking creature,' Dinah told her. As she spoke, her fingers stroked Melissa's curves. Jo guessed it was meant to be some sort of examination but, although Dinah's features were twisted with concentration, her hands gave away the real pleasure she was extracting. Rather than simply touch the naked blonde, Dinah used the tips of her fingers to caress. She explored Melissa's narrow waist, then lingered over her hips before moving her hands upwards. All the time Dinah was watching the path that her fingers followed but her faraway smile looked as though it was only there to disguise her growing excitement.

Jo caught a breath when she saw Dinah cup Melissa's breast. The air in the church seemed to have thickened and the tension was almost palpable. Dinah scrupulously examined Melissa's left breast, then her right, before stepping behind her. Able to study Melissa's nudity, Jo stopped herself from licking her lips, but she couldn't drag her gaze away. Melissa had a buxom chest with a narrow waist that tapered down to the fluffy mound of her pubic curls. While Dinah continued to stroke and study her back, Melissa kept her eyes tightly shut and Jo wondered if this was because of pleasure or embarrassment. She could read a combination of the two emotions in Melissa's face and it was difficult to say which took precedence.

'Have you found anything?' Steve asked.

Dinah gave no reply. She appeared from behind Melissa, squatted down and smoothed her hands against the blonde's hip. Her face was inches away from Melissa's flesh and her sombre frown was enough of a reply to show that her search had so far been fruitless.

Jo was tempted to ask what she was looking for but she knew the time for that question would come eventually.

Dinah moved her hands over Melissa's other hip before continuing downwards. Jo watched her caresses slide towards the blonde's inner thigh, edging close to the crease between her legs.

Melissa's eyes remained tightly shut and her cheeks glowed crimson in the candlelight. But still Jo couldn't believe her response was wholly attributable to embarrassment. There was a telltale lilt to her lips that Jo felt sure was a smile of anticipation.

'No sign of it,' Dinah whispered. Although she spoke quietly, her voice was clear enough to be heard over the droning incantations of the priests and priestesses. She eased herself from the floor, taking her hands from Melissa's body with an obvious reluctance.

'If it's not her then it must be this one,' Steve said, pointing at Jo.

Jo met Dinah's speculative gaze with her own cool one.

'It could still be either or neither of them,' Dinah said, stepping closer to Jo. The dagger had returned to her hand and she raised the blade as she approached. 'I'll need to carry out the same meticulous study of this one to find out one way or the other.'

'You're not using that knife on me,' Jo warned her. It was difficult not to feel intimidated by the group but she was determined that they wouldn't see her worries. Struggling to maintain a defiant posture, Jo pointed at the knife and said, 'You can keep that bloody thing away from me.'

'I know what I'm doing. I've never cut a living creature with this yet.'

'I don't care about living creatures,' Jo replied haughtily. 'These jeans are my favourite Calvin Kleins and no one's taking a knife to them.'

'I need to have you naked, to see if you have the mark.'

'Then you'll wait for me to undress, rather than cutting the clothes off me.'

Dinah nodded, allowing this with only the slightest pout of her lower lip to show that she was put out by Jo's objections.

Unhappy at having to undress in the imposing atmosphere, Jo tried to distance herself from the coven's pent-up air of expectancy. She bent down to unfasten her boots and realised that Dinah was standing too close to allow her this freedom. The woman's pubic mound was on Jo's eye level. Although she wasn't wanting to look, Jo could see that the blonde curls around the woman's pussy lips were still smattered with the remnants of Steve's seed. The intimacy she had previously witnessed wasn't a memory she wanted to revisit right now. She was already fearful of having to endure Dinah's caress and didn't want to put up with that indignity while betraying the symptoms of arousal. She tugged one boot off her foot and glanced up at the figure that towered over her.

Dinah stared down, her face peeking between the valley of her cleavage.

'What exactly will you be looking for?' Jo asked.

'I'm looking for a sign.'

'What sort of sign? No entry? Stop? Maximum height two metres?'

Dinah shook her head. 'I'm going to search your body for the mark of a witch.'

Jo nodded as she stepped out of her jeans. 'Thanks for explaining that,' she said, folding the Calvins and placing them tidily on the floor. She started working on the buttons of her blouse, aware that Dinah was growing impatient. 'I don't think you're likely to find a sign on me, but, if it helps to get me away from this lunatic asylum you call a coven, then I'm more than willing to let you have a look.' She shrugged the blouse from her shoulders and placed the garment on top of her jeans. Trying to show that she wouldn't be bullied, Jo held Dinah's gaze as the woman stepped closer.

'You're still wearing your bra and panties,' Dinah reminded her. 'I asked you to undress.'

Jo glanced down at the clothes, not sure she wanted to expose herself so fully. Admittedly, Melissa had been stripped, Dinah was already naked and the remainder of the coven were wearing nothing but their cloaks, but she was still uncomfortable with the idea of stripping completely. 'There are no signs of my being a witch under my bra and panties,' she said quickly. 'I checked myself before I came out this evening and I've given myself the all-clear.'

Dinah lifted the blade to cut between the two cups and Jo's breasts were released into the chill air of the abandoned church. Before Jo could raise a word of protest, Dinah was using the silver dagger to slice through the hip of her panties. The flimsy fabric fell on either side of the blade and Jo watched her underwear drop to the floor. She glared at Dinah but the woman seemed unmindful of her antagonism.

'I can conduct my search properly now,' she explained.

'You're not coming anywhere near me until you say exactly what you're looking for,' Jo told her. She glanced from Dinah to Steve, not sure which of them would respond better to her defiance. Deciding that Dinah, with her silver dagger and malicious smile, was the more immediate threat, Jo met the woman's gaze and repeated the words. 'I mean it. You're not coming anywhere near me until you say exactly what you're looking for.'

Dinah's smile was disarming. 'I'm looking for a third nipple,' she explained. 'It's known as the true mark of a witch. If you have one of those, we'll know that you are our rightful leader.'

'A third nipple?' Jo couldn't stop herself from sounding sceptical. 'Don't you think I'd have noticed one of those if I had one? I count them regularly and I've never managed to get the number up to three. Trust me, I don't have a third nipple, just the usual brace.'

Dinah's smile turned cold. 'You will still be searched, just so that we can be sure.' She stepped closer, placing her naked body unnervingly close to Jo's.

Glancing down at herself, Jo could see their breasts were almost touching. 'No one has a third nipple,' Jo told her. She had wanted to say the words as though she was dismissing the topic, but mounting excitement had made her tone husky. 'That's just myth, or fable or complete bullshit, isn't it?'

'It's not a total myth,' Dinah replied. She half turned, then raised her arm.

For an instant Jo wondered if she was about to be struck by the knife. She dismissed the irrational thought before it had fully formulated or given rise to panic. Dinah passed the dagger to Steve, then pointed to her side, behind her right breast.

Studying the small protrusion, Jo tried not to gasp when she realised what she was looking at. It was easy to understand why she hadn't seen it before because Dinah's arm would have normally concealed it. She remembered thinking that Dinah had been extracting inordinate pleasure from simply touching her side and this certainly seemed to explain that peculiarity. As Dinah pointed a sensibly short finger-nail against the ring of darkened flesh, Jo realised she was staring at a third nipple.

'That's not real, is it?'

'It's incredibly real,' Dinah explained.

Jo stared at it with slack-jawed amazement. Unable to stop herself, and suddenly forgetting all those fears that had been tormenting her, she bent closer.

'It's incredibly real,' Dinah repeated. 'And, because it's such a beautiful gift, I use it whenever I'm able.'

The words went over Jo's head. 'Use it how?'

'It's exceptionally responsive,' Dinah told her. To illustrate, she stroked a finger against herself, then shivered as though she was being swept up by waves of immense pleasure.

Watching her, Jo couldn't quell a whisper of envy.

The nub of skin was as dark as the cherry nipples tipping Dinah's breasts but only about half the size. There was no areola and Jo supposed it could just have been a mole or a skin tag, but she felt sure that neither of those explanations was correct. As bizarre as it seemed, as difficult to accept as she found it, Jo had to concede that Dinah really did have a third nipple.

'Both of these are responsive too,' Dinah told her. To show what she meant she crossed her arms over her chest and tweaked at the tips of her breasts. Her smile grew broader but it was clear to Jo that the woman wasn't receiving the same intensity of stimulation that she had enjoyed before. 'I love having these touched,' she went on. 'But I've brought myself to orgasm just by teasing this third one.'

Unable to stop herself, Jo reached forward. She flashed a questioning gaze into the mother goddess's eyes and was rewarded with a nod of assent. Dinah raised her arm higher and Jo was afforded free access to caress her flesh. Her fingers traced over the rigid nodule and she was only mildly surprised when Dinah shivered beneath the touch. If the bud was as sensitive as Dinah maintained then Jo realised any stimulation would be deeply felt.

Without moving her fingers away, Jo asked, 'If you've already got the mark of a true witch, why are you looking for a replacement?'

Dinah blinked, looking briefly surprised by the question. Her eyes had a faraway gleam in them, and Jo wondered how intense her momentary thrill had been. 'I have to leave the village soon,' Dinah told her, 'and that means I can't lead the coven.'

'Can't you promote someone from within the ranks?' Jo asked, nodding at the chanting priests and priestesses. 'Couldn't one of them be the new leader?'

Dinah shook her head. 'Our brand of Wicca doesn't work that way. We believe there is an order to things. Some of us are born with three nipples, and others are born to suck on them.' Without another word, she grabbed Jo's hair and forced her face towards the thrusting nub.

Unable to stop herself, and not sure she would have wanted to anyway, Jo pushed out her tongue. She and Sam had enjoyed similar games in the past and this wasn't the first time she had held a woman's nipple between her lips. However, it had to rate as the most unusual. The perversity of the situation only added to her arousal. Caught up by her own welling appetite, Jo dared to suck.

Releasing her hold on Jo's head, Dinah growled a low murmur of approval. Given the freedom to move, Jo kept her lips where they were. She teased the rigid bud with delicate nibbles, then raised one hand to caress Dinah's breasts. The woman's responsiveness was exhilarating and her excited cries echoed through the church. Encouraged by her reaction, Jo worked her mouth more forcefully.

'Isn't there a true reason for our being here?' Steve's voice crashed through Jo's arousal and encouraged Dinah to step away.

'That's right,' Dinah agreed. Her voice was heavy with resignation. 'We do have a true reason for being here.' She grinned sheepishly in Jo's direction, then seemed to regain her composure with a sigh and the shaking of her shoulders.

Jo resumed her position in one point of the pentagram and allowed Dinah to step close to her. Her shoulders and arms were stroked and investigated while Dinah held her gaze. The woman's attention was disquieting and Jo wished she could distance herself from the eye contact. She came close to sighing with relief when Dinah broke their gaze and turned her attention to the search. But, even then, the threat of stimulation wasn't far away. Dinah kept her face myopically close to Jo's body, as though she was fearful of overlooking the tiniest detail. Her warm breath whispered against Jo's bare flesh, each exhalation evoking a promise of future pleasures. She hadn't intended submitting to the same meticulous study that Dinah had conducted on Melissa, but now the memory of her planned refusal seemed a thousand miles away. As her breasts, hips and sides were caressed, the idea of trying to stop Dinah seemed plainly ridiculous. The thrill of the woman's intimate examination was a joy that Jo wouldn't have wanted to miss.

Dinah dropped to her haunches, her inspection leading her over Jo's buttocks and round to her hips. Her fingers continued to trail along unimagined erogenous zones, stoking the fuels of Jo's need. As her hands reached Jo's inner thighs, the electric sensation of being stimulated became overwhelming. If this had been an evening for the two of them together, Jo knew this would have been that magical moment when she and Dinah first shared proper sexual intimacy. The idea was too exciting and Jo released a shiver.

Dinah stood up, snatching herself away from Jo's body. 'No mark,' she said, glancing angrily at Steve. 'No mark at all.'

The goat's-head mask turned away and a sigh of exasperation came from its nostrils. 'Then what are we supposed to do now? Could it still be either of them, or does this prove it's neither?'

Dinah frowned, considering this. She glanced at Verity and a sly smile stole across her lips. 'Neophyte,' she snapped.

Verity glanced up.

'I need two poppets, wicker ones if you can make them. Quickly, neophyte.'

Verity rushed to the bag the coven had brought with them and began rummaging through its contents. Jo guessed that most of its possessions had been depleted for the altar and she wondered why Verity was making such a long chore of searching for whatever items Dinah had requested. She wasn't sure she liked the sound of the word 'poppet', although she knew the mother goddess could have probably requested many things that sounded far more intimidating.

Verity returned to the pentagram with a sheaf of slender, flexible twigs in one hand. She separated the sheaf into two even handfuls and quickly began to bend and shape the first.

Jo watched intently. She wanted to make some comment about this evening becoming a craftwork demonstration, but she knew such a remark would break the solemn mood. She thought of doing it anyway, just to ease her own growing fears, but, before she could say anything, she realised Verity had finished making her first poppet.

'It's a dolly,' Jo said, surprised that Dinah had requested something so simple. She glanced at Verity and saw the neophyte was working quickly to form and shape a second one. 'She's just making dollies,' Jo gasped. 'How is this supposed to help you decide which of us is your next leader?'

Dinah was glaring but Jo was able to ignore her and the coven. The appearance of the dolls seemed so puerile that the witches no longer struck her as being ominous or threatening.

'It's not your place to ask such questions,' Dinah snapped.

'I just want to know how you think dollies will help you to make such an important decision.'

Dinah glared at her. 'The religion of Wicca has been mocked and persecuted for centuries,' she began.

'I'm not surprised, if it's filled with grown women like you still playing with dollies.'

'Don't think we'll be upset by your ridicule and sarcasm,' Dinah hissed.

'You can't perform this spell while you're angry,' Steve warned her.

Dinah turned on him. 'I'm well aware of that,' she spat. 'And I'm telling you now, I'm not angry.'

Verity passed her the second poppet and Dinah accepted it with a mumbled thank-you. She flashed her angry gaze at Jo, retrieved her dagger, and turned to Melissa. Her movements were quick, as though anger still had some hand in her actions despite her protestations. She caught a strand of Melissa's blonde locks between her fingers and cut it from her with the knife.

Melissa gasped, putting a hand to her head where the hair had been severed.

Nimbly, Dinah tied the strands of hair around the head of one doll before passing it to Steve. She turned on Jo and, before the private investigator could stop her, Dinah had cut a length of brunette hair from her head.

'Why did you have to do that?' Jo demanded. 'My hairdresser won't be happy when he sees you've spoiled my fringe.'

Dinah wrapped the hair around the head of the second poppet and ignored Jo's whining. She tied the hair tight, smiling only when her work was finished.

'What's the point of this?' Jo asked.

'A true witch can't be controlled by her effigy,' Dinah explained. 'Steve and I are going to "play with the dollies", as you put it. If one of you is really our leader you'll remain unmoved by what we do to your doll.'

'And, if this is all a load of hokum, we'll both remain unmoved by what you do with the dolls,' Jo said dryly.

Dinah sniffed the comment away. She kept hold of the brunette poppet and gestured for Steve to bring his blonde doll into the pentagram. The pair closed their eyes and mumbled an incantation that was louder than the chants of the priests and priestesses.

Jo glanced at Melissa and saw that the naked blonde was growing more and more unnerved by the turn of events. She understood how the woman felt.

'Behold your effigy,' Dinah said, pushing the brunette doll in front of Jo's face.

'Behold, your effigy,' Steve repeated, shoving Melissa's doll in front of her.

Jo studied the doll sceptically. 'And what's supposed to happen?' she asked, hoping she sounded braver than she felt. Now the coven was acting mystically again she could feel her fears returning. Trying to mask her unease with bravado, she asked, 'If you pull its leg away would mine drop off?'

'I don't think you'd want me to put that to the test, would you?'

As she spoke, Dinah rubbed her fingers over the doll's chest.

Jo watched and was shocked to feel her body suffering what felt like an echo of that friction. If she

108

hadn't known it was impossible – if she hadn't known there was no one touching her – she would have sworn Dinah's caress had brushed over her own bared breasts rather than the doll's. She glanced down at her chest and saw that her nipples were rigid with excitement.

'We could test your effigy in a number of ways,' Dinah smiled. She still held the dagger and she placed its tip against the chest of the brunette doll. 'We could test it with Steve's divining rod, we could test it with pleasure, or we could test it with pain.' After saying this final word, she pushed the tip of her dagger hard against the poppet.

Jo coughed, startled to feel a corresponding weight against her chest. Determined to hide her feelings from Dinah she forced herself to return the mother goddess's smile as though she was unperturbed. It was a difficult act to perform with panic and pain vying for control of her emotions. Using a resolute effort, she maintained her composure until Dinah turned her head away and placed the dagger back on the altar.

As soon as the blade was moved from the poppet, Jo snatched a breath of air. She was surprised her lungs needed it so badly. Her chest felt sore and bruised and she tried to find some way to rationalise the unexpected bolt of discomfort that she had just suffered. An excited tingle in her nipples made her glance up, and she saw Dinah dancing her fingertips over the chest of the brunette poppet.

'Personally, I find the responses of pleasure are easier to detect,' Dinah grinned. 'Unbelievers like you always find it difficult to conceal arousal when their effigy is being excited.'

Jo heard and understood the words but she was loath to accept them. Her mind suggested the word 'psychosomatic', and she snatched at it as though it was a talisman. This was all kidology, she assured herself. It was the power of suggestion, her own mind being so weak that it was drawn in by the mystical mumbo-jumbo that Steve and Dinah had been spouting. She tried to cling on to those thoughts when Dinah rubbed her hand over the doll again. It was difficult to stay focused on the thought because her body was revelling in an unbidden thrill of arousal.

'The true leader of our coven would be beyond the powers of our effigies,' Dinah explained. She teased her fingers on the front of the brunette doll and Jo saw she was touching the spots that correspond with her nipples. Ripples of pleasure were emanating from her breasts and Jo willed herself not to believe that Dinah was magically stimulating her. She wanted to place her hands protectively around herself but she knew that doing so would show Dinah that she had been affected. Not wanting to lose this battle of wills, Jo tried to remain unmoved as her body was mysteriously stimulated.

Steve was working on Melissa's doll with a painstaking effort. He held the poppet with loose fingers, using his other hand to press and squeeze against the doll's thighs and chest.

Melissa looked as though she was trying to remain unmoved but Jo could see it was a difficult act. Her cheeks were flushed and she stared at the members of the coven with startled respect. The tips of her breasts were darkening and Jo knew it was the flush of arousal that coloured them. Melissa's chest rose and fell with drawn-out sighs that were clearly brought on by excitement.

Glancing at Steve, Jo saw he was pushing his index finger between the poppet's legs.

'Fight it, if you think you have to,' Dinah grinned. She danced the tip of her fingers against the brunette doll, then moved her hand lower.

Shivers of unbidden excitement were tickling through Jo's body even though she kept telling herself they were impossible. She tried to hold Dinah's gaze, then looked away, fearful that such an exchange would show her arousal. Ripples of pleasure were coursing from every nerve and Jo knew that if she and Dinah made eye contact the secret of her stimulation would be revealed.

'Perhaps that's how the true leader resists being controlled by her effigy,' Dinah suggested. 'Perhaps we witches have been fooled into thinking a coven's leader is beyond the reach of our magic when she's just strong enough to resist showing it.'

Jo said nothing, sure that any word she spoke would be carried by a groan of delight. Dinah used a slender finger to tease between the legs of her poppet and Jo's body was responding as though she was experiencing the caress at first-hand. Her pussy lips tingled as if they were being teased and her clitoris had become an aching ball that throbbed with its need for fulfilment.

Melissa cried out and Jo watched the blonde press a hand over her pubic mound. Because she was facing her, Jo thought it looked as if Melissa was playing with herself. Her cheeks were flushed and her frame quivered. However, because Jo was suffering the same surreal stimulation, she knew Melissa's arousal hadn't come from her own hand.

Dinah and Steve both smiled at Melissa, watching the blonde fall to her knees as she tried to contain her response.

With their attention distracted, Jo wondered if she dared to give in to the pleasure for just a moment. The sensation was infuriatingly exciting and her libido craved the indulgence. She stopped the thought when Steve and Dinah turned back to face her.

'It must be her,' Steve said. The glassy eyes of the goat's-head mask glared blindly at Jo.

'She's fighting it well,' Dinah mused.

Behind them, Melissa writhed on the floor, her legs kicking out languidly as she succumbed to waves of pleasure. Steve was still teasing between the legs of the blonde poppet and Jo wanted to tell him to stop. She didn't say the words, knowing that it would confirm her acceptance of the magic that was being used.

'It's her,' Steve insisted, nodding towards Jo.

'It could still be either of them,' Dinah told him. 'Watch.' She took the poppet and pressed it between her breasts. Her eyes fluttered closed, and a smile of bliss stole across her lips. With her grin growing broader, she rubbed the poppet against her left breast and shivered.

Jo groaned, not sure where the wave of pleasure had come from, only aware of the affect it had on her.

Encouraged by the sound, Dinah shifted the doll to her right breast. She pressed it hard against herself and this time Jo struggled not to scream in response. The idea of begging the coven to stop now seemed like the most sensible thing to do but, before Jo could manage to voice her cry, Dinah had pressed the poppet over her third nipple.

The sensation was exquisite. An unimagined thrill of pleasure stole through Jo's body, effectively silencing any exclamation she had been about to make. Waves of joy washed over her and she wondered how it was possible to enjoy this much stimulation without being touched. She stared incredulously at Dinah and watched her eyes blink slowly open.

'This one is just as aroused,' Dinah said. Her voice was low and her words sounded ever so slightly laboured. 'This one is just as easily controlled by the effigy.' She moved the poppet away from her third nipple and slid it down, over her stomach.

Jo caught her breath when she saw the doll's head combing through the thatch of Dinah's curls. She could see where the doll was going and, while she didn't know what effect this next stage of the spell would have, she wasn't sure she wanted to find out. The pleasure had already been far greater than she would have believed possible and she dreaded the idea of its becoming any more intense.

When Dinah brushed the doll's head against her sex, Jo was stung by a debilitating joy. She closed her eyes and tried to shake off the arousal. Distantly she knew this was a futile struggle. Every inhalation was flavoured with the musky taste of arousal and she knew that in some unbelievable way she was inhaling the perfume of Dinah's sex.

Dinah released a small moan and Jo envied her the ability to make that sound. Screams of pleasure were building inside her but she didn't dare release them for fear of how the coven might react. She realised that even if she had wanted to shout her cries she wouldn't have been able to because it suddenly seemed impossible to find the necessary air.

Dinah wanked herself gently with the poppet's head.

From her point in the pentagram, Jo watched the mother goddess slip the wicker doll between the yielding lips of her pussy. The head slid in and out of her sex and the brunette hairs on the poppet grew darker and slicker.

Each time the head plunged inside, Jo felt a claustrophobic sensation tightening her chest. Arousal still burned through her body and it grew stronger as her airless lungs made her more aware of every sensation. When the poppet's head was pulled

113

out of Dinah, Jo snatched greedy breaths, trying to ignore the musky flavour of every one of them.

'This one is really fighting hard,' Dinah whispered. 'But I'm sure the poppet's controlling her.'

Hating her for being so accurate, Jo groaned and fell to her knees. She was on eye level with Dinah's sex and she watched the poppet being pushed hard against the mother goddess's wetness. Its head slid inside her for a final time and Dinah rolled it gently inside herself. She released her own soft sigh of joy before snatching the doll away.

As Jo gasped hungrily for breath, she glanced up and watched Dinah take the doll to her face.

Grinning wickedly, Dinah pushed her tongue towards the poppet's sex.

The orgasm washed over Jo with crippling force. She couldn't say where the pleasure had come from but that no longer worried her. All that mattered was giving herself over to the cascading ripples of pleasure. She fell to the floor, writhing beside Melissa as her lungs finally found the air to release gratified sobs.

'This is proof that we should wait for Samhain,' Steve said. 'Neither of these women is our leader. We should take this as a sign.'

Dinah sniffed. She placed the brunette poppet on the altar and took the blonde one from Steve to place that there too. After she snapped her fingers, Jo watched Verity rush to Dinah's side, asking what was needed.

'You received the message, didn't you? The flame told you that our new leader would be here, in this church?'

'That's right.'

'Then concentrate now and tell me, is our leader still here?'

114

Verity closed her eyes and, although she was only half watching, still trying to collect her thoughts after the unexpected pleasure she had just endured, Jo could see that Verity was concentrating furiously hard.

'Yes,' Verity whispered. She opened her eyes and stared lovingly into Dinah's face. 'Our leader is still here.'

Dinah nodded, as though this confirmed everything she had already thought. She turned to Steve and gave him a reassuring wink. 'There could be reasons for these two failing our test,' she declared. 'A poppet can never control a true witch but maybe neither of these two is a true witch yet. Maybe the coven is about to be led by someone who isn't a witch, or maybe that condition only works once a witch has been initiated.'

'Or maybe Verity is wrong and we should be waiting for Samhain,' Steve ventured. 'It's only six months away.'

'We're not waiting for Samhain. I have a way of finding out which of them is real.'

Jo eased herself from the floor, suddenly embarrassed that the coven had watched as she thrashed before them with orgasmic pleasure. 'Why don't you just let us go?' she suggested. 'Melissa and I have done everything you asked, and then some more. Why don't you let us both go?'

Dinah shook her head. She snatched a cloak from one of the pews and wrapped it around her body. 'Don't you worry,' Dinah smiled, starting away from the altar. 'I have a way of finding out which of you is our true leader. I don't think either of you will like it, but I'm beyond caring about that right now.'

Jo could tell the woman was trying to intimidate her and she tightened her resolve to show no fear.

'You're not going to see *him*, are you?' Steve asked.

Jo glanced in his direction, wondering why he placed such a peculiar emphasis on the word.

'I have no other option, have I?'

'I've already told you my thoughts on that,' he reminded her.

'We're going to get this resolved tonight,' Dinah said firmly. She cast her gaze between Jo and Melissa and her smile twisted cruelly. 'I doubt that these two ladies will enjoy it, but, with *his* help, we'll have this dilemma sorted out before morning light.'

As Dinah turned her back and walked towards the vestry, Jo realised her fears were no longer groundless. On a purely intuitive level she knew that whatever she had already endured this evening would be nothing compared with the torment that lay ahead.

Five

The only light in the van came from the black-and-white monitor. Those parts of their bodies that weren't concealed by shadows were bathed with blue-grey light. It reminded Sam of those times that she and Jo had made love with the lights off in front of the TV set.

Todd kissed her, his tongue twining with hers and promising more intimate penetrations. She welcomed the intrusion, silently encouraging him to be bolder. His hand had been squeezing her narrow waist, but it moved upwards now, finding the swell of her breast. As he rolled her stiff nipple between two calloused fingers, Sam groaned. She moved her hand to his bulge and rubbed at him through his combat pants.

'God, but you're sexy,' he whispered.

'I know,' she giggled. She broke the kiss only for the instant it took to breathe both words. As soon as they were spoken she pushed her mouth back over his.

'I want you,' he told her.

'I want you too,' she agreed. She glanced at the van door, then said the words louder, hoping Jo was standing just outside and able to hear them. 'I really, really want you,' she assured him.

Her words were encouragement for Todd. He moved his mouth to her breast and sucked hard. She gasped, thrilled by the sensation and excited by the image they would present if Jo chose that moment to return. They would be caught in tableau, her hand on his groin, his mouth at her breast and their intentions as blatant as scarlet nail polish. She could picture Jo's face, the expression turning from comprehension to fury, and then she could imagine the punishment that was bound to follow. The prospect was thrilling because it would mean an end to the argument and a return to their previous relationship of pleasure and pain.

The van door remained obstinately closed and the only movement came from the figures on the black-and-white screen. Todd teased and tongued her breast, sparking pleasurable tingles that were almost strong enough to distract her from the thought of having Jo return.

She had wanted Todd from the first moment she saw him. On a Friday, two weeks earlier, he had been sitting in Jo's office, explaining his credentials as she interviewed him. Dressed in faded jeans and a slightly scruffy T-shirt, he hadn't looked like a typical inter-viewee and it was that glimpse of individuality that had sparked her interest. When they made eye contact Sam had seen a promise in his smile and found herself instantaneously needing him.

As Jo was fond of telling her, it was a case of lust at first sight.

But immediately after the interview, before Sam could comment on how cute he was, or say how much fun she thought they could have with him, Jo had warned her off. She had gone to great lengths to catalogue some of Sam's previous interoffice relation-ships and had illustrated the discussion with two dozen records from the file marked 'Former Person-nel'. By the time Jo had finished, Sam had learned that the Flowers & Valentine Detective Agency was going to continue trading only if she obeyed a rule of no fraternisation.

It was a demeaning condition, made worse because it spoiled so many of the pleasures that life at the agency had to offer. If there was a new face on the payroll, Sam usually looked forward to exploiting it as she prepared for work on a morning. She chose her underwear for the day with images of how it would be stripped from her by the new lover they were employing.

But Jo had insisted and eventually – and with more than a little reluctance – Sam had agreed. They had decided the rule could be broken only if fraternisation was vital to the progress of a case but, even as they agreed to this one exception, Sam knew such criteria were unlikely to be met. She had left Jo's office feeling hurt and miserable, viewing the world as though it was a shop window that now displayed goods she was no longer allowed to purchase.

The long week after that meeting had been an exercise in frustration.

Sam had easily avoided Todd – he was occupied with Jo on a surveillance project – but there was still her receptionist and Jo's secretary in the office. Both were former conquests and the more she thought about not being able to have them, the greater Sam's longing grew. Trying hard to keep her promise to Jo, she valiantly ignored the subtle temptations they offered as they went about their work.

She had tried to take her mind away from the frustrations of the office by visiting a couple of her favourite haunts but, without the excuse that she was looking for new staff, the trips just seemed like tacky exercises for the sake of her own libido.

However, after seven days of obeying the no-fraternisation rule, Sam was on the verge of accepting

119

nine-to-five celibacy as part of her office routine. It was a perplexing lifestyle, completely devoid of meaning and purpose, she thought; but, if it meant Jo was happy, then it was something that Sam was prepared to tolerate. The following Friday, a week after she had first seen Todd, Sam burst into Jo's office, intending to announce that she was a convert to the ethos of keeping work and play as two separate issues. A part of her was hoping they could celebrate this good news with an elevenses diversion that might possibly have involved Jo's secretary but she never got to find out if something like that could have happened.

When she burst into the room, Sam caught Todd and Jo holding each other.

Their mouths were locked together, he cupping her breast through her jacket, she working her fingers down to his groin. The scene was so obvious that Sam hadn't needed any explanation to know what was happening. She turned and fled, deciding the most mature way of dealing with the whole episode was to walk away and stop talking to Jo.

Since then their only communication had been through sentences that sounded like the beginnings of an argument. Each of these had been stopped when she or Jo reminded the other that they weren't talking. As far as Sam was concerned, that was the way things would stay until Jo apologised.

Todd moved his mouth to her other breast and Sam groaned. She glanced beyond him and groaned louder. 'You suck tits really well,' she told him. She wasn't looking at Todd as she spoke. Her face was directed towards the closed van door and she was hoping her voice would carry through its panelled walls.

When the door remained obstinately closed, Sam realised that Jo wasn't outside listening to them and she cursed her partner for not having the decency to eavesdrop. She pushed Todd's head away and folded her arms across her chest before glaring moodily at the monitor.

'What's wrong?'

She shook her head, not sure she could answer the question. She had wanted him on the first day she saw him and she still wanted him now, but for entirely different reasons.

'Did I do something wrong? Or is it the case?'

She frowned, then remembered they were there on surveillance. Focusing an uninterested eye on the screen, she saw that Dr Grady and Jasmin were just off camera. There was something that looked like a bare backside in one small corner of the screen but Sam figured that was just an optical illusion brought on by her own licentious imagination. If it really was a backside, she knew it would have to belong to a kneeling Jasmin and her position suggested she was bent over Dr Grady's lap. Sam believed she might have been able to see things more clearly if she had retrieved her glasses but she knew they always made her face look vulnerable and that wasn't an image she wanted to go for this evening.

Deciding there was nothing of interest happening on screen, she turned back to Todd. 'What were you doing with Jo?'

He blushed and looked away.

'Last Friday, when I caught the pair of you in her office,' she reminded him. 'What were you doing?'

'Jo said I shouldn't talk to you about that. She said if you wanted to know what was going on you'd have to talk to her.'

'Jo and I aren't talking,' Sam pointed out. 'So, if I'm going to get an explanation, you'll have to give it to me.'

He shook his head. Glancing at the monitor, he attempted an expression of intrigue but Sam saw it was a façade. 'Hey, look,' he said, pointing at the screen. 'They got naked. Do you think we might already have the footage we need?'

'Tell me what you were doing.'

He turned back to her and frowned. 'I can't.'

She nodded as though she had expected such a denial, then reached for the waistband of her jeans and began to unfasten them. 'I never did get to show you where that chastity belt chafed me, did I?' Turning her back to him, she knelt on her seat and pulled the jeans down. She thrust her bare backside towards his face and asked, 'Can you see it clearly?' Reaching under herself, she pointed a finger between her legs and said, 'It's just there.'

Todd made no attempt to turn on the van's internal light. He pushed his face so close she could feel the heat of his blushing cheeks against her inner thighs. If he had moved any nearer, Sam knew she would have felt the delicious friction of his razor stubble grazing her buttocks.

'That must have hurt really bad,' Todd muttered sympathetically. His voice had lowered to a husky whisper.

'It did,' Sam agreed. 'It rubbed and rubbed at my pussy lips until they were unbearably sore.'

He moved his face closer and this time she could feel him against her. The hairs on his cheek scratched between her buttocks, sending shockwaves of excitement hurtling through her body. Glancing back at him, she saw that his eyes were gleaming with a reflection from the monitor.

'It must be the light in here,' Todd told her. 'But it doesn't actually look marked at the moment. From what I can see, you look perfect down there.'

'It's healed now,' she admitted, inching herself away from the scrub of his face. 'But it was terrible at the time. It was all red and tender for hours.'

Todd ran his fingers along the line where Sam pointed. He managed to caress a couple of the ginger tendrils that had escaped her last bikini waxing and she shivered. The sensation made her want to experience more and it took a phenomenal effort not to wriggle closer.

'And why were you wearing the chastity belt? Did you say it was for a bet, or was it something to do with a case?'

'Of course it wasn't a bet,' Sam laughed. 'Jo was deadly serious when she made me wear it. She said I'd been playing around too much.'

Todd licked his lips. His excitement was obvious and he continued trying to stimulate her. His finger stroked back and forth against her sex and Sam struggled to suppress her response.

He teased more forcefully and asked, 'Had you been playing around too much?'

Sam shrugged and shivered in the same instant. She considered asking him to stop, then decided she could endure another moment of his teasing. Bravely, she remained on all fours, trying not sway with the slow rhythm of his moving fingers. 'I guess I had been a bit naughty,' she confessed. 'I was quite happy to go out on an evening and pick up any man or woman that caught my eye. You wouldn't believe some of the things I did behind Jo's back.'

His fingers moved to the edge of her cleft and he casually stroked those hairs that remained there. A tingling thrill was being transmitted from each follicle he touched and Sam fought hard to resist the temptation he was offering.

'Maybe I would believe you,' he pressed. 'Why don't you tell me some of the things that you did?'

123

'It wasn't just on an evening,' Sam told him. 'I suppose that was one of the main reasons why Jo bought the chastity belt. I was being unprofessional with members of staff and Jo hates anything that lacks professionalism. Especially during office hours.'

'Unprofessional how?' He stroked the curls away from her labia and caressed the pout of her sex.

Sam stiffened and finally found the strength to pull away. It wasn't that she wanted to take herself out of his reach but she knew that she had exposed herself to temptation for too long. Another moment and she didn't doubt that passion would override common sense. She still wanted Todd. Judging by the pulse of her arousal she supposed she needed him. But, without the chance of Jo's catching her, Sam expected it would be an empty experience.

She sat down on the chair and folded her legs so that her sex was still facing him. It was one thing to deny herself the promise of pleasure but she thought it might work to her advantage if she kept Todd believing that something might happen between them. 'Perhaps we could exchange information,' she suggested. 'Perhaps I could tell you some of the things I was doing, in exchange for you telling me what was happening between you and Jo.'

He frowned and she could see he was going to say no. His mouth had started shaping the word and his head was tilting to one side in preparation for his shaking his head.

Speaking quickly, trying to make the offer seem more tempting and attractive, she said, 'Perhaps I could show you some of those things in exchange for that information.'

'What do you want to know?'

'What were you and Jo doing when I caught you in her office on Friday?'

He opened his mouth and Sam's heart skipped a beat. She could see that in spite of his reluctance he was going to give her an answer and she shifted position in her chair and leaned closer.

On screen, Dr Grady groaned. It was the sound of climactic release and it was sufficient to distract Sam and Todd from their conversation. They turned to the monitor in unison and watched the scene being played out there.

Dr Grady was standing in front of the camera, his shirt open and his trousers at his ankles. Jasmin knelt before him, one hand on his erection, guiding it towards her mouth. With Dr Grady's groan a white spray spurted from the end of his shaft. Jasmin chose that moment to move the length away from her lips and his seed spattered her face. Unconsciously, she turned to the camera and allowed herself to be caught with droplets of semen beading her forehead. Tears of his white spend trailed down her cheeks.

'That's enough,' Dr Grady gasped. 'You've done well for me.'

'I need to come,' Jasmin whispered. Her voice was almost too quiet for the hidden microphones to detect but Todd had done a good job of preparing the surveillance equipment. Her nearness to frustrated tears was replayed through the speakers in the van.

'You know our condition. You're paying a penance and that's not one of the ways that you're allowed to do it.'

'But I –'

'You have to leave now – you've already been here too long. You have to go to the church and cause chaos among the pagans.'

'Pagans?' Todd whispered. 'What's he talking about?'

Sam shrugged, not allowing her attention to be distracted.

'Before you leave,' Dr Grady continued, 'you may go to the bathroom. But you are only allowed there to wash. I will be angry if I think you've been pleasuring yourself.' He dragged Jasmin from the floor and started pushing her towards the door. He held her by the hair and seemed to be controlling her like an inept puppeteer. 'In fact,' he went on. 'I think it will probably be most prudent if I come with you.'

'I can go on my own,' she wailed.

'It's not that I don't trust you, but I think you'll be less likely to succumb to temptation if I'm there with you.' Roughly, he pushed the snuffling brunette through the doorway.

As it closed on their egress, Sam and Todd were left to study an empty room.

'I wonder what that was about.' Sam frowned.

Todd shook his head and sighed. 'I'd best call Jo and tell her we might have the footage she wanted.' He started moving forward in his seat, reaching for the mobile phone clipped to his waist.

'The footage she wanted?' Sam echoed. 'What exactly is our remit for this operation?'

He glanced at her with a flicker of impatience.

Sam pouted, ready to defend her ignorance by saying there was little point in all three agents on a surveillance team knowing every detail. Admittedly, prior to any covert operation, Jo usually briefed everyone concerned on the case's remit. But, because they weren't talking, Sam had seen little point in attending the preoperation meeting for this one.

Instead of berating her, Todd said, 'We're supposed to catch Dr Grady doing something embarrassing. I'm assuming that most conventional lay preachers would agree that film of themselves being sucked by a uni student comes under that category.'

'That's our remit for this case?' Sam frowned. 'It's not like Jo to take that sort of work.'

Todd shrugged. 'I did voice some doubts myself,' he admitted. 'But Jo assured me this was all on the level. She said she trusted the client implicitly.'

'Was it a male client?' Todd nodded. 'It wasn't the really hunky one who called in two days ago, was it? The muscular, gymnasium type?'

Todd frowned and then nodded once the memory was clearer. 'That sounds like him.'

Sam curled her hand into a fist and struck the side of her chair. 'She's getting to be worse than I ever was.'

Todd glanced at her doubtfully and then pressed a button on his mobile phone. The dial became a luminous green and the keys chirruped musically as he pressed them. 'I think I'd better just call Jo and tell her what's happened.'

Sam shook her head. 'You can't do that,' she said quickly. 'You can't do that because Jo hasn't got a mobile with her, and I think we were discussing something before Dr Grady came into our conversation.'

He depressed another button on his mobile and the keypad turned dark. A perplexed frown creased his forehead and Sam knew it had little to do with his not being able to communicate with Jo. He was studying her as she sat next to him and although his gaze switched between her bare breasts and the crease of her sex she could see he was now mastering those impulses that had brought him close to giving in and answering her questions.

'I'm not sure that I –'

'Weren't we going to have an exchange of information?'

He shook his head. 'Should we be doing that? Here and now?'

Sam leaned forward in her chair and placed an arm around his shoulder. Her lips hovered close to his mouth and she smiled into the growing shine in his eyes. 'I think it's vital that we have that exchange here and now.' She cupped the bulge at his groin and said, 'It's what I want, and I think it's what you want, too.'

'I'd feel like a cheat if I betrayed Jo's trust in me,' Todd told her. 'She did say that I shouldn't tell you what was happening and that if you wanted to know –'

Sam stopped his words with a kiss. Her mouth covered his and she silenced his squirming tongue with her own. She waited until he had started responding to her passion before easing her lips away. 'You were kissing her, weren't you? You and Jo were kissing each other.'

'Yes.'

'Why were you kissing her?'

'Do people need a reason to kiss?'

She pushed her mouth back over his. Between his legs, she worked her hand more firmly against his erection. His stiffness swelled at the front of his pants and she wriggled her fingers against him with an unspoken promise of what lay ahead. His hardness grew in her palm and she knew she was on the verge of recapturing his interest.

'Why were you kissing her?' Sam repeated.

'Jo asked me not to say.'

'What else did you plan on doing?'

'You should be asking Jo these questions.'

'You know that Jo and I aren't talking, so *you'll* have to supply the answers. What else did you plan on doing?'

'I'd have done whatever she let me,' Todd confessed. 'I'd have done whatever she told me, but that's not the issue here, is it?'

Frowning, Sam sat back in her chair and realised he was right. It didn't matter how Todd thought that morning might have progressed for himself and Jo. The important points were knowing why Jo was doing it and how far she would have gone.

'I have to know why you were kissing.'

'Jo should be the one answering questions like this.'

Sam nodded angrily, working her thoughts quickly towards a way of making him tell her. 'If you can't say what you were doing, can you *show* me?'

'Say again.'

'If you can't *say* what you were doing, can you show me? Can you show me how you were kissing? Can you show me how you were holding her?'

'I don't know if –'.

Sam wasn't listening. She dragged him from his chair and stood up so they were face to face. The jeans were still around her calves, making her posture precarious and unladylike, but she knew it would sour the promise of arousal if she pulled them back up. To keep his interest at a premium, Sam knew she couldn't spoil that emotion. She cast her mind back to the Friday morning when she had caught the pair and tried to remember exactly how Jo had been holding him. The image had been replayed in her mind's eye so many times it wasn't difficult to capture the pose. She snaked one arm around his waist and placed her other hand over his groin.

Todd fell naturally into position, embracing her waist with his left arm and cupping the swell of her breast with his right hand. His fingertips casually stimulated her nipple, and Sam stiffened.

'This is what the scene looked like to me,' she told him. Her voice had deepened to a husky pant and excitement came close to making her croak the words. 'Would you say we've reconstructed the scene fairly accurately?'

His erection twitched beneath her fingertips. 'It was pretty much like this,' he agreed. He was trying to feign nonchalance but his growing need for her gleamed in his eyes.

'What happened just before this?'

'How do you mean?'

'In the moment that led up to this? What had the pair of you been doing or saying?'

Todd sighed heavily. His face was so close she could see his unhappiness at having to break a confidence. 'I shouldn't be telling you this. You should really be asking Jo.'

'What had the pair of you been doing in the moment that led up to this?'

'Jo asked me if I wanted to kiss her, to confirm our date.'

'Date?' Sam took a step back and almost fell because of the jeans at her ankles. 'You and Jo have been on a date?'

He shook his head and held his hands out to steady her. Sam tried to brush him away but he was determined to stop her from falling. 'We haven't been on a date. We were sorting out the details for our first one when you burst in.'

'Where were you going to go?'

He shook his head. 'I've said enough already. I've probably said too much.'

'You haven't said nearly enough.'

'I've said as much as I'm going to say.'

She resisted the urge to growl with frustration and eased herself from his embrace. Settling herself back in the chair, she said, 'Jo and I used to interview potential staff together. Do you know what I used to do during those interviews?'

He said nothing and she could see he was fighting not to get caught by his arousal again.

Determined that he wouldn't win the battle of wills, Sam said, 'I'd go to the interview wearing a short skirt and no knickers. I'd sit in front of the interviewee and slyly flash myself at them.'

In the van's thickening silence, she heard Todd swallow. He glanced at her and she supposed that with proper lighting she would have seen his excited blush.

'I did it very discreetly,' she explained. 'Jo and I would be sitting behind an open-backed desk and the interviewee would be placed so they had the perfect view. It was fun to watch some of them squirm as they pretended not to notice. It was more fun to watch the others as they tried to answer Jo's probing questions while I discreetly touched myself.'

To illustrate what she meant, Sam licked her index finger and stroked it against her sex. She shivered as she caressed her own flesh and widened her grin for him. 'Occasionally, if we got a good-looking one and got them really horny, Jo and I would share them. It didn't happen often from interviews, but Jo and I used to share our best lovers a lot. We usually did it together so we could help each other to achieve the best results.'

'I'm not telling you any more about what went on that morning,' he said determinedly.

She continued as though he hadn't spoken. She licked the tip of her finger again, not sure whether she was trying to moisten it for when she next touched herself, or savour the scent that lingered there. Her arousal was fragrant and sweet and the perfume of her own musk always excited her. 'I'm sure you could share a couple more details with me. Where were you going on your date?'

'Ask Jo.'

She returned her finger back to her sex and stroked back and forth over the folds of flesh. He was watching intently and Sam realised she had recaptured his interest. The thought was confirmed when she watched him lick his lips. 'Jo's not here, so I'm asking you. What would have happened if I hadn't arrived when I did?'

'I don't know.'

'You'd have done anything she asked, wouldn't you?'

'I might have.'

She eased the tip of her finger inside herself, surprised by how easily it slid in there. When she removed it, the end was glistening with her dewy excitement. 'How much longer would your kiss have gone on if I hadn't burst in?'

'I don't know.'

'How much further would it have gone?'

His blush was so severe she could even see it now in spite of the van's poor lighting. 'I don't know what you mean.'

She shook her head. 'You know exactly what I mean. It wasn't just the lips on her face that you wanted to kiss, was it?'

'I suppose not.'

'If she'd said "tongue my pussy", what would you have done?'

He licked his lips again. His hand went to the front of his pants and he rubbed at his hardness as though it was an annoying itch.

'Answer me, Todd,' Sam pressed. 'We've just re-enacted that kiss for you. Was it as exciting as the way Jo kissed?'

'Yes.'

'Did it make you feel the same as when Jo kissed you?'

'Yes.'

'So, if I now said "tongue my pussy", what would you do?'

Before she could stop him he had dropped to his knees. He placed a hand on each thigh and rubbed his tongue over the pulsing nub of her clitoris. His mouth was the skilled tool she had known it would be and the sensations he evoked were debilitating. She arched her back against the chair and squirmed on to his face.

It occurred to her that this would be the ideal moment for Jo to return. The idea had the appeal of perfect revenge and she could imagine the hurt on her partner's face as she stepped into the van and saw what was happening.

'*What the hell are you doing?*' she knew Jo would ask.

She pictured herself smiling through a haze of bliss brought on by Todd's tongue. She imagined herself pushing his face back to her pussy and waiting until he resumed his kisses before she deigned to reply.

'*We're not doing anything that you weren't planning on doing last Friday,*' she would respond. '*But don't worry. This is the same brand of no fraternisation that you use.*'

It was a satisfying scenario because in it Sam had the best of all worlds. She had Todd's tongue exactly where she wanted it and she was exacting a beautiful revenge on her adulterous partner. The scenario would have been perfection if it could have ended with Jo spanking and punishing her. That mental image alone would have been enough to bring her close to orgasm. With the addition of Todd's writhing tongue at her pussy lips, Sam wondered how she was managing to contain her base needs. Remembering there was one other piece of information she required before she could properly surrender herself, she tried to catch the breath that was needed for a final question.

Todd gripped her thighs hard and tugged her so his mouth could work more adeptly. His tongue burrowed deep inside and the wet friction sent her dizzy with growing desire.

She swallowed and forced her arousal to the back of her mind. 'Where were you going on your date?'

Instead of answering, he snatched his mouth from her pussy and placed it over her breast. His groin pressed against her sex and the weight of his erection pulsed through the fabric of his zip.

'Was she going to take you to our favourite restaurant?' Sam gasped. 'Is that why you aren't telling me?'

He moved his mouth to her other breast and shards of delicious pleasure erupted from it. She panted to ask another question, contemplated not bothering, then bristled as he clamped her nipple between his teeth.

'Was she going to take you to the pictures or the theatre? Was she going to take you to see one of our favourite films or shows?'

Todd said nothing. His hands slipped from her thighs and when she glanced down at him she saw he was unfastening his trousers. His erection was briefly illuminated in the dim light, then it was cloaked in shadows as he pushed towards her needy hole.

Sam gasped, biting back a hungry cry.

Todd guided his shaft towards her, holding the head over her gaping lips. He continued biting and sucking her breasts, then returned one hand to hold her leg in the air. She could feel herself being spread for him and knew that his urgent desire matched her own.

'You have to tell me,' Sam whispered. 'Where were you going on your date?'

He glared down at her with an exasperated frown. His shaft rested over her pussy lips and when he spoke she could feel every word's vibration tingling at her sex. 'Ask Jo. When she comes back here, why don't you ask Jo?'

'I'm asking you,' Sam told him.

'Can't you think of better things for us to do than ask questions that I'm not going to answer?' He nudged his pelvis forward and his cock nuzzled closer.

The head was on the verge of penetrating her and Sam considered thrusting herself on to him. It would take only a small push of her hips and she would be welcoming his shaft between her greedy labia. His penetration was something she wanted badly and Sam could almost savour its entry before he had begun. She wanted to have him on top of her and yearned to feel him pounding between her legs.

Surprising herself, she whispered, 'No, Todd.'

'Say again.'

The idea of having him suddenly seemed all wrong. Her body still craved his penetration but her mind was screeching that it wouldn't be right. Throughout the week that she obeyed Jo's no-fraternisation rule she had wanted to give in to every temptation imaginable, but, out of deference to Jo, she had suppressed those urges. After seeing her and Todd kiss, Sam had wanted to have some sort of revenge but she didn't want it like this. If she allowed Todd to take her now it wouldn't be the culmination of her plans that she had wanted. Of course, she could give Jo a blow-by-blow account of what had happened, but that would be a cheap alternative to the way she wanted things to progress. Weighing up all the options, Sam thought it would be far more satisfying for Jo to catch her and Todd together. That was what she had been planning all evening and she was determined not to spoil that scenario just because of her demanding lust.

Common sense and the lateness of the hour were telling her that Jo wasn't going to interrupt and, when she listened to that voice, Sam realised a part of her mind was starting to worry about why her partner had been away for so long. She sighed heavily and tried to pull herself away from him. 'No, Todd,' Sam repeated, surprising herself with her sudden display of willpower. 'We can't do this. I promised Jo that I wouldn't.'

She could see from his injured frown that he wanted to raise a million reasons as to why she could do this. He had struggled with his own conscience before coming this close to having her and she could see he had convinced himself it was a logical progression of events. Wanting to speak over his objections before he could raise them, Sam glanced at the monitor and saw a new face there that she hadn't seen before. It was a striking blonde woman and it struck Sam as peculiar that she seemed to be wearing a cowl. 'There's something happening in the house,' she told Todd. 'And I think Jo's been gone for too long now.'

'Maybe she's giving us a little time together,' Todd suggested. He lowered his mouth back to her pussy and planted a delicate kiss against her clitoris.

It had taken a lot of effort to resist him and Sam almost gave in when he tongued her again. His mouth warmed her sex and the gentle stimulation promised fulfilment of the unsatisfied needs she was harbouring. Sam suppressed the urge to give in and pulled herself properly out of his reach. 'Maybe she's in trouble,' she said seriously. She tugged her jeans back on, ignoring her body's protests at this turn of events. 'There's something weird going on in that house and a good investigator wouldn't just stay here waiting to see it happen on the CCTV monitor.'

Still naked, Todd held his erection with one hand and frowned as she started to dress. She could see he was hurt by her sudden refusal to surrender and a part of her wanted to assure him that it wasn't because she didn't want him. She decided not to give him that comfort, knowing it would only lead them back into each other's arms.

'What are you planning on doing?' he asked.

'Like I said, a good investigator would get out there and find out what's happening,' she told him.

He grunted sourly, not concealing his obvious resentment. 'A good investigator has already done that. Isn't that where Jo went?'

'Jo Valentine isn't the only good investigator in this agency,' Sam sniffed. She was secretly satisfied by his jibe against her because it stopped her from thinking how sexy he looked with his shaft in his hand and her pussy honey glistening against his chin. She glanced at the console of monitors and electrical boxes and asked, 'Will this stuff continue to record even if we're not here to play with it?'

Todd nodded.

'Good.' Sam fastened her waistband and pulled the T-shirt back over her head. 'If that's the case, we should go and see what's happening in Dr Grady's house.'

'Hold on a second.' Todd placed a hand against her arm as she made for the door. At first she thought he was going to try to embrace her, or kiss her, or do something else that might stimulate her thoughts back to the direction where they had just been. She contemplated brushing his hand away, not sure she could resist him if he did that. However, instead of looking at her, Todd was watching the screen intently. 'There's more activity in the room. Something's happening with the new arrival.'

Forgetting her ideas about prowling around in the night outside, Sam sat down in front of the black-and-white monitor and watched.

Six

The tall blonde woman entered the room and Jasmin was struck by her air of self-assurance. She was barefoot and wearing only a shapeless cowl, but she held herself with a majesty that was inspiring. Each step revealed she was naked beneath her cloak – the garment wasn't fastened and her long legs stepped through the split – but the striking blonde seemed either oblivious or unmindful. It didn't seem to trouble her that her breasts were close to spilling from the coarse hessian wrapped around her chest. When she released her hold on the fabric around her waist, she didn't seem bothered by the glimpse of dark blonde curls she was exposing. She stepped close to Dr Grady, pressed a dry kiss against his cheek and said, 'Hello darling. I've come to ask you a favour.'

'Dinah!' He looked shocked and Jasmin could see he was struggling to disguise his surprise. 'You're here earlier than I . . .' He paused and drew a deep breath before correcting himself. 'I mean, this is an early hour for you to be calling.'

'I have a dilemma. I thought perhaps you could help me resolve it.'

He frowned. 'I thought you and your fellow heathens would be desecrating the abandoned church by now.'

'We're not desecrating the church: we're only making use of it. But yes. That's where I've just come from.' She stared at him quizzically. 'How did you know that?'

'It's the first of May,' he snapped. 'Even I know that your godless horde celebrate Beltane on the first of May.'

Uncomfortable, Jasmin shifted from foot to foot. There was an undercurrent of antipathy between the pair and while their words had the ring of an oft-repeated argument she sensed it had the potential to turn ugly. Dinah's deportment and obvious strong will gave Jasmin the impression of an independent spirit who didn't tolerate rudeness or insults. Not bothering to disguise his contempt, Dr Grady was being as confrontational as possible and Jasmin felt sure this combination was a volatile blend.

'We're not godless,' Dinah told him firmly. 'We just worship in a different way from how you do it.' She shook her head as though making that point was an unnecessary distraction. 'But that's not what I meant. How did you know we'd be at the abandoned church?'

He shrugged. 'I assumed you'd be choosing your replacement. Your more important ceremonies invariably end up there.'

Dinah grunted humourless laughter. 'That's exactly what Steve said.'

'I'd rather you didn't mention his name in here,' Dr Grady sneered. 'It's bad enough that I'm suffering a witch without having to suffer the name of her consort as well. What's your dilemma, Dinah? If you're here to ask me to reconsider the transfer, my original answer still stands.'

Dinah glanced at Jasmin and graced her with a cool appraisal. Her expression was so shrewd that

140

Jasmin felt grateful that Dr Grady had allowed her the chance to clean up after his final climax. Even feeling confident that she no longer bore any trace of what had gone between them, Dinah's discriminating stare made Jasmin feel as though rivulets of his semen still coated her face. The woman was studying her as though she knew exactly what had gone on before she arrived.

'Who is this?'

Dr Grady glanced at Jasmin and frowned. 'Formal introductions,' he grumbled sarcastically. 'How remiss of me to forget such niceties at nearly half past one in the morning. Dinah, I'd like you to meet Jasmin Atkinson, the youngest daughter of our employer Major Atkinson. Jasmin, I'd like to introduce my estranged wife, and leader of the local band of heathens, Dr Dinah Grady.'

Jasmin stepped forward and offered a polite hand. She didn't want to be polite – every instinct in her body was demanding she run from the room and get away from the confrontational atmosphere – but she had already decided her position was inescapable and she didn't want to remain and have Dr Dinah Grady think she was rude. 'You two share the village practice that Daddy owns, don't you?'

'Until the end of the week,' Dinah told her, 'yes.'

Her voice was crisp and Jasmin realised she had touched on a sensitive subject.

Dinah glared at Dr Grady and added, 'After the end of the week, one of us is expected to leave our practice in the hands of the other and take up residence in the inner-city health centre that your father's just acquired. And that's two hundred miles away.'

Jasmin wished she could retract the words that had brought this topic into the open. 'Daddy mentioned something about that,' she mumbled.

Dr Grady's grin widened. 'You'll be a natural for the role,' he assured Dinah.

Dinah continued to glare at him. Beneath her air of serenity she looked to be struggling to contain an angry outburst. She turned back to Jasmin and asked, 'What on earth are you doing here at this time of night?'

Before Jasmin could reply, Dr Grady was answering the question. 'Major Atkinson asked me to help Jasmin deal with an issue at her university,' he said quickly. 'I don't think the details would interest you.'

Dinah sniffed and shook her head. 'I can already imagine how you're dealing with it,' she told him. With a forced smile, she turned back to Jasmin and said, 'You have a sister, don't you? Is she still at the university, or is she here as well?'

Again, before Jasmin could reply, Dr Grady was speaking for her.

'Did you just visit to discuss social issues with Jasmin? Or did you say that a dilemma had brought you here?'

It was another of his confrontational statements, delivered in a tone that killed Dinah's attempts at polite conversation.

Jasmin glanced at him, aware from his frown that he didn't want her to answer Dinah's questions. Knowing there would be punishment for going against his wishes, she held her tongue and stepped back against the wall to distance herself from the conversation.

Dinah fixed her gaze on Dr Grady, a flash of her eyes conveying the fact that she was reluctant to discuss her business in front of Jasmin. Dr Grady saw the expression but he was obviously gleaning too much satisfaction from her discomfort. Clearly happy to grasp a further opportunity to make his estranged wife feel even more ill at ease, he said, 'You can say whatever you like in front of Jasmin. If you've come here to discuss your pagan colleagues you'll only embarrass yourself, not her.'

Dinah passed Jasmin an untrusting scowl and then turned back to him. 'My coven is trying to choose a new leader,' she began. 'We have two potential choices and we can't decide which of them should be invested. I was hoping that with you being the keeper of the village's Christian faith –'

'*Two* potential choices,' Dr Grady broke in. 'How did that happen?'

Watching him, Jasmin wondered why his behaviour was so odd. Before Dinah turned up he had confided that he was expecting his estranged wife's arrival but, when she entered the house, he had tried to pretend her visit was unexpected. As he had also predicted, Dinah was asking him to resolve a dilemma but he now looked genuinely surprised that she had such a problem for him to deal with. She wondered if there was some element in his schemes that he hadn't calculated for and she listened intently, trying to work out what was happening.

Dinah seemed oblivious to her estranged husband's odd behaviour and pressed on with what she had been trying to say. She drew a deep breath and said, 'I was hoping, that with you being the keeper of the village's Christian faith, you could help us in the traditional way.'

'Two potential choices,' he repeated.

'Yes.' Dinah sounded on the verge of becoming irritable.

'And you want me to help in the traditional way?'

'You always claimed it was one of your abilities.'

He sniffed dismissively. 'It is. You know I can trace my genealogy straight back to the Witchfinder General, Matthew Hopkins.'

Dinah shook her head as though this information disappointed her. 'I see it's still something you're proud of. But will you do it?'

He stepped away from her and Jasmin watched his confidence return. If there had been an aspect of this evening that he hadn't accounted for, Jasmin could see he was still happy with the way things were working out. He glanced at Dinah's half-shrouded body, his smile a wide leer. 'You want my help in return for what?'

Dinah chewed on her lower lip and glanced at Jasmin again.

Jasmin blushed and wondered whether she should offer to leave the room. She didn't make the suggestion, scared that Dr Grady might refuse or, even worse, use the opportunity to mention her shameful need to masturbate. The idea of having that urge exposed in front of a stranger was unsettling enough to make her stay silent.

'I've told you that, whatever you have to say, you can say it in front of Jasmin. It's late, Dinah. Just get on with it and tell me what you're offering.'

'Can't you just do it for old times' sake?' she asked. 'Can't you just do it as an act of kindness for all those years we shared together?'

His grin was twisted with cruel mirth. 'No,' he said eventually. 'I can't do it for those reasons. If you need my help you'll have to offer a better inducement than that.'

Dinah frowned but Jasmin couldn't see any surprise in the woman's face. 'I assume your appetites are still as dark as ever. I assume you still get your pleasure from the suffering of others. I assume you still have the heart of a flagellant.'

Jasmin stared down at the carpet. Memories of what she and Dr Grady had done earlier flitted through her mind and the shame turned her cheeks crimson. She contemplated rubbing a consoling hand over her backside, sure that the act of recollection was rekindling the dull glow that burned there. Judiciously, she decided that wouldn't be a sensible thing to do. The punishment hadn't been without its pleasures and she feared the pressure of her own hand might provide too much comfort and excite her need once again.

Dr Grady laughed, the sound echoing from the walls. 'If that's how you'd like to phrase it, then yes, I still have the heart of a flagellant. What are you offering me, Dinah?'

'I'm offering you the chance to thrash two feminine backsides.'

He sniffed. 'It's not enough.'

She frowned, then blundered on as though he hadn't spoken. 'I'm offering you the chance to take your cat-o'-nine-tails and indulge yourself with two supine young creatures as you try to determine which of them belongs at the head of my coven.'

'I said it's not enough.'

Her air of serenity looked close to being destroyed. An expression of bewilderment flushed her cheeks and she shook her head. 'Your appetites can't have changed that much. What more could you want?'

His smile was rapacious. 'There's one backside that I've been longing to chastise for the last year. Perhaps, if you offered me that one, I might agree to help.'

'No.' She took a step backwards. 'You're not doing that.'

'There's one backside that I've been wanting to thrash since you left me,' Dr Grady mused. 'I've tried to picture it each time I've had the opportunity to mete out chastisement, but I'm sure that the reality would be far better than anything my imagination can conjure up. If you want me to help you find your replacement, that's the price you'll have to pay.'

'No,' she said. 'I won't do that.' She was shaking her head vehemently, her eyes no longer meeting his. When she had entered the room she had displayed her nudity like a badge of courage. Now she cinched her cloak tight around her waist, concealing her naked body from his lewd appraisal. She seemed unaware that this accentuated her figure, revealing the inviting swell of her backside and the roundness of her breasts. Her entire body language seemed focused on trying to impart the message that she wanted nothing to do with his suggestion. 'Not that,' she repeated. 'I won't do that.'

'If you want me to help find your replacement you will do it.'

Dinah stared at him with obvious desperation. 'Isn't it enough that I'm giving up my practice? Isn't it enough that you're forcing me to leave the village? Isn't it enough that I'm forsaking my position as a religious leader?'

'Your paganism is hardly a religion,' he sneered. 'And those other things are just fortuitous bonuses. If you want my help, you will do it.'

'Is that your final word?'

'Unless you think you can persuade me otherwise, yes, it is my final word.' He delivered the sentence as though it was a challenge.

Jasmin watched the pair, not sure what sort of relationship they had enjoyed when they were husband and wife, only certain that it must have been passionate. For two people to harbour so much antipathy, she believed they must have once shared a very strong need for each other. She could see options being considered and discounted in the openness of

Dinah's face and she was struck by the woman's discomfort at having to have this conversation in front of a stranger. Dinah clearly had no problems about publicly displaying her beliefs or her body but it seemed that discussing her private life left her feeling exposed and vulnerable.

Nevertheless, as though she was trying to defy Dr Grady and rise to his challenge, Dinah shrugged off her cowl. It fell from her shoulders and pooled at her ankles.

Jasmin gasped, surprised by the woman's brazen display and impressed in the same instant. With the hessian wrapped tight around her it had been clear Dinah possessed an enviable figure. Revealed, she was an image of feminine perfection. Jasmin had never considered herself so prudish that she couldn't admire another woman's body, but looking at Dinah she felt the tug of another emotion. There was something about the firmness of the woman's breasts and the stiffness of her nipples that made Jasmin want to touch Dinah. Shocked by the sudden rush of desire, she turned away and fixed her gaze on the floor.

Dinah stepped close to Dr Grady and traced her fingers down the front of his shirt. 'Perhaps I could offer you something else,' she whispered. 'We always enjoyed a wonderfully physical relationship before our marriage broke up. Perhaps we could revisit one of those moments in exchange for your helping me.'

He shook his head from side to side. 'You no longer excite me the way you used to,' he said coldly. 'I don't think that would work.'

Dinah continued in spite of his rude rebuke. 'I've always been able to excite you in the past.'

'I've grown impervious to your charms,' he chuckled. He glanced at Jasmin and she blushed before looking away.

Dinah missed the exchange, her fingers snaking down to his groin. 'Are you sure I can't offer you something other than the price you're suggesting?'

'If you want my services to help you choose your new leader you know what I want from you. You can either agree to have your backside thrashed, or you can go. It's all the same to me.'

Jasmin couldn't decide whether to watch or turn away. Dr Grady stood with his back to the fireplace as a naked Dinah made more attempts to arouse him. She unzipped his trousers and took his flaccid shaft from his pants before working on him with a vigorous movement of her wrist.

'You no longer have your hold over me,' Dr Grady informed her. His voice was cold and distant. 'The arousal you inspired is a disease to which I am now immune.'

Jasmin saw a flicker of panic on Dinah's face. The woman fell to her knees and started licking at his soft length.

Dr Grady was grinning as though his own lack of response was giving him enormous pleasure. He stretched his fingers until the knuckles cracked. 'You're wasting your time trying to excite me, Dinah,' he said cheerfully. 'I'm beyond the reach of your witchcraft now. Either pay the price I'm demanding, or take your heathen charms and leave here.'

Dinah continued as though he hadn't spoken. She moved her mouth over his shaft and sucked so furiously her cheeks dimpled. When her lips moved away from his length he was glistening with saliva but he remained soft and unerect. The circumcised head was a bloodless lilac, the same pallid colour as the rest of his shaft.

'Should I make the decision for you?' Dr Grady suggested. 'You needed my help badly enough to come here for it. You were prepared to pay one price in exchange for my services. I'm sure the circumstances at your coven haven't changed while you've been here, so you'd better be ready to do as I've asked.'

'There must be something else.' She whispered the words with a tone of desperation.

Dr Grady shook his head. His eyes were shining with unconcealed triumph.

Reluctantly, Dinah eased herself away from him. She placed his flaccid shaft back inside his trousers, then zipped him up. She stepped gracefully back to her feet and glared at him unhappily. 'You want to thrash my backside.'

'That's right.'

'And in return you'll help my coven with their dilemma?'

'That's the arrangement I offered.'

She sighed heavily and glanced at Jasmin. 'If I'm going to suffer that, I want it to happen while we're alone. I don't want her watching.'

Jasmin wanted to sigh with relief. Her body still ached with the pent-up tension of not having achieved climax and she was thankful that Dinah was creating an excuse for her to leave the room. Her arousal for the woman was disturbing enough and she didn't think she could cope with the additional excitement of watching the blonde's backside being punished. Until this evening she hadn't known there were pleasures to be gleaned from such discipline but after suffering Dr Grady's brief introduction she was scared by the world of delights he had shown her. Taking his dismissal for granted, she started towards the door.

'Jasmin stays,' he said firmly. His smile tightened a notch as both women began to protest. 'She may leave the room briefly.' He glanced at Jasmin and said, 'I have a Gladstone bag in my bedroom. You can go and retrieve that for me. But when you return you will stay and, if I insist, you will help.'

Meekly, Jasmin nodded.

She heard Dinah spluttering oaths at Dr Grady but the words had the sound of something mystical and distance made them inaudible as she rushed out of the room and tried to find his bedroom. She navigated the house's geography easily enough and found the Gladstone bag at the foot of his bed. She briefly toyed with the idea of exorcising the orgasm her body needed, then decided she didn't dare to do that. It was a tempting idea, and she could picture herself sprawled on his bed, touching herself, then shivering as the desperate pleasure racked its way through her frame. Her nearness to climax was so close she didn't doubt it would take more than the pressure of a single finger to have her shrieking with relief. However, she knew that if she took a moment longer than was necessary Dr Grady would know what she had been up to. Even if he only suspected it, she believed he would see it as grounds to punish her and she was loath to suffer that indignity again.

She glanced out of the bedroom window, wondering where Melissa had gone and how quickly she and her sister would be able to be reunited and put this terrible night behind them. Aside from the large Transit van she had noticed when she and Melissa entered the priest's house, the street was deserted. Her hopes for a sudden end to the ordeal began to plummet and she hurried quickly back to where Dr Grady and Dinah were waiting.

'I don't want her to watch this,' Dinah insisted.

'You don't have a say in what happens,' Dr Grady reminded her. 'And, if you keep trying to lay down your demands, she won't just be watching. I can always give her an active part in this.'

Dinah was bent over with her backside held high in the air. Jasmin felt a wave of sympathy for the woman's plight, knowing how humiliating the posture was. She knew she would have died from embarrassment if Dr Grady had made someone else stand in attendance while she endured her chastisement and she thanked circumstances for saving her from that indignity.

Dr Grady took the Gladstone bag and unfastened its clasp before reaching inside. His solemn features brightened as he retrieved first one whip, then a second and finally a third.

Glancing uneasily at them, Jasmin saw each was slightly different: a short one with thin tendrils; a longer one, with thick leather fingers; and the final one with its long, thin strands knotted at the end. She didn't know anything about whips but she suspected that each of these could rightly be called a cat-o'-nine-tails. Dr Grady reached for the shortest of the three and tested it through the air. The whip sighed like a startled breath and Jasmin and Dinah flinched in unison.

He stepped towards Dinah's bare backside and reached out to stroke her flesh. His broad hands cupped one cheek, then the other, and his fingers rested briefly over the curls covering her sex. 'Beg for my forgiveness,' Dr Grady muttered. His fingers wriggled against her cleft and Jasmin wondered whether he wasn't deliberately trying to stimulate his estranged wife. 'Beg for my forgiveness, and perhaps this won't be as intolerable as you're anticipating.'

'It's already intolerable,' Dinah grunted. 'But the idea of begging you for anything is more unbearable. Get this over and done with, so we can get up to the church.'

His frown returned. Jasmin pitied Dinah's position as she saw how much worse the woman had just made her situation. Dr Grady had been intent on punishing her before but now it was clear that he was going to make the indignity as demeaning as possible. The whip hurtled down against her arse and landed with a dozen wet slapping sounds. Dinah stiffened but made no noise in protest and Dr Grady raised the whip for a second time.

Jasmin watched the scene, wishing she could drag her gaze away. She could see that Dr Grady's erection was threatening to resurface and she wondered whether he was aware that he was rubbing at his growing stiffness. The bulge wasn't that noticeable but it prodded against the front of his trousers like a lame finger and it seemed to stiffen each time his left hand worked against it. His right hand held the whip and he raised it again before throwing it down with a furious weight that scoured both Dinah's buttocks.

The blow struck with enough force to make her grunt with dissatisfaction.

'Was that you begging for forgiveness?'

Dinah shook her head.

Dr Grady threw another blow against her backside. 'Beg for my forgiveness and I might show some leniency.'

She was squirming to maintain her posture, clearly suffering beneath the sting of the whip. Her breathing was coming in guttural rasps but when she turned to stare at him her eyes shone with defiance. 'Do you know, if I didn't think it was impossible, I'd swear that you'd engineered this whole scenario.'

Dr Grady looked as though he was trying to feign ignorance. He attempted to laugh off the suggestion, then stopped, as though he realised how artificial the sound was. 'Whatever do you mean?'

Dinah fixed him with her stare. 'I left you because of your whipping games and now it looks like you're having your ultimate revenge on me.'

This time his laughter was derisory and not forced. 'You're reading too much into this, Dinah,' he assured her. 'You didn't just leave me because of my whipping games. Part of our separation was due to religious differences, and a greater part of it was down to your growing relationship with Steve.'

Dinah said nothing as she tolerated another blow to her offered cheeks. He sliced a second one before she could catch her breath and she sucked air nosily through her teeth.

'If I'd really engineered this whole thing, don't you think there'd be other events happening to make my revenge perfect? Don't you think I'd be forcing you to break up your relationship with Steve? Don't you think I'd be trying to destroy your coven, or force you to work in one of the vilest areas in this country?'

'But all of those things are happening,' Dinah wailed.

He chuckled. 'So they are. Isn't that just the meanest of coincidences? It's almost as though the good Lord has had a hand in trying to end your unholy ways.'

Dinah turned to face him. The shine of tears glistened in her eyes. 'If I ever learn that you've been behind all of this . . .'

'You're being irrational, Dinah.'

'If I ever learn that you're responsible for –'

'Your dilemma is that you're trying to choose between two potential leaders for your coven,' he reminded her. 'How could I have organised for one of them to be at the church when you arrived there, let alone two?'

'– I'd pay you back for this and more,' she growled.

He hurled the whip at her backside for a final time, forcing her to squeal with surprise. Her arse cheeks were peppered with red speckles where the cat had bitten hardest. The moonlike buttocks were a flustered blush underneath those marks and, watching the scene, Jasmin empathised with Dinah's suffering. Earlier Dr Grady had reddened her own backside with the palm of his hand and she knew that the punishment was made more severe because it wasn't all discomfort. The rouging of her bottom had fuelled the warmth at her sex and the whole episode had caused her need for relief to grow enormously. Watching Dinah suffer blow after blow, Jasmin felt the resurgence of her carnal appetite as she longed to participate more fully.

'I think we've warmed you up sufficiently,' he said. He reached for a longer whip, selecting the cat with the thicker tails. 'You should really start begging for my forgiveness now,' he warned her. 'It will really start hurting after this.'

Dinah turned away from him and studied the floor.

Dr Grady snapped his fingers and Jasmin realised he was summoning her.

'Check Dinah's backside,' he barked. 'Make sure that the chastisement has properly warmed her.'

'I don't know what to . . .'

'Just do it,' he growled.

Not sure what she was meant to be doing, Jasmin stepped behind Dinah and reached a tentative hand towards her buttocks. She stroked the reddened flesh, allowing her fingers to brush the darkest pimples where the cat had made its worst marks. She was aware of the woman flinching beneath her touch but, more than that, she was aware of the sensation of warmth. Stroking her fingers over Dinah's backside she felt the electric crackle that was always there when she caressed a lover's body. The temptation to snatch her hands away was almost irresistible but she knew Dr Grady would be displeased if she did that.

Continuing to touch and explore, Jasmin tried not to wonder if Dinah had felt the same tingle pass between them. From the corner of her eye she could see that the blonde was looking at her, but Jasmin deliberately stopped herself from meeting her gaze.

'Has she been warmed?'

'I think so,' Jasmin mumbled. She took her hands away, grateful for the excuse to break the contact. Her fingertips tingled as though they were carrying the heat of Dinah's excitement, and that thought was a spur to her arousal.

Dr Grady stepped past her and plunged two fingers into Dinah's sex. He was brusque and plundered her with scant regard for her feelings. As he pushed his fingers deeper, he rested a hand against her buttocks and squeezed the ravaged flesh.

Dinah drew a shuddering breath.

Jasmin heard herself echo the unspoken sentiment.

'She's more than warm,' Dr Grady grinned. 'She's close to melting.'

Dinah blushed. She stared coldly at the floor as her face turned the colour of her reddened backside. She shook her head as though she was repudiating Dr Grady's suggestion, but there was something in the flush of her face that told Jasmin she was denying the truth.

Dr Grady slid his fingers free and raised his whip again. 'Beg for forgiveness,' he commanded, striking hard against her backside.

Dinah grunted. 'Never.'

'Say that you were wrong to leave me,' he insisted. He flicked the cat against her buttocks and it landed with a crackle. The sound was so blistering that Jasmin flinched as though she was the one being struck.

Unmindful of the force he was using, Dr Grady hurled the whip again and again. The sounds of the leather descending became a blur as his pace increased to a frenetic tempo.

Dinah's muttered protests turned into a ragged sigh as she lost the capacity to articulate her discomfort. Bent over, with her hair almost veiling her face, she looked close to tears. Her cheeks were a flushed purple that could have been caused by embarrassment but Jasmin sensed there was more to the woman's blushes than that. She could hear the rasp of Dinah's breath and, studying the rigid tips of her nipples, she knew Dinah's condition wasn't wholly the result of discomfort and humiliation.

Dr Grady stepped back, sighing as he put the second whip down. He snapped his fingers for Jasmin again and pointed at Dinah's raw backside. 'Check again,' he barked. 'See that she's been properly warmed.'

Jasmin considered saying no, then thought better of it. She took a hesitant step towards Dinah and brushed reluctant fingers over her backside. The tingle she had felt before was nothing compared with the sensation her hand now encountered. As she touched Dinah's burning flesh it was almost as though a spark of electricity had shocked her. Not wanting to share the intimacy, but unable to stop herself, Jasmin caressed the orbs with the palms of her hands.

Dinah groaned beneath her touch. She glanced back over her shoulder and Jasmin met her gaze. Her hands remained cupping and stroking at Dinah's cheeks and she defiantly held eye contact with the woman. A bolt of arousal struck her as they exchanged glances. Dinah's piercing blue eyes were glassy with the threat of tears but, beyond that anguish, there was the promise of something more.

Frightened by the expression, Jasmin moved her hands away.

'Test her for warmth the way that I just did,' Dr Grady growled.

Jasmin flushed and started to shake her head. She met his menacing scowl and realised he wasn't going to allow her the opportunity to refuse. Knowing better than to court his punishment, she placed a tentative hand over Dinah's cleft and tried to summon the courage to do as he was asking.

'Do it,' Dr Grady snapped.

Trying to distance herself from the actions of her own body, Jasmin stroked two fingers through the curls over Dinah's sex. The slippery wetness was a cool balm against her fingertips and, as the dewy folds began to yield beneath her touch, she realised the enormity of what she was doing.

She glanced down into Dinah's face, not sure whether she expected to be met by an expression of loathing or refusal. Seeing neither of those emotions, she watched Dinah's mouth pout wantonly. Her lips were parted in a silent sigh of bliss and her eyelids fluttered as though she was in the realms of unimagined joy. Encouraged by the response, Jasmin pushed her fingers into Dinah's wetness.

Her sex muscles gripped hungrily, their rhythmic tempo hinting at a greedy passion that demanded satisfaction. Staring into her face, Jasmin saw that Dinah was beyond the humiliation of her predicament. She had been taken past the point of embarrassment and was now residing at a pinnacle where nothing existed other than her need to spend her climax. It was easy to read the emotions on her face because Jasmin knew they were the mirror image of the ones she was enduring.

'Is she wet?'

Dr Grady's voice was so low that Jasmin didn't realise he was talking to her at first. She kept her fingers inside Dinah's sex, trying to slide them deeper as the tube of slippery muscles pressed around her hand.

'Is she melting?'

Swallowing thickly, Jasmin turned to face him. She drew her fingers slowly from Dinah and met Dr Grady's gaze with a flustered frown. 'She's been warmed.'

He chuckled quietly. Pushing Jasmin to one side, he reached for the third whip, then knelt beside his estranged wife.

'Are you ready to beg for my forgiveness now?' he asked.

'I've done nothing that needs your forgiveness,' she growled. Her voice was husky and her need was audible.

'Are you ready to tell me you were wrong for leaving me?'

Dinah shook her head.

He placed his hand over her buttocks and squeezed hard.

Dinah flinched but she made no sound to show her discomfort. 'I wasn't wrong for leaving you,' she hissed. 'Leaving you was the best thing I ever did.'

'I thought you'd say that,' he said sweetly. 'But you can't blame me for trying to score points, can you? I don't doubt you'd have done the same if our roles had been reversed. I'll just have one final thrash at your backside before we go to the church and resolve your coven's dilemma.' He paused to draw breath and Jasmin could hear he was excited by his own accomplishments. 'But, while I'm thrashing, I want you to think about the way things have worked out. You said before that this was close to being my perfect revenge. But you said that before I'd whipped your backside.'

Dinah looked to be regaining some of her composure. 'What's your point?'

'My point is that you overlooked something. My perfect revenge would include getting you out of my practice, breaking up your coven and getting you out of the village, but it would only be perfect if I could show that I'd broken the spell you had on me.'

'What spell?' Dinah demanded. 'What are you talking about?'

He laughed. 'Isn't it obvious? Or are you just trying to hide from an unpleasant truth? You've shown yourself incapable of arousing me, Dinah. Despite your best efforts at cocksucking, despite the fact that you've submitted to enduring my chastisement, you haven't managed to make me want you.'

'You bastard.'

Grinning happily, he ignored the insult. 'That alone would make this almost perfect for me. But this has been even better. I've shown myself capable of exciting you, even though you were fighting the sensation.'

'You lousy, despicable bastard.'

'You've always prided yourself on your ability to arouse men, whether they wanted to feel that emotion or not. I've shown you that your ability is not infallible. I've got you on a point where your body is craving orgasm.'

She glared at him furiously.

He laughed and stepped back. 'Dwell on that while you suffer this last cat,' he told her. 'Dwell on that and remember that you haven't sparked a single pulse of arousal in my body.'

Despite his words, Jasmin noticed he was now sporting a full erection and she wondered whether he was aware of it. He was no longer touching himself as he had been before but the length pushed urgently

159

against the front panel of his trousers. She knew better than to draw attention to it as she watched him raise the whip and hurl it down for a final time.

He scourged Dinah's backside seven times – three for each cheek and a final one across both. The knotted tips landed hard and Jasmin pitied Dinah's predicament as she suffered each of the blows. Dinah struggled against tears but by the time the final one had landed she was sobbing freely.

'We'll give you a moment alone,' Dr Grady said quietly. He snapped his fingers and summoned Jasmin to follow him into the hall. As soon as they had closed the door on Dinah, he reached for Jasmin's skirt and pulled it up. His other hand was working at the zip on his trousers and she saw he was trying to free his erection.

She started to raise a defensive hand, then stopped herself. It wasn't that she wanted the attention he was forcing on her but her lingering need for orgasm made her hope that he might be about to give the relief she craved. She inhaled the scent of his nearness and her nostrils were filled with the taste of his excited sweat. The aroma was bitter and dark and it heightened her arousal. She glanced down to where his hands were fumbling and saw his shaft was now hard and the end had become a deep, engorged purple. The thick blue veins traversing his length pulsed with their urgent need. She glanced away from his shaft and stared into his eyes.

'Stay quiet,' he whispered.

Jasmin nodded and allowed him to push her against the wall. She sensed his urgency and knew it was as desperate as her own. She felt sure the weight of his erection at her hole would be enough to give her the relief she wanted, and she yielded to his instructions.

He lowered his pelvis and thrust himself inside with brutal force. His hands gripped hard at her hips and, although his embrace was cold and uncaring, Jasmin felt herself responding as though he was the most sensitive of lovers. She closed her muscles around him, certain it would take only two more thrusts and her body would be able to revel in the climactic bliss that she yearned for.

His ejaculation came straightaway. Instead of thrusting, his cock pulsed into her and he climaxed with a grunt. His hot, white spend shot deep inside her and she could feel herself growing wet with his seed.

She wanted to groan with frustration but he had already warned her against making a sound. Bitterly, she swallowed the sob and allowed him to slide his spent shaft from her confines.

'You do that so well it will almost be a shame to send you back to the university,' he told her.

Jasmin said nothing, unable to think of anything except her body's unfulfilled desires.

After zipping himself back up, Dr Grady led her into the room where Dinah was fastening herself inside her cloak. She glared at them both with a look of sullen contempt but said nothing about where they had been or what they might have been doing.

'I think you've suffered enough,' Dr Grady grinned. He started folding the whips into the carpetbag he had been packing earlier and told Jasmin to get his coat from the door. She retrieved her own coat and was met by his frown when he saw what she had done.

'Where do you think you're going?'

'I thought I would be going with you.'

He shook his head. 'You can stay here and pray for forgiveness.'

'But what about Mel—'

'You'll stay here and pray for forgiveness,' he broke in. He snatched a fat, carved church candle from the mantelpiece and thrust into her hands. 'Meditate on this while I'm gone. It may help you to remember my instruction of the one thing that you're not supposed to do.'

He glanced slyly at Dinah and in that expression Jasmin saw he was being discreet. She didn't know whether it was for her sake or his own purposes, but she was grateful that he hadn't mentioned her shameful need in front of his estranged wife. Even after the intimacies that the three of them had shared, she was still mortified by the idea of having her urge to masturbate being spoken of out loud.

'If I come back here and discover you've broken that condition, I'll have to chastise you again,' he told her. 'Do you understand?'

'Yes, Dr Grady,' she whispered.

He nodded crisply, snatched the carpetbag from the floor and started out of the door. Without bothering to look at Jasmin, Dinah hurried after him. When they slammed the door closed on their egress, she realised she was alone and forbidden from giving her body the release it craved.

Seven

'Which one of you is it?' Steve demanded. 'Which one of you is supposed to be our new leader?'

Melissa exchanged a glance with the woman who had introduced herself as Jo, but neither of them spoke. They were cross-legged in the centre of the pentagram, both naked, and trying to make their bare backsides comfortable on the abrasive, wooden floor. They each had their ankles and wrists bound and sat silently beneath the horned one's imposing frown.

The priests and priestesses continued to circle, holding hands and chanting their incantation: '. . . The candle will show us the way. The candle will show us the way . . .' They were naked and lit only by the candlelight. Shadows from the long, yellow flames fluttered as each one of their bare bodies danced by. In the empty acoustics of the church, their voices weren't quite musical and the result was something that looked and sounded unnaturally eerie.

'If one of you is the new leader, you really ought to say,' Steve insisted. He switched his gaze back and forth between Melissa and Jo. 'If one of you knows that it's *not* you, you should tell us that now.'

The glass eyes of his mask glinted menacingly as he glowered down at them. His ceremonial cloak hung open and Melissa could see every sculpted curve of his body. His chest was broad, smooth and hairless and his stomach was washboard flat, but her gaze travelled lower than that. The sight of his manliness was frustrating because it reminded her that the night had been spent fuelling urges that she still needed satisfying. Not wanting to brood on those desires Melissa lowered her eyes and stared at the pockmarked wooden floor.

'I don't think either of you is the next mother goddess,' he said gruffly. 'But, if one of you knows that you're our next leader, you'd better speak up now. You'd better speak up before Dinah returns with this friend of hers because he won't be asking nicely.' Steve chewed on his lower lip, the only part of his face that was visible, and looked momentarily pensive. Almost as though he was speaking to himself, he said, 'He won't be asking nicely at all.'

'I know you from somewhere, don't I?' Jo broke in.

Steve glared at her, clearly annoyed with the distraction. 'Yes. We've met before.'

'Where do I know you from?'

'That's not important right now.'

'I think it is,' Jo insisted. 'I think it's vitally important. Who are you when you're not acting the goat?'

The question infuriated him. He raised his hand as though he was going to strike her, then shook his head with exasperation. A snort of annoyance came from beneath his mask and he said, 'I don't think either of you is the leader that we're looking for and I don't know why we're wasting our time. There's no sense in me trying to save you from your impending misery.' Turning his back on them both, he pushed through the circling priests and priestesses and stormed away from the pentagram.

Melissa raised her gaze from the floor, sad to watch him go.

In spite of his brash manner there was something comforting about Steve's presence. Melissa couldn't decide whether it was a facet of his personality that shone through from beneath his mask and costume, or simply the animal arousal that he stirred in her. A part of her wanted to read more into it, suggesting she enjoyed Steve's company because she was destined to be his consort, but she hurriedly told herself that the idea was ludicrous. She knew it was a combination of Dr Grady's sermon and then the mysticism of the coven that had made her open to such a suggestion. But even when she had rationalised it so plainly the idea lost none of its weight in her mind. The more that she dwelled on that thought, the more certain she became that she was the horned one's intended consort: she was the leader they were looking for.

'I know that I know him,' Jo said quietly. 'I just wish I knew who he was.'

Lost in her own thoughts, Melissa didn't reply.

There had always been an attraction to the village that she had never been able to understand or resist. It was the impulse that had urged her to return during every break from boarding school. Foreign holidays had always seemed less appealing than returning to the family home, and coming back hadn't seemed like such a bad option after her expulsion from university. Thinking about that driving force, Melissa wondered whether it was governed by something more than a basic need to return to the familiar surroundings of the village. The rational part of her mind told her she was reading too much into the situation. It was just unfortunate circumstances that had landed her in the company of the coven this evening and common sense insisted it had nothing to do with kismet or divine intervention. But the argument that she had been guided by destiny's hand was a compelling one. It was an explanation that made a lot of sense about the things that had happened in her life and she wondered whether she was on the brink of discovering her true vocation.

'Do you think you're the witch that they're looking for?' she asked Jo. 'They seem convinced that it must be one of us. Do you think it's you?'

Jo grunted dour laughter and shook her head. She was plucking at the twine that bound her ankles and looked near to unfastening one of the complicated knots with which Verity had secured her. Raising her head, she glanced at the circle of priests and priestesses before turning to Melissa. 'I don't think it is me,' she said quietly. 'It's not often I can use this as an excuse,' she confided, 'but it seems I don't have enough nipples.'

Her reply added reason to Melissa's growing belief but it puzzled her as well. 'If you're so sure that you're not their leader, why don't you just tell them that?'

Jo shook her head. 'I'm not telling this lot anything until I've learned more about them.' In a confidential whisper, she added, 'I don't think you should tell them anything, either.'

'Why the hell not?' Melissa sniffed haughtily. 'Why can't I tell them whatever I want? They seem friendly enough.'

Jo laughed rudely. 'You have an interesting interpretation of the word "friendly". These people have stripped our clothes off, touched us up and left us tied and naked on this cold floor. But, that aside, I think our safety here might depend on their not choosing one of us.'

'I don't understand what you mean.'

'I mean we don't know what they're going to do with the one of us that they don't want. We don't even know what they're going to do with the one that they *do* want. Until we've discovered what their intentions are, I think it would be wiser to keep quiet about why we're here.'

Melissa brushed Jo's worries aside with an impatient flick of her wrist. 'You're being very unfair on the coven. You're treating them as though they're up to something sinister. And what are you doing here, anyway?' she asked suddenly. 'Who are you? I know that you came into the church just after I did. You weren't following me, were you?'

Jo considered her levelly. 'You tell me why you're here and then I'll tell you why I'm here.'

Melissa blushed, then looked away. 'I can't say why I'm here. I was told not to.'

'Then neither can I.'

Melissa ground her teeth together, annoyed by the distraction of talking with Jo and frustrated that it had broken her chain of thought. If Jo wasn't the coven's new leader, then the laws of simple deduction meant it must be she. The idea explained her persistent return to the village and it gave direction to all the seemingly irrational choices she had ever made. She had messed around at university because it wasn't intended for her to be there. Her expulsion had been governed by a fate that had driven her to the abandoned church for a time when the coven needed her. Coupled with her intuitive nature, and the fact that fellow students had said she and Jasmin were like a pair of witches in the making, the argument began to develop more weight inside her mind. It was an explanation that fitted all the facts and, the more she thought about it, the more she began to believe it was right.

She turned to Jo and placed her bound hands on the woman's thigh. Jo's skin was inviting and smooth and the throb of a deep-seated pulse beat beneath Melissa's fingertips. The silky friction surprised her and she swallowed thickly before speaking. 'I think it's me,' she confided. 'I'm beginning to think I might be the leader that they're looking for.'

Jo's smile wasn't unkind but it was edged with cynicism. 'You shouldn't put too much credence on your thoughts about this,' she said seriously. 'I think we're both quite susceptible to their suggestions at the moment.'

'What does that mean?'

'It means that I'm not trusting my own observations right now,' Jo said quietly. 'And I don't think you should trust yours. These people have shown they can exert an influence over us physically. Didn't we both respond when they were using those effigies?'

Melissa blushed but she didn't lower her gaze. She wasn't ashamed of how she had reacted when her effigy had been manipulated but Jo's bluntness made her feel embarrassed. 'That just proves that the coven is for real, doesn't it? That just proves they're real witches using real magic, doesn't it?'

'Maybe,' Jo said, blinking her consideration away. 'But, if they can exert a physical influence over us, who's to say they can't exert some sort of mental influence as well?'

It wasn't an argument she wanted to hear and Melissa brushed it aside. She pressed her fingers more firmly against Jo's thigh, unconsciously enjoying the way that the firm flesh yielded. 'But what if I *am* the chosen one?' she asked. 'What if it *is* me? Have you considered that?'

'What if we're just a pair of poor bitches who ended up in the wrong place at the wrong time?' Jo countered. 'Have you considered that?'

Melissa sighed with exasperation. It was easy to understand why the coven appeared secretive if they expected to face scepticism like this when they revealed their beliefs. Jo had seen the same inexplicable things that she had seen, and experienced the same impossible arousal, yet still she was trying to find an explanation that came within the realm of her understanding. Considering that degree of disbelief, Melissa found herself beginning to admire the coven for maintaining their convictions. 'Maybe we *are* just a pair of poor bitches who ended up in the wrong place at the wrong time,' she agreed. 'But don't you think that's unlikely? Don't you think there's more to it than that? They came to an abandoned church, in the middle of the night, expecting to find a new leader. What were the odds on them finding anyone here?'

Jo nodded. 'That's the one thing that's been troubling me about all this. That's the one thing that doesn't seem to make any sense.'

'So, you think I could be right?' Melissa asked quickly. 'You think I could be the chosen one?'

'I think there's more going on here than either of us knows about.'

'But do you think there's a chance I might be right? Do you think it might be me?'

Jo considered her flatly and said nothing.

Seeing the glint in her eye, Melissa knew that she was wasting her time. She removed her hands from Jo's lap, unhappy at breaking the contact but sure that there would be no point in explaining herself further.

The priests and priestesses continued to circle without paying her any attention, and Melissa scoured the rest of the church for someone who might listen. She wanted to catch Steve's eye but he had disappeared into one of the shaded corners near the vestry. Hardly aware that she was speaking out loud, she repeated her conviction purposefully. 'It *is* me,' she decided. 'I really think it *is* me.'

The mousy girl, Verity, rushed through the circle of priests and priestesses. She lowered herself to her knees and pressed her mouth close to Melissa's ear. The pressure of her lips tickled Melissa's lower lobe and the warmth of her breath was a subtle, intoxicating caress.

'You've been instructed to be silent,' Verity whispered. 'The horned one will be angry if you don't obey that rule.' She glanced nervously in Steve's direction and added, 'You don't want to make the horned one angry. He has a vicious streak in him when he's roused.'

Melissa shook her head, unable to contain a growing smile. 'How did you first know that you were meant to be a witch? What made you first believe?'

Verity moved back from her exuberance looking uneasy with the question. 'I'm not a witch,' she said quickly. She glanced at the priests and priestesses, as though she was fearful they would condemn her if she didn't answer properly. 'I'm not a witch,' Verity said. 'I practise Wicca. I've spent a year and a day as a probationer and tonight I became a neophyte. I haven't been practising long enough yet to be properly called a witch.'

'Why did you come here tonight?' Jo asked. 'Not just you,' she added hurriedly. 'Why did your entire coven come here? What brought you to this place?'

Melissa frowned at the interruption, then decided there was no harm in hearing the answer. If she was destined to be the leader of the coven she supposed it would be to her advantage to know as much about its workings as was possible.

Verity glanced from one face to the other before beginning. 'I brought the coven here,' she explained. 'We had the ritual of the black flame and –'

'The black flame?' Jo broke in. 'What's that?'

Melissa frowned at her again but Verity seemed quite pleased to share her knowledge. 'The black flame is one of our most potent rituals,' she said. 'Dinah says, like with all of our magic, it's particularly effective during Beltane and Samhain –'

'Beltane and Samhain?' Jo broke in again. 'What are they?'

'Beltane is our May Day celebration. Samhain is how we practise Hallowe'en.' She paused and in her open expression it was clear that she was backtracking and trying to remember the point she had been about to make.

'You were telling us about the ritual of the black flame,' Jo prompted.

Verity flashed her with a grateful smile before continuing. 'The black flame is a powerful spell,' she confided. 'I was proud to be a part of it. I was tied naked in a pentagram and I had to present myself for the horned one's ceremonial adultery.'

Melissa caught an excited breath in her throat, thankful that she didn't embarrass herself and release the sound. The idea of having to endure Steve's ceremonial adultery sounded infuriatingly appealing and she envied Verity the pleasure that she had obviously enjoyed.

'The mother goddess and the horned one shared me,' Verity explained. 'But it wasn't just sex. There was the magic and the chanting and Dinah taught me all about the rule of three. There was much more to it than just sex. It was a proper ceremony for our religion.'

'I'm sure it was,' Melissa agreed. She paused for a moment, waiting for Jo to make some similar comment. When the brunette remained obstinately silent, Melissa repeated her reassurance for Verity. 'I'm sure it was a proper ritual.'

'The ritual of the black flame was the symbolic representation of the mother goddess and the horned one's parting,' Verity said. 'At the peak of our pleasure, the flame from the candle turned black.' She glared from Melissa to Jo, trying to impress on them that the magic really had happened. 'It really did turn black,' she insisted. 'I saw it with my own eyes. It really did.'

Melissa placed a reassuring hand on Verity's. 'I believe you,' she said.

'It really happened,' Verity repeated. 'Dinah's having to leave the coven, and the ritual of the black flame showed us where to find her replacement.'

'Does your coven do anything that doesn't involve a ritual?' Jo asked. She leaned forward on her haunches, seeming to have forgotten that she was trying to unfasten the twine that bound her ankles. 'Does your coven do anything at all that doesn't involve a ritual?' she repeated.

Verity frowned. 'I don't understand what you mean.'

'You have a ritual to get rid of your current leader, and a ritual to find the location of her replacement. You have rituals to test which of us might be that lucky replacement –' she nodded at the circle of chanting priests '– and rituals to keep the foot soldiers happy while nothing's happening. Am I likely to get out of here without having to endure another one of your bloody rituals? Or have you got others lined up for me this evening?'

Verity glared at her. 'There will be a ritual welcoming for the new leader this evening and a ritual cleansing for whichever one of you is just a pretender. The coven won't disband tonight until we've done that much.'

Jo rolled her eyes and sat heavily back on the floor. 'I thought that would be the case,' she grunted.

'But it's all true,' Verity said suddenly. 'I don't know why you won't believe it. The black flame brought us here.'

'The black flame brought *you* here?' Jo repeated. 'But how –'

Impatiently, Melissa shook her head. 'This is all immaterial, and none of it answers my question.' Ignoring Jo, she turned to Verity and said, 'How did you know that this was what was meant for you? How did you know that this was what you wanted from life?'

Verity considered the question earnestly before replying. She cast another glance over her shoulder and then seemed to come to some internal decision. She seemed happier to be discussing her beliefs with Melissa rather than Jo, and her entire demeanour softened when she eventually replied. 'I felt it here,' she said eventually. She reached for Melissa's bound hands and pressed them beneath her cloak.

Melissa's fingers touched a small, pert breast and an inexplicable charge soared through her. She told herself it was more than the simple excitement of touching another woman. Even when Verity's nipple began to stiffen in the palm of her hand, Melissa's mind insisted that her arousal was governed by something more profound than simple sexual stimulation.

'I felt something deep in here,' Verity went on. She spoke as though she was oblivious to the arousal she was inspiring. 'I don't know if you'd call it a vocation or a calling, but this is where I felt it.'

'I can feel it too,' Melissa told her.

She didn't know whether she was talking about Verity's breast, or an echo of the revelation that they were discussing. Aside from the weight of the stiffening nipple Melissa was aware of a tingling warmth emanating from the woman's body. Her flesh was as inviting as Jo's had been but this contact seemed more vital and magical. As she cupped and squeezed Verity's breast, Melissa was dizzied by the excitement of the moment.

'I think I'm the leader your coven is looking for,' Melissa confided. 'I really think it's me.'

Verity's tiny face was too guileless to hide her doubts. The uncertainty was even clear in her voice when she asked, 'Do you really think that you're our new leader?'

'I feel a warmth, here,' Melissa explained. Reluctantly she removed her fingers and reached for Verity's hand. Guiding the neophyte's touch to her own chest, she allowed Verity to hold her breast as their eyes met. 'I feel a warmth in here,' she repeated. 'And it's telling me that I'm the chosen one.'

The moment lingered for a glorious eternity. Melissa's nipple grew hard with the warmth of Verity's hand and the pulse of her arousal began to beat with renewed haste.

Rather than keep her hand still, Verity rolled and kneaded Melissa's flesh.

Her caress was an intimate pleasure that Melissa hadn't been expecting and she shivered in response. She opened her mouth to say something but the only sound to come out was a long, lingering sigh.

'I can feel something,' Verity told her. She leaned closer and shifted the weight of her hand. Instead of continuing to massage, she traced the shape and swell of Melissa's breast with the tip of one finger. It was an evocative touch that trailed dwindling circles around Melissa's areola. As the circles drew smaller, and the tip of Verity's finger slipped unbearably close to the puckered skin, Melissa shivered.

'I'm sure I can feel something,' Verity insisted.

She was on the verge of touching the nipple and Melissa held herself still in anticipation. When the contact finally came a thrill of pleasure bristled from her breast. She drew startled breath, considering Verity with a combination of excitement and respect.

'I think it could be you,' Verity decided.

Her eyes were glistening and Melissa thought she could see the prospect of reverence in her expression.

'It could very well be you,' Verity told her. She snatched her hand away and a guilty flush darkened her cheeks. Without saying another word she lurched through the circle of priests and priestesses and ran into the darkness of the church.

Melissa was left in a dizzying haze of arousal.

'I was right,' she whispered. 'It *is* me.'

She heard Jo grunt disdainfully but, having already encountered her scepticism, Melissa found the woman's disbelief easy to ignore. Her conviction was growing just as her excitement had flourished a moment earlier. She watched Verity rush towards the vestry and her heart began to pound faster when she saw Steve turn to glance in her direction. Their conversation didn't last for more than a terse exchange before he was following the neophyte and storming into the pentagram.

'Verity thinks you're the chosen one,' Steve said.

His mask continued to make him look dour and frightening but Melissa was beyond being intimidated. 'I'm sure it's me,' she told him.

He dragged her from the floor with one effortless sweep of his arm. For an instant her feet were dangling above the floorboards as she was lifted out of the pentagram. Steve placed her by the side of the coven's makeshift altar and continued to hold her until she had balanced herself on her bound feet.

She could see the lower half of his jaw beneath the mask and she realised his lips were tilted at the same cynical angle that she had seen on Jo's face. Not that his doubts mattered, she told herself. She was convinced that she would be proved right and felt certain that she could convince him as she had convinced Verity.

Steve placed a hand on her breast and the unexpected intimacy sliced through her thoughts. His hold on her was vicious and uncompromising, squeezing hard without deference to her feelings. 'What makes you so sure it's you?' he demanded.

'Destiny sent me here,' she replied. She had expected the words to sound trite or shallow but they resounded throughout the church with absolute sincerity. 'Destiny guided me here when the coven needed me.'

Steve nodded at Jo. 'Destiny guided her to the same place at the same time.'

'Leave me out of this,' Jo said quickly. 'I've already been told that I don't have enough nipples.'

Melissa allowed her smile to glint with triumph. Jo's roundabout denial seemed to prove that she was right and she wondered why Steve couldn't draw the same logical conclusion.

Below his mask he was frowning. 'Do you know what it would entail to be our leader?'

'Not yet,' Melissa replied honestly. 'But I can learn.'

He shook his head. 'You'd have to guide the coven,' he told her. 'That's quite a responsibility.'

She nodded, having already expected this much. 'I could do that.'

'You'd have to practise Wicca.'

'That doesn't worry me.'

'And you'd have to be my lover.'

Her heart skipped a beat. She studied the glass eyes of his mask and could have sworn they were glinting lasciviously. There was a cruel set to his mouth but her gaze travelled lower than that. His cloak was open and she could see that his length had turned thick and hard.

'I could cope with that,' she said thickly.

'I'm a demanding lover,' he warned.

She met the challenge of his voice with a resolute expression. 'I wouldn't expect anything else,' she told him. 'In fact, if I was leader of the coven, I think I'd insist on that.'

He grabbed hold of her hands and snatched the ceremonial knife from the altar. The blade slipped between her wrists, the cold steel chilling her flesh as he severed the twine. Before she had a chance to rub the circulation back into her fingers, Steve had dropped to his knees and was cutting through the twine at her ankles. The top of his masked head was disturbingly close to her sex and she was struck by the exciting image of having him as a lover. She could picture their bodies naked and entwined and the prospect sent a rush of anticipation tingling between her legs. The idea was still at the forefront of her thoughts when he stood up and placed the knife back among the other artefacts.

'You'd insist on that, would you?'

'Yes,' she breathed softly.

He considered her for a moment, then hurled an arm around her waist and drew her body close to his. The weight of his length pressed against her thigh and she was sure that the heat was branding her. Her breasts were crushed against his chest and the earthy flavours of his sweat and nearness filled her nostrils.

'You really believe you're our new leader?'

The vibration of his words trembled through her chest. It reminded her of how near he was and hinted at the intimacy that was about to come. Melissa swallowed twice before finding her voice and even then she thought her tone sounded weak with anticipation. 'Yes,' she told him. 'Yes. I believe I am.'

'And, you think you could cope with the conditions I've just spelled out?'

She could see what he was insinuating and the prospect thrilled her. He nudged his hips forward and the weight of his shaft nuzzled between her legs. Her pussy lips were brushed by his burning heat and the promise of passion sparked through her body. She had shivered before but this time she trembled.

'Well? Do you think you could cope with the conditions I've just spelled out?'

'I think I could do more than cope with them,' she told him. She lowered her hand to his groin and took his thick shaft in her palm. His stiffness was darkly exciting and she struggled to keep her hand steady as she held him. Guiding his erection to the centre of her need, she rubbed his swollen end back and forth against her sex.

Steve sighed.

It was a small sound that told her he was experiencing a thrill that was equal to the one visiting her. A part of her wished she could see his face, and judge his response properly, but another part of her was happy for the perversity to continue. The abandoned church, the candlelit atmosphere and the chanting of the omnipresent priests and priestesses all made for a heady blend. The addition of Steve's mask and cloak completed the surreal setting and made the moment feel like something truly unimagined and potentially memorable.

Slowly, determined not seem too eager, Melissa rubbed his length repeatedly over the lips of her pussy. She wanted to tease him and possibly tempt him with the threat of penetration. She wanted to bring him to the point of desperately needing her but her body's urges were too strong to resist. Unable to stop herself, she guided the head of his shaft to her sex and thrust herself on to him.

They both groaned loudly.

His thickness spread her wide as he plunged deep inside.

A shock of pleasure slapped her and she was thankful that he still had an arm around her waist. If he hadn't been holding her, Melissa believed she would have fallen back into the pentagram in a sobbing, satisfied heap.

'You could tolerate this through all of our ceremonies, could you?' Steve asked.

His voice was a breathless grunt and Melissa knew that when she replied her own tone would be rich with the same hue. She considered her response carefully as he began to ride in and out. Their standing position allowed her to control the rhythm but she found that wasn't what she wanted. Instead of dominating the pace, she was happy to let him take charge of that responsibility. His shaft was long and broad and it satisfied the aching need that had been filling her since she was subjected to Dr Grady's caning. The idea of controlling the horned one was alien and unwanted and she was happy to give herself over to whatever demands he had.

'You could tolerate this through all of our ceremonies?' Steve repeated.

Melissa believed she could have happily tolerated his lovemaking through anything and she struggled to say as much. 'Yes,' she gasped. The word came out strangled with emotion. 'Yes. Of course. Yes.'

He seemed to ruminate on her answer while adjusting his hold. He moved the hand from her waist and edged his grip between her buttocks. Melissa was shocked to feel a finger pressing against the rim of her anus and even more startled when he pressed deliberately against the puckered muscle. Her sphincter resisted, but even that forbidden sensation wasn't without some pleasure. The threat of intrusion spiked her with a bolt of unexpected excitement and she squealed happily. The noise turned into an elated sigh when his finger finally squirmed into her taboo orifice.

Studying the shaded line of his jaw, Melissa saw that Steve's smile was tinged with cruel satisfaction. 'Could you tolerate this?' he grunted. Snatching his shaft free from her sex, and pulling his finger out of her backside, he spun her around and then clutched her hips.

For an instant Melissa felt dizzy and lost. The satisfaction he was administering was taken away and all that was left in its place was a hollow, empty space. Before she had a chance to think that the prospect of a climax had gone, Steve was pressing himself back against her. Rather than push at the lips of her sex, his bulbous dome probed her anus.

She chewed her lip to stifle a demure protest.

'Could you tolerate this?' he demanded.

She didn't know whether she could tolerate it, or even stretch to accommodate it, but her body yearned to find out. Writhing against him, trying to wriggle on to the offered threat of his erection, Melissa nodded her head up and down. 'Yes,' she growled softly. 'I could tolerate that. Yes.'

It was all the encouragement he needed.

Whereas Melissa had taken the initiative before, Steve took it this time. He placed the end of his erection against her anus and then secured his hold on her hips. Pulling her backwards, he forced himself firmly between her buttocks.

Melissa screamed.

There was no pain in the sound, only a cry of pure, unparalleled pleasure. Her muscle was stretched wide by his thick girth and she supposed, if it hadn't been for the distraction of her euphoria, there could have been some discomfort. But that wasn't something she could be bothered to think about. Wrapped up in the nearness of her impending orgasm, she allowed Steve to plunge deeper as the forbidden penetration took her ever closer to the moment of release.

'You're enjoying this,' he noted.

She sighed, unable to think of how to reply to such an obvious statement.

'And you could tolerate this sort of treatment at each of our ceremonies?'

Melissa nodded, then wondered if he had seen the silent reply. He had bent her double so he could slide his shaft further into her anus and she suspected that her head was bobbing up and down with the rhythm of his incessant pounding. Releasing her words in time to his entry and egress she said, 'I could tolerate this whenever and wherever you wanted.'

'Here in an abandoned church?' Steve pressed.

'That's what we're doing, isn't it?'

'What about in the centre of the village's stone circle?'

The idea of being had by him out of doors was animal and powerful. It gave a dark flavour to her excitement and that in turn added a perversity to her arousal. The flush of a full orgasm was blossoming in her stomach and she had physically to concentrate to reply. 'Wherever you wanted,' she gasped. 'Whenever you want. Here in an abandoned church. Or even in the village's stone circle. Anywhere. Everywhere.'

'What about in the pentagram?' Steve pressed.

He placed a peculiar emphasis on the question but she didn't think it was important. It was certainly nowhere near as important as the promise of satisfaction he had created deep inside her, and she answered him without thinking. 'Anywhere,' she insisted. 'Everywhere. Whenever and wherever you tell me.'

He pushed hard into her and the force drove her stumbling forwards.

Glancing down at the floor, she realised she was on the brink of standing in the pentagram and she wondered whether the chalk lines were supposed to have some significance. Clearly, the symbol was important to the coven. From what she had already seen this evening the witches regarded the five-pointed star in the same way that Dr Grady revered his crucifixes. But Melissa could see it only as a chalk drawing on the dusty floor. A part of her thought that it might be important to Steve but that consideration was overridden by the rush of her arousal.

Inspired by his quickening tempo, Melissa rubbed herself happily on his length. The flurry of her orgasm was building quickly and she knew that when it did come the joy was going to be tremendous. She braced herself for the onslaught of the pleasure and revelled in the power of his deep, penetrating thrusts.

Steve adjusted his hold on her waist, pulling her closer and allowing his hands to reach beneath her and cup her breasts. He squashed them mercilessly, catching her nipples between his fingers and squeezing with unnecessary force. The brutal treatment was unexpected and took her closer to the point of release.

'You can do this for our ceremonies?' he asked.

'Yes.'

'And you've no problems doing it inside the pentagram?'

She shook her head, knowing that her climax was only a whisper away. Again, she thought his emphasis on the question was peculiar but that worry seemed far less immediate than the satisfaction of her need. 'No,' she breathed. 'I have no problems with doing this inside a pentagram.'

He thrust firmly into her and she stumbled forward with the force. Staring at the floor, she watched one bare foot fall into the pentagram, followed quickly by the other. Her orgasm was a single thrust away and she drew a deep breath, preparing to vent her release with a scream to match its magnitude.

Steve pulled his length out of her anus and shook his head disparagingly. 'That proves that you're not our leader,' he growled. 'That proves that you're not our leader and that you never will be.'

Melissa stared at him, unable to comprehend how or why his mood had suddenly changed. It was clear from his surly demeanour that their lovemaking had ended and she wondered what she had done wrong to bring things to such an unsatisfactory conclusion. 'Why have you stopped?' she whispered.

The glass eyes of the goat's head mask glared at her.

The promise of orgasm had been so close that Melissa could still taste its bittersweet flavour. The emptiness between her legs felt as though something vital had been torn from inside her and she could feel herself on the brink of being consumed by frustrated tears. Confused and weak with exertion, she fell to her knees and stared miserably up at him. 'Why have you stopped?' she asked again. 'Why?'

'I've stopped because you're not the chosen one,' he said bluntly.

Melissa shook her head, convinced that he was wrong. 'I believe I am,' she insisted. 'I really believe I am.'

'The chosen one would happily give her body during a ceremony,' Steve explained. 'But not the way that you've just done.' His lips had curled into a sneer of contempt. 'The chosen one would never allow herself to be used in such a low and vulgar fashion. And she would never submit to that in the centre of a sacred pentagram.'

His disdain made her feel mortified and she closed her eyes against the threat of tears. 'I am the chosen one,' she insisted. Whereas before her words had sounded believable and convincing, they now came out like a petulant whine. 'I am the chosen one,' she said again. 'I really am.'

He shook his head and the eyes of his mask continued to glare at her. A sound at the church door made him turn and his jaw hardened with distaste. 'You're not our leader,' he said, turning back to Melissa. 'And you'd do well to remember that. You'd do well to put the idea out of your mind for the sake of the coven. And you'd do well to put the idea out of your mind before this lunatic gets to hear what you've been saying.'

Starting to cry, Melissa placed her hands over her face and hid her tears of disappointment and frustration.

Beyond the sound of her sobs, she heard Jo ask, 'Is this Dinah's friend?'

'That's the legendary Dr Grady,' Steve explained.

There was so much revulsion in his voice that Melissa wiped her eyes and tried to catch a glimpse of the new arrival.

Steve glanced at Jo, then at Melissa. 'Regardless of whether you're here by accident, or whether you were meant to be here, he's the one who's going to make you wish you were somewhere else.'

Jo shook her head. Her brow was furrowed into a deep frown. 'I wonder,' she began hesitantly. 'I wonder why I'm not surprised to see him here.'

Eight

Jasmin sat in the glow of the firelight and clutched the church candle tight between her legs. Her hands were clammy with sweat and its thick length slipped stiffly in her grasp. Her arousal continued to smoulder like the cherry coals at the base of the fire and she twisted her thoughts in every direction so as not to dwell on that. Reflections from the orange flames flickered over her scowl but it was the only illumination in the room. The rest of Dr Grady's study was held in long, impenetrable shadows.

She felt drained, and not a little nervous with being alone in the house, but she believed the solitude was helping her to put things in perspective. Dr Grady had made her pay her penance for the sins she had committed at university, and Jasmin suspected he had made Melissa pay for hers, too. His promise to talk to Principal Dean gave her hope that the future wouldn't be as bleak as she had anticipated and, with any luck, she believed he would return with Melissa, make a brief call to their father, and then allow them to go home. In the morning he might even have news that Principal Dean had agreed to give them one more chance. It was a lot to hope for but Jasmin didn't think any of it was outside Dr Grady's capabilities.

And yet, much as she wanted to be comforted by the way things were working out, none of it helped to release her pent-up sexual tension. Barely aware that she was doing it, Jasmin rocked her hips back and forth. The base of the candle was tight against her cleft and, each time she nudged her body forward, her sex was rubbed by the stout length of wax. Her arousal remained so potent that the dull thud of pleasure didn't register as a new sensation. It was more like a continuation of all those unsatisfied desires that continued to boil within her loins.

Licking her parched lips, Jasmin was reminded of Dr Grady's final climax. His flavour, and all of the recollections it evoked, made her shiver. She didn't like to think of the taste of his semen, or remember the feel of his manliness on and in her body. It wasn't that she was repulsed by what they had done – while it had been shameful, she knew the whole experience could have been enjoyable if she had been allowed to indulge herself further – but the memories threatened to rekindle her arousal to an unbearable degree. Rather than brood on what had happened, and so worsen those desires that still gnawed inside her stomach, she tried turning her thoughts to the prospect of returning to university.

Unconsciously, she pushed the base of the candle beneath her skirt. Her sex lips were wet and eager and they parted as soon as the wax touched her hole. A nuance in the carved girth rested against her clitoris and Jasmin was spiked by a delicious bolt. A tremor racked her body and the spasm finally forced her to look down and see what she was doing.

For an instant she couldn't decide whether to be elated or disgusted.

Her skirt had been hitched up to reveal the pallid splendour of her thighs and the glow from the fire made her flesh amber. She could see that the base of the candle sat inside her pussy lips and its thickness promised to satisfy her lingering needs. The lowest carving pressed on her clitoris and every shift in pressure triggered another tingling thrill.

Her first thought was that she was committing an act of unforgivable sacrilege. Dr Grady had given her the candle and, because it was an ornately carved church artefact, Jasmin couldn't have been more upset if she had found herself rubbing her cleft with a crucifix. However, it was not so much the thought of the unintentional profanity but the memory of Dr Grady's warning that made her hesitate. He had told Jasmin not to satisfy her urges and had said there would be repercussions if she did. There had been a finality in his tone that left her with no doubt that his command had been made in earnest and she wondered whether she should stop herself before she deliberately disobeyed his instruction.

But her need to climax was greater than any remembered warning. It overrode her self-disgust and pushed aside her fear of Dr Grady's recriminations. Forcing the candle against herself, she released a small moan and allowed her body to revel in enjoyment. In an instant she was wallowing in the waves of joy that flooded from her sex. As she allowed the length of wax to glide slowly in and out, the onset of orgasm began to tremble in her toes and fingers. Her unsatisfied need blossomed from the pit of her stomach and shook its way through every nerve ending. The nearness of climax was so close that Jasmin knew nothing would stop her from finally attaining that goal.

With renewed determination, she pushed herself back and forth. The candle's fat base opened her wide and heightened her need for more. The ridges of the carving gave the penetration an unusual texture and she had a moment to think that the implement might have been specifically designed for this task. It was only a fleeting thought, swept away by a rising tide of passion. The electric flavour of excitement filled her mouth and the pounding of adrenaline thudded in her temples.

'There's no one in here. All the lights are off.'

The whisper of approaching voices forced Jasmin to stop what she was doing.

She slipped the candle from her hole, unable to stop its sticky coating from covering her fingers. A part of her wanted to continue, not caring whether anyone, even Dr Grady, caught her frigging herself to climax. If it was him returning, Jasmin thought she might purposefully defy his instruction and satisfy her needs with the remaining handful of thrusts that were required. She could visualise herself doing it while he watched and she could see herself thrashing with euphoria as he called her a depraved and godless harlot.

It was an exhilarating image and, almost certainly, there would be punishment. He would be livid at her defiance and outraged by the irreverence of her using his church candle. But she remembered that even his punishments hadn't been without some pleasure and the chance of experiencing them again wasn't an unwelcome prospect.

The whole scene had built so quickly in her mind that it added fuel to her unsatisfied need. The candle felt warm and greasy in her grasp and she itched to return it to the spot where she needed it most.

But Jasmin resisted the impulse. So far, the details of her debasement were known only to Dr Grady and his estranged wife and, as long as it was within her power to control such things, Jasmin was determined to keep the events a secret among the three of them.

'I tell you she's still in here. She'll be able to tell us where they've gone.'

Jasmin could hear it was a man's voice but it didn't sound like Dr Grady. She didn't rise from her seat in front of the fire, wary that it might be a ploy to test her or catch her off her guard. Her hands trembled as she brushed down the hem of her skirt and she tried to steady them by clutching the candle tighter.

'She can't be in there.' This was a woman speaking but Jasmin didn't think it sounded like Dinah. 'There's no light on, Todd. She wouldn't just be sitting in the dark.'

'He'd told her to stay where she was and I think she was going to obey him.'

'And what would you know about the way that women think?'

The light in Dr Grady's study burst on and Jasmin blinked, her eyes having become used to the gloom. She stared solemnly at the couple as they stepped into the room, not surprised that they were complete strangers. He was an untidy yet not unattractive man, close to her own age. The woman was a vibrant redhead, a couple of years older. She would have been exceptionally pretty if not for her surly lower lip and the scowl lines creasing her brow. 'See.' The man was pointing at Jasmin. His smile looked triumphant. 'I told you she'd still be here.'

The redhead tossed her hair so that her Titian curls gave a dismissive wave. 'So, you were right,' she grunted. 'That still doesn't tell us where Jo is.'

'Ask her,' Todd said. 'I'll retrieve the equipment.'

'Who are you?' Jasmin asked. 'This is Dr Grady's house and he didn't say anyone would be visiting.'

The redhead sat on the arm of Jasmin's chair and grinned down at her. 'I'm Sam and this is Todd,' she said, extending a hand.

Jasmin kept her fingers wrapped tightly around the candle. She didn't want to shake the woman's hand because she was aware that her fingers would still be embarrassingly wet. 'Has Dr Grady sent you?'

'Not exactly.'

'Then what are you doing here?'

Todd had walked over to the mirror and seemed to be trying to lift it from its hooks. Without glancing back at her he said, 'We just came here to remove some stuff and ask you a couple of questions.'

Jasmin flashed her gaze from one to the other. 'You're not burglars, are you?'

Todd laughed but Sam seemed offended.

'No. We're not burglars,' she said stiffly. 'We're pri– we're detectives.'

Jasmin thought the explanation sounded credible enough, although she felt sure that Sam was hiding something. Before she had a chance to work out what it was, Todd had lifted the mirror from the wall. Behind the glass, staring directly at her, was the lens of a camera.

Horrified, Jasmin placed a hand over her mouth.

'Where's Dr Grady gone?' Sam asked.

Jasmin shook her head. Instead of looking at Sam she stared at the camera as Todd uncoupled it and placed it in the large canvas bag he had brought. 'You've been filming him?' she whispered. 'You've been filming us?'

'This has been one aspect of our surveillance operation,' Sam said pompously. 'And we can get on with the rest of it if you'd tell us where Dr Grady has –'

'Did you film me?' Jasmin demanded. Her calm evaporated like steam on a griddle. She clutched at the lapels of Sam's jacket, dragging the redhead close as she levered herself out of her chair. 'Did you film me?' she repeated.

Sam's smile turned briefly cruel. 'I think you might appear on some of the footage,' she said coyly. 'That's not a problem, is it? You're very photogenic.'

Panic and despair threatened to overwhelm her. Jasmin glanced towards Todd, but he was busy unfastening electrical leads and placing them neatly inside his holdall. Turning back to Sam, Jasmin realised the redhead was studying her with a twisted lilt to her smile.

'You have to destroy it,' Jasmin whispered urgently. 'You have to destroy the tape.'

Sam shook her head and sucked noisy breath through her teeth. 'I don't think I can do that,' she said softly. 'I don't think I can do that at all.'

'But you have to,' Jasmin insisted.

When she had thought the events of the evening were a secret – a secret that would remain between herself, Dr Grady and Dinah – Jasmin had been able to come to terms with the whole, shameful ordeal. But the discovery that her punishment had been filmed was too shocking to cope with. There was the irrational worry that her friends at university might see what she had been doing, and the more pressing fear that the tape could be shown to her family. But regardless of who saw the tape – and in Jasmin's mind it was already a certainty that someone would see it – its existence promised absolute ruination.

'You have to destroy it,' she insisted.

Sam shook her head. 'I couldn't do that. It would spoil the fruits of a very intensive surveillance operation.'

'But you *have* to,' Jasmin told her. She renewed her grip on the redhead's lapels and pulled her closer. 'No one must see that tape. No one.'

'You've got nothing to worry about,' Todd assured her. 'We're very professional and very discreet about this sort of thing. It's not like we're going to make copies and stick them on the shelves at Blockbuster.'

Jasmin wasn't listening to him as she met Sam's green eyes. They glinted with the same salacious need that she had seen in Dr Grady's expression and Jasmin felt sure there was a chance to bargain with the woman. Putting her principles to one side, ignoring the small voice at the back of her mind that insisted what she was contemplating was wrong, Jasmin said, 'I'll do whatever you ask if you promise to destroy that tape.'

'Now, that sounds like a tempting offer,' Todd said cheerfully. 'But there's no need for you to worry yourself. We're professional and discreet and we're not going to let this tape fall into the public domain.'

He still had his back to them and Jasmin was aware that he couldn't see the shift in Sam's grin. The redhead's smile had hinted at a cruel streak before but now it was etched with predatory intrigue.

'You must really want to see that tape destroyed,' Sam observed.

'I do,' Jasmin told her. 'And I'll do anything if you do that for me.'

'Anything?' Sam injected so much intimation into the single word that Jasmin had no doubt about what was being implied. She didn't need to see the way the redhead's green eyes widened, or notice that her gaze dropped briefly to appraise what was being offered.

Todd dropped his holdall heavily to the floor. The resounding thud broke the tense silence that had thickened the room's air. 'Sam?' he gasped. 'You can't seriously be thinking of –'

'Fuck off, Todd,' Sam said coolly.

The words struck Jasmin like an unexpected slap to the face and she gaped at Sam's fiery turn of phrase.

Todd remained stoical, as though he had expected this response. 'What about Jo?' he asked calmly.

'What about the fact that she's gone missing? And don't you think we're going to need that tape for –'

'Go back to the van and wait for me there,' Sam told him.

She half turned and Jasmin noticed the truculent way that the redhead held herself. It was like watching a spoiled teenager throw an understated tantrum. 'If Jo had played fair with me, she might rank higher on my current priority list,' Sam decided. 'If you'd done the decent thing and told me what you two were doing –'

'Jo asked me not to –'

He didn't get to finish. Sam waved a silencing hand through his argument and continued as though he wasn't speaking. 'If you'd done the decent thing and told me what you and Jo were doing, I might have let you stay to watch this. I might even have suggested that you join in.'

Jasmin was simultaneously sickened and enthralled by the redhead's words. Sam was talking about her as though she was nothing more than an object to be used or shared. Her casual tone and manner suggested the redhead was used to abusing people in such an offhand way and, much as she wanted to be repulsed, Jasmin couldn't help but be won over by a rush of dark excitement. Her sexual need had been strong before but now it returned with a gut-wrenching force.

Sam continued to glare at Todd, oblivious to Jasmin's escalating arousal. 'You could have had all that,' she told him. 'But, because the pair of you have treated me like I don't matter, I think it's time I did the same to you.'

He opened his mouth, looking ready to argue his point, but Sam was into a forceful stride. She held up a warning finger and said, 'Whatever it is, I don't want to hear it, Todd. If you're not out of here in the next five seconds I'll terminate your employment with the Flowers & Valentine Detective Agency.'

'You aren't serious,' he whispered.

'Do you want to try me?'

His cheeks were spotted by a flush of anger and for the briefest instant it looked like he was going to defy her. Sam met his frown with her jaw set squarely and that seemed to be the thing that finally told him he wasn't going to win this argument. Snatching his holdall from the floor, Todd shook his head despairingly and left.

Sam turned back to Jasmin as soon as the door had slammed closed. 'Now. Where were we?'

A block of ice-cold fear pierced Jasmin's chest. She didn't want to be in Dr Grady's study, and she definitely didn't want to be subjugating herself to an unknown deviant like Sam, but there were no other choices available. If she wanted to keep the night's events a secret, she knew that she had to do something, and submitting to Sam seemed like the only option. 'You were going to destroy that tape,' she replied.

Sam's cruel smile returned. She brushed a stray lock of hair from Jasmin's brow, allowing her touch to linger. 'I think you were going to do something for me first, weren't you?'

'What would you want me to do?' Jasmin asked.

'I think you can start by letting me kiss you.'

It was all the warning that Sam gave before she acted. She slid into Jasmin's chair, pinning her to the seat. Her mouth was open as she pushed her face closer and she crushed her with greedy kisses. Sam tugged eagerly at Jasmin's blouse buttons, making no attempt to disguise the immediacy of her desires.

It crossed Jasmin's mind that she should struggle but she could see no point in doing that. She didn't want Sam's kisses, fearful that if she did accept them it might indicate something adverse about her sexuality. She had been excited when Dr Grady gave her the chance to touch Dinah but that had been her first opportunity to try such a thing. At university she had never considered looking at another woman and had been happy with every male lover she had known. There had been occasions when she and Melissa had shared a guy but that had always been done with strict deference to unspoken rules about not touching or even looking at each other. Regardless of what they had been doing, or how involved they had been in the moment, neither had explored the other's nudity. But, since returning to the village, Jasmin had caressed one woman intimately and was now being kissed by another. Worst of all, she thought, each experience seemed far more intense and exciting than the best of her previous encounters.

'Do you promise that you'll destroy the tape?' Jasmin mumbled.

Sam broke their kiss and leaned back. She reached for the front of Jasmin's open blouse and pushed her hand beneath the fabric. Her fingers found the shape of a bare breast and she cupped and kneaded the flesh. The ball of her thumb rolled against the fat bud of Jasmin's nipple and sparked a memorable bolt of friction. 'I'm a woman of my word,' she said quietly. 'I always do what I promise. Can you say the same thing?'

Jasmin blinked her mind away from the pleasure at her breast. Forcing herself to concentrate on the conversation, she asked, 'How do you mean?'

'You promised to do anything I said,' Sam reminded her. 'Are you going to do that?'

Jasmin studied her warily. 'What do you want me to do?'

Sam crossed her arms over her waist and quickly pulled the T-shirt away from her chest. She was braless and thrust her exposed breasts enticingly close to Jasmin's face. 'First, I want you to excite me,' she said thickly. 'Do you think you can do that?'

Jasmin's silence lasted for only a few seconds but inside her mind it continued for an eternity. A part of her wanted to refuse Sam's breathless command but there was another part of her that was eager to do whatever the woman asked. Torn between a need to do what she believed was right and a desire to do what her body wanted, Jasmin hesitated.

'Well?' Sam pressed. 'Do you think you can excite me?'

'I think I can do that,' Jasmin decided eventually.

Not allowing her doubts to make her linger any more, she embraced the redhead and pressed her mouth around her breast. The nipple was only small but it began to stiffen between her lips and grew thicker the more she moved her tongue against it.

Sam gasped and groaned loudly.

She made no attempt to disguise her enjoyment and Jasmin wondered whether she should give herself over to the same libidinous response. There was far more pleasure to be had from the experience than she would have thought possible and she alternated her hungry kisses from one breast to the other.

The knee of Sam's jeans pressed between her legs.

The pressure was hard and Jasmin rubbed her sex firmly against it. Her skirt was brushed aside and she experienced the rough weft of denim caressing her bare pussy lips. The pleasure was electric and the promise of her yearned-for orgasm returned with blistering force. Jasmin was briefly struck by the wealth of enjoyment and moved her mouth from the succulent treat of Sam's nipples.

Using a surprisingly gentle degree of force, Sam guided her head back to where it was needed. The weight of the woman's hands controlling her inspired a resurgence in Jasmin's arousal. She sucked furiously on the offered breast, occasionally daring to nibble at the delicate flesh. Her hunger for the task grew so strong that she didn't even consider stopping when Sam begged her to wait.

Sam had to prise herself from Jasmin's embrace before she could eventually free her breast and catch her breath. 'You're not the only one who can do that,' she grunted. Not elaborating on the cryptic comment, the redhead eased herself out of the chair and knelt between Jasmin's legs. Her hands clutched fistfuls of Jasmin's blouse and, with an unexpected wrench, she ripped the garment open.

Jasmin gasped as her breasts were exposed.

Sam's eyes shone with lascivious excitement.

Jasmin was thrilled to see appreciation and lust on the woman's face, and then the expression was hidden from view as Sam pushed her mouth over one orb.

The rush of pleasure was exquisite.

Jasmin steeled herself against the thrill, gripping the sides of the chair and burying her fingernails deep into the padded arms. She was aware of Sam's naked torso pressing against her and the contact threatened to be more than she could handle. Her body had never known so much pleasure and she was fearful that when her release finally did come it would be more than she could bear. Nevertheless, she found herself frowning with disappointment when Sam eased herself away.

'Did I do something wrong?' Jasmin asked.

Sam shook her head and started to unfasten the buttons on her jeans. 'You haven't done a thing wrong,' she assured her. 'I'm just taking these off so we can enjoy ourselves more.'

'Your friend seemed to think you shouldn't be doing this,' Jasmin mumbled.

Sam sniffed dismissively as she stepped out of her jeans and panties. 'My friend might be right,' she agreed. 'But that's not going to stop me. I've had a bellyfull of people telling me what to do and when to do it. I've decided now that I'm going to be the one in control.' She paused and frowned down at Jasmin. 'You are aware that I'm the one in control, aren't you?'

Jasmin hadn't heard a word.

The sight of Dinah's naked body had excited her but Dr Grady's estranged wife hadn't possessed the same beautiful poise that Sam was blessed with. The redhead's petite figure was slender and desirable, from the pert mounds of her breasts right down to the neatly trimmed tuft of ginger curls that concealed her sex. Standing with her legs apart and her hands on her hips, she looked dangerously exciting and Jasmin could feel the full force of her arousal swelling between her legs.

'You are aware that I'm the one in control, aren't you?' Sam repeated.

Eagerly, Jasmin nodded. 'I'm very aware of that,' she mumbled.

Sam seemed satisfied with the answer. She raised a commanding finger and turned it into a beckoning hook. 'In that case, if you're aware that I'm in control, you can crawl over here and lick my pussy.'

It was a thrilling command and Jasmin responded without any hesitation. She slipped out of the chair and lowered herself to her hands and knees. There was no hint of reservation as she crawled across the floor and she acted as though this sort of gameplay was second nature. As she neared the redhead, Jasmin became aware of Sam's excited musk. The fragrance was intoxicating and Jasmin sniffed the air greedily as she pushed her face closer. With growing excitement, determined only to savour the moment and not think about the consequences, she pushed her mouth against Sam's sex and began to lick.

Sam squealed ecstatically. She lowered her hands to Jasmin's head and held herself steady as the pleasure plundered her hole.

Like so many of the night's events, it was a new experience for Jasmin. The taste and texture of the woman's sex were a discovery of pleasure that she had never imagined. Sam's sex lips were smooth and responsive. The flesh was malleable beneath her tongue as she stroked back and forth and up and down. The urge to push inside crossed Jasmin's mind but she made herself hesitate, not wanting to rush the experience. She swallowed the sweet, intimate flavour of Sam's arousal, drinking greedily as the redhead's wetness grew more copious.

Unable to stop herself, Jasmin reached between her own legs. Her clitoris was an aching ball that demanded attention and she squeezed it lightly. The subtle touch almost crippled her as an exquisite shock erupted from her cleft. Briefly, she moved her head from the chore of tasting Sam, then she was burying her face back and nuzzling the ginger curls with renewed ferocity.

'You dirty bitch!' Sam exclaimed.

In spite of her shocked tone there was no real malice in her voice. Jasmin grinned up at the redhead and was met by her encouraging smile.

'We should do that properly for you, shouldn't we?' Sam suggested.

Jasmin wasn't sure what was being implied but she didn't shy away from the suggestion this time. She smiled up the length of Sam's body, happy to nod agreement to whatever lay ahead.

Sam's gaze darted around the room before falling on the forgotten church candle in the chair by the fireside. 'That'll do,' she said crisply. Her smile turned lascivious when she said, 'That'll do just fine. I wonder why you didn't see it before.'

Jasmin frowned, wondering whether she was being teased and if Sam knew what she had been doing with the candle. She thought the comment sounded innocent enough but she had already guessed that Sam was something of an unpredictable commodity. 'What are you going to do with that?' Jasmin asked, retrieving the candle for her.

Sam encouraged Jasmin to return to the chair. 'You just sit down and I'll show you.'

Jasmin didn't need telling twice. She returned to the chair and allowed Sam to position her so that she was sitting with her legs spread apart and her calves resting over the arms. It was a wanton pose that left no part of her body hidden, but Jasmin knew they were already beyond such inhibitions. She allowed Sam to kneel in front of her and thought only of the impending pleasure as the redhead teased the candle around her hole.

'That's a church candle,' she said quietly, wondering whether Sam would think it made a difference.

Sam shrugged. 'I'll remember that the next time I'm out shopping.' Without another word, she pressed the rounded base against Jasmin's sex and rolled the length of wax between her pussy lips.

Jasmin swallowed a small scream of protest, suddenly struck by the fear that the candle would be too large for her this time. She started to tell Sam that she wouldn't be able to manage this, then stopped herself from uttering the words for fear that they would break the moment.

Slowly, employing infinite patience and care, Sam began to work the base of the candle deeper.

Jasmin's sex was stretched wider as the candle began to fill her. Her pussy lips were strained taut as the thick girth of wax plunged inside. She was brushed by hot and cold sweats as she tried to acclimatise her body to the delightful combination of pleasure and pain. Jasmin balled her hands into fists, then clutched at her own ankles with the need to hold on to something. Pulling her legs further apart, she inched her hips forward, encouraging her sex to meet Sam's penetration.

'Does that feel good?' Sam asked. 'Or does that feel good?'

Struck mute with pleasure, Jasmin didn't reply. She wanted to tell Sam that there weren't sufficient words to describe the wonder that was visiting between her legs but she knew there would be no point. The thick girth was filling her, and sliding ever deeper, while the ridges and bumps of the carvings teased the mouth of her sex. A million blistering joys scorched from her hole and each one brought her millimetres closer to the triumph of release. She was on the verge of shrieking with her joy when Sam snatched the candle from her sex and slapped it into Jasmin's hand.

'My turn now,' Sam said cheerfully.

Jasmin stared at her with a combination of adoration and dark fury. Before she could raise an argument or protest, Sam was speaking over her.

'You said you'd do anything I told you,' Sam reminded her. 'I've just told you that it's my turn and you're not going to argue, are you?'

It was suddenly clear to Jasmin that Sam and Dr Grady were both carved from the same mould. Admittedly, the redhead was more honest about her desires and how they would be attained but, just like Dr Grady, Sam was single-minded in her quest for satisfaction. The discovery that she could be so easily controlled by such people wasn't the unsettling revelation that Jasmin thought it might be. Contrarily, she decided that if the rest of her life was meant to be played out as the submissive in a dominatrix's fantasies, it was a far rosier future than some of those she had imagined for herself.

'I've just told you that it's my turn,' Sam repeated. 'You aren't going to argue, are you?'

Reluctantly, Jasmin shook her head. She climbed out of the chair and allowed Sam to take her place in the seat in front of the fire. A part of her expected her satisfaction to diminish instantaneously but instead she found that her excitement continued unabated. There was an unarguable thrill to having another woman ride her with the church candle but there was an unexpected amount of enjoyment to be gleaned from doing the same for someone else.

She licked and nibbled at Sam's pussy before starting to tease her with the candle. Rolling the base slowly around the redhead's sex, she tried to squeeze the thickness between the slippery lips. She concentrated on the task, not hurrying even when Sam begged to feel more. Extracting malicious pleasure from the control she now had, Jasmin allowed Sam only small tastes of the length. She inched the candle gently forward, then snatched it away before the penetration could become too much.

'You teasing little bitch,' Sam growled. 'What are you doing?'

'I'm playing,' Jasmin replied coquettishly.

Sam threw herself back in the chair and tried easing herself on to the candle.

Jasmin contemplated prolonging the redhead's torment, then decided that she had suffered enough of that sort of misguided treatment herself for one evening. She pushed the length into Sam's cleft and was rewarded by the squeal of her climax.

'More,' Sam demanded. Her voice was a guttural command. 'I want more. And I want it faster. Much faster.'

Caught up in the passion of the moment, Jasmin wished there was a way they could share the bliss of release together. The idea came to her when she realised that half the candle was sticking out, with no hope of ever squeezing inside Sam's tightly packed hole. She raised herself to her haunches, thrust her sex to meet the untouched wick of the candle and guided it inside her sex. The phallic length of wax was penetrating them both and Jasmin pushed herself on to it without letting it slide from Sam's sex.

Sam screamed for a second time. She shifted in her chair and pulled Jasmin into her embrace. Her manicured nails clawed at Jasmin's back and she thrust her pelvis forward in a long and eager lunge. Her hands were alternately caressing gloves and cruel talons. She stroked the curve of Jasmin's waist, then buried her nails into the cheeks of Jasmin's backside. Resting back in her chair, shoving her hips forward, Sam pulled them both together. The action was done with enough finality to let their shared explosion flow from between them.

It was the release that her body had been craving and Jasmin was close to fainting with relief. Her abdomen was crippled by paroxysms of pleasure and it was all caught up in a discovery of new and exciting smells, sounds and sights. Her gaze went momentarily blurry and then she was falling away from Sam's embrace as the blistering enjoyment began to dwindle.

Unable to stop herself, Jasmin collapsed on the floor in a trembling, satisfied heap. The blissful pain of her climax continued to wash through her in slowly receding eddies. The study, which she had first considered to be gloomy and sinister, was now tinted by the rose-hued filter of her most satisfying orgasm.

'That was quite a satisfying show,' Todd grunted.

Jasmin was too drained to be bothered to glare at him, or ask how long he had been watching, but Sam seemed to have more than enough energy for that task.

'What the hell are you doing back here?' she demanded.

His crooked grin only turned wider in the face of her fury. 'I came back to tell you what you so desperately wanted to know,' he drawled.

The words made Sam flounder.

Jasmin had thought Sam was as wrapped up in their lovemaking as she had been but that misconception was quickly cast aside. Sam rushed to Todd, seeming to forget Jasmin in her haste to resolve something that was obviously far more important.

'You're going to tell me what you and Jo were up to?'

'You've been bursting to know, haven't you?'

She punched her arms back into her blouse and then stepped back into her panties as she waited for his reply. 'You know I want to know,' she insisted. 'Go on.'

'Jo was planning a surprise for you. She'd been planning it for over a month.'

'What surprise?'

'A surprise for you. A surprise that involved Jo, you, me and possibly a couple of other bodies from the office.'

Jasmin could see a flurry of expressions on Sam's face but it was difficult to decide which took precedence. There was disbelief, disgust and something that looked like mounting anger.

'Jo wouldn't have been planning a party. She'd set up rules to stop me from doing things like that.'

'The simple pleasure of denial,' Todd said, shaking his head. 'She'd set up those rules so that you'd enjoy it more. Haven't you ever noticed how nice a beer tastes when you haven't had one in a week or two? Haven't you ever noticed how delicious chocolate can be when it's been a fortnight since you've had a piece?'

'It's been more than a fortnight since I last had any,' Sam grumbled.

From the truculent tone of her voice, Jasmin suspected the redhead wasn't just talking about chocolate.

'She was just doing it to control me, wasn't she?' Sam whispered. Todd shrugged. 'She was using her damned rules to control me, just like she'd used that damned chastity belt.'

A sullen smile crept over her face and Jasmin was pained by the expression she saw there. Regardless of what they had shared, it was clearly inconsequential compared with the feelings that Sam held for her friend Jo.

'That's nasty,' Sam grinned. Admiration and annoyance fought for control of her face, leaving her smile twisted with grudging respect. 'That's really nasty,' she grinned. Seeming to come to a sudden decision, she said, 'That's nasty, and it needs paying back.' She turned a hard glare on Todd and asked, 'Why are you telling me this now?'

He tossed his glance between Sam and Jasmin. An almost bashful blush crept from beneath the collar of his khaki T-shirt as he began his explanation. 'You hinted that we might be able to do things if I told you. I thought I'd get back here before you'd finished.'

'You were too full of integrity to tell me before.'

He shrugged again. 'What do you want me to tell you? They say that you can buy anyone with the right bribe. I guess you found my price.'

Sam glanced back at Jasmin, her smile faltering briefly. Jasmin thought that expression had taken on a stern quality that seemed far removed from the dreamy look of passion she had worn before.

'Where did they all go?' Sam asked. 'Dr Grady, the naked blonde woman and your sister. Where did they all go?'

Jasmin opened her mouth and then hesitated. The night had been an emotional roller coaster filled with fears for her future and explorations into the unknown. Now, finally satisfied and beyond caring about any of those things that had seemed so important earlier, she wanted to be sure of only one thing before she answered.

'Are you going to destroy that tape if I tell you?'

'I promised that I would,' Sam assured her. 'But you have to tell me where the others have gone before I'll do it.'

Jasmin nodded, confident that her ordeal had finally ended. Dr Grady's punishments were distant memories, fuel only for any masturbatory fantasies she might want to indulge in at a later date. Her experiences with Sam and Dinah were indicators that there were more pleasures to be had from the world than she had ever considered before. And, most importantly, judging from the honest expression she could see in Sam's eyes, the threat of her indiscretions being discovered was now well and truly over.

'Come on,' Sam encouraged, stepping into her jeans and fastening them. 'Where did they all go to?'

'They all went to the same place,' Jasmin said quietly. 'They went to the old, abandoned church just behind this house.'

The answer had Sam lurching to the door without even saying goodbye. Jasmin caught her parting words and was shocked by the relief they gave, even though they weren't directed at her.

'I'm going to the abandoned church,' she told Todd. 'You can join me after you've been back to the van and destroyed those tapes that we've made.'

Nine

Dr Grady towered over them both, his frown austere and foreboding.

Staring into his coal-black eyes, Melissa felt small, exposed and vulnerable. She hadn't expected him to come to the abandoned church and she didn't know what he would make of the fact that she was now naked and in the company of a coven of witches. His anger had been bad enough when he was punishing her only for a handful of misdemeanours at university. She thought that these circumstances might be sufficient to make his wrath seem biblical.

'Two potential candidates,' he muttered. He turned his back on them and faced Dinah. 'I take it you've renounced your leadership?'

Dinah glared at him. Steve had come to her side but she didn't look as though she needed the comfort of his hand on her arm. 'You know I've renounced my leadership,' she said tiredly. 'You know the workings of our coven better than most of the priests and priestesses here. Do you think you'll be able to work out which of these is my replacement?'

Dr Grady nodded sagely. 'I can test them both,' he allowed generously. 'But I'm not promising anything.'

Dinah made an angry face and Steve's posture stiffened. 'Why did you have to bring this pompous fool here?' he demanded. 'What good do you think this twisted, no-good –'

'He's here to help,' Dinah reminded him.

'It's a brand of help that we can well do without,' Steve returned. 'The man's a manipulative piece of shite.'

By her side, Melissa heard Jo gasp with surprise. 'Of course,' Jo whispered. 'That's where I know him from.'

'I didn't come here to be insulted by your fellow pagans,' Dr Grady told Dinah. 'If you don't want my assistance I can go now.'

Dinah placed a hand on his arm. 'Don't go,' she pleaded. She fixed Steve with an impatient scowl that seemed to silence any further interruptions he might make. 'Please don't go,' she begged the lay preacher. 'I'm only asking this one small favour before I leave. Is it really too much for you to do for me?'

Dr Grady considered his reply before nodding consent. 'Just this one small favour,' he said eventually. 'But I'm warning you now: it could be that neither of these two is the witch that you're looking for. It could be that your spells haven't worked, and then what will happen?'

'You know what will happen,' Dinah said quietly. She lowered her gaze to study the floor. 'If neither of these is meant as my replacement then the coven will have to disband.'

He shook his head sadly and Melissa could see that he was struggling to contain a smirk. 'And we wouldn't want that to happen, would we?' he said sweetly. Not waiting for a response, he reached inside his bag and produced two black, rubber ball gags. He tossed them both towards Steve and snapped his fingers. 'Gag the pair of them,' he commanded. 'I have work to do.'

'Gag?' Jo began. She twisted at her ankles and wrists in an attempt to free herself. 'I don't think I want –'

She never got to complete the sentence.

Melissa watched two of the priests lift her from the floor as Steve wedged one of the ball gags into her mouth. Jo struggled but she was a lone, bound woman fighting against three strong, determined men. Her resistance was overcome and the gag was secured tightly in her mouth. As soon as it was fastened at the back of her head they pushed her back to the floor.

'I want them both gagging,' Dr Grady said fiercely. 'If either of them is a witch I don't want to suffer their curses.'

'You decry our religion,' Steve mumbled. 'But you believe in it enough to fear our magic.'

Dr Grady didn't bother looking at him. 'If I go back home I don't have to listen to that rambling pagan of yours,' he told Dinah. 'Is that what you want?'

Dinah pulled Steve to one side and began to hiss an angry rebuttal at him.

Remembering she had been instructed not to talk while she was in the church, Melissa didn't protest when she was forced to accept her gag. She allowed the ball of rubber to wedge her mouth open and tried not to think about what was going to follow.

'Take that one aside,' Dr Grady said, pointing at Melissa. 'I think we'll start on the other one first.'

Jo glared at him but Melissa knew from past experience that the expression wouldn't have any effect. She allowed the two priestesses to lead her to one side as Jo was lifted to her feet and then turned to face the altar.

'How are you going to test them?' Dinah asked.

Melissa was thankful that the woman had voiced the question because it was the same one she wanted answering. She listened attentively for Dr Grady's reply, torn between wanting to hear it and not wanting to know the suffering that was bound to be promised.

Dr Grady reached into his bag and produced a short, stubby cane. He held it in one fist, smiling grimly at its wicked length. 'My forebear, Mr Hopkins, had several effective methods of testing witches,' he began. 'But most of those would be unsuitable here. They were ultimate tests, based on pain and suffering, and they seldom gave anything to a witch's longevity. What I'm proposing will work along the same brand of pain and suffering, but we can manage it without a funeral pyre or a ducking stool.'

'What exactly are you planning?' Steve growled.

'I'm planning to test them,' Dr Grady replied. 'I'm planning to test them like this.' Without another word he hurled his cane against Jo's backside. The blow was sudden and severe, leaving a slim red line across both her buttocks.

Jo squealed around her gag.

Melissa began to tremble as she watched. Her earlier punishment at his hands had been brutal but she knew that Dr Grady hadn't used anything like the force he was now employing. A part of her wanted to sympathise with Jo's plight but she couldn't think beyond the fear that she would be the next to receive a thrashing.

'I'm planning to test them like this, and this, and this,' Dr Grady grunted.

He punctuated each phrasing with another slice across Jo's bottom. The cane snapped sharply but its crisp report was drowned out by Jo's muffled cries.

'I'll test them until one of them confesses that they're the witch.'

'How can either of them confess?' Steve demanded. 'You've got them gagged so they can't speak.'

'I know what I'm doing,' Dr Grady growled. He held up the cane as a warning and fixed his angry glare on Steve. 'I know exactly what I'm doing and I won't ask you again to stop interrupting me. If I have to hear one more of your impertinent, ignorant questions, I'll leave.'

The two men faced each other in a confrontation that looked set to turn ugly. Steve had brushed his cloak to one side so that the taut bulge of his muscles was obvious. He looked lean, athletic and physically capable but Melissa thought that Dr Grady looked equally imposing and he was brandishing a weapon. If their argument resulted in a fight, she thought it would be a bloody one and she didn't think Steve would be able to win against Dr Grady's malevolence.

'Please, Steve,' Dinah begged. She tugged at his arm, trying to pull him away. 'Please, leave him to do as I've asked.'

'It's not right,' Steve grumbled. 'If one of these women is meant to be your replacement, this is a piss-poor way of welcoming her to the coven.'

Although Dinah looked to be listening to his argument she didn't seem to hear. 'Please, Steve,' she repeated. 'Just leave him to do his job.'

Not disguising his frustration, Steve stepped back. 'I still don't think this is right,' he growled. Dinah tried to put a placating hand on his arm but Steve brushed it away as he pushed past her and walked to the back of the church.

'You can keep him out of my way until I'm finished,' Dr Grady told Dinah. 'I need to concentrate to do this properly and interruptions like him aren't helping.' Not giving her the chance to respond, he turned back to Jo and slapped the cane three times across her buttocks.

She stiffened beneath the onslaught and, by the time he had landed the last blow, Jo had begun to sob freely.

'Is she the one?' Dinah asked.

'I haven't even begun to test them yet,' Dr Grady snapped. 'This is nothing more than a warm-up exercise, just to get them prepared for what's going to come.' He summoned the priestesses with a snap of his fingers and got them to drag Jo out of the pentagram. Responding to his instructions as though Dr Grady was the coven's leader, the priests led Melissa to where Jo had stood and made her bend over for him.

She was aware of Dr Grady stepping closer, the aromatic scent of incense and masculine sweat reminding her of the punishment he had administered before. His mouth moved to her ear and he whispered, 'I gave you an instruction not to say a word while you're in here. I trust you're going to remember that.'

Melissa wanted to assure him that she would but she couldn't get the words around the gag. Realising he was only reiterating the warning, and that she wasn't supposed to answer, she simply nodded as he moved away. She tried not to tremble in anticipation of the pain that was going to come but it was difficult to exert the necessary control over her body. A part of her was scared that he would inflict more suffering than she could endure. Her fears were proved right because she almost fainted when the first blow struck. A weal of agony blazed across her buttocks, its burning sting penetrating deep beneath the flesh.

'Stay still,' Dr Grady barked. 'I want to make sure you're prepared for my tests. And I'm not going to

manage that while you're squirming like a dervish.'
He threw the cane down fiercely, striking again and
again and making each lash more punishing than the
last.

Melissa wanted to crumple to her knees. She
wanted to beg him to stop and then flee from the
church, but she knew that was impossible. Even if she
hadn't been gagged and bound she wouldn't have
been able to leave until Dr Grady gave her permission
and said that he had sorted things so that she could
return to her family. The only alternative available
was to stand miserably in the pentagram and endure
the chastisement that he was meting out.

By the time he had finished, her skin felt flayed. She
had begun to cry but she didn't know where the tears
came from or why she had released them. A dull,
shameful warmth was spreading between her legs and
she supposed that the base desire for pleasure was
one of the reasons why she had eventually started
sobbing. Not wanting to dwell on that thought,
anxious only to put an end to this torment as soon as
she could, Melissa allowed the two priests to lead her
from the pentagram.

'They seem sufficiently prepared,' Dr Grady said
cheerfully. He tucked the cane back into his bag and
produced a small, silver dagger. Its blade glinted
menacingly in the gloom of the church's candlelight.
'I suppose we should now begin our test properly.' He
took one of the candles from a priest and used it to
light the black one that stood on the witch's
makeshift altar. 'Bring me the brunette,' he said
coldly. 'It's time for her ordeal by the flame.'

Jo was shaking her head but no one acknowledged
her protest. Her struggling body was dragged into the
centre of the pentagram, where she was laid helplessly
on the floor.

'Move and I'll make your suffering all the more painful,' Dr Grady hissed.

He kept his words quiet, so they wouldn't be heard by the rest of coven, but Melissa could see his mouth shaping the threat and she caught the whispered echo of his meaning.

Jo clearly understood what he was saying because she remained completely still in the centre of the pentagram. The only part of her that moved were her eyes. They grew wider and rounder with fear.

Watching from the side, Melissa wondered why Jo looked so fearful. She supposed that Jo was unnerved by having someone so cruel standing over her with a knife but, she thought, it seemed obvious that Dr Grady wasn't going to use it to cut her. From what Melissa could see, it didn't even look as if he was going to use it to inflict pain. He held the dagger close to the spluttering flame of the black candle but it was never actually licked by the length of orange fire. For those in front of the altar, and for Jo laid beneath him, Melissa guessed it would look as if he was heating the blade, ready to test the brunette and discover if she was a witch. But Melissa could see his actions were a clever piece of misdirection and nothing more than a deceptive charade that was being played to mislead the coven.

'Are you ready for your ordeal by the flame?' Dr Grady demanded.

Jo shook her head from side to side as he made a pretence of drawing the dagger through the flame for one final time. She looked ready to roll away from him and try to make some doomed escape attempt, but he was pinning her to the floor before she could move. Extracting malicious pleasure from her fear, he placed the flat of the blade over her breast and pressed it across her nipple.

Jo looked set to howl, and then stopped herself. She stared up at Dr Grady with an expression of unfeigned confusion. She was clearly wondering why the blade hadn't branded her and Melissa suspected that she had already tortured herself by anticipating the agony. Knowing that she was going to be next to suffer this torment, Melissa had already imagined the pain of a searing heat burning through her own breast and decided that the punishment would be enough to have her screaming. Perversely, the idea left her torn between cold revulsion and a hot sweat of desire. The thought of being so horrifically abused was inflammatory to all the suppressed urges she still harboured. For an instant she found herself envying Jo, until she remembered that the woman wasn't really suffering any discomfort at all.

'See how this one is immune to the heat?' Dr Grady observed. 'She's able to take the test of the flame better than any normal woman. I think she could be the heathen you're looking for.' He snatched the ball gag from Jo's mouth. 'Are you a witch?' he demanded. 'And if you are, are you ready to confess?'

'You're a bloody lunatic,' Jo spat.

She shaped the words awkwardly, as though her mouth remained uncomfortable after the ball gag. Her speech was a rush of indecipherable syllables and the only reason Melissa understood was because she thought Jo was saying the same things that she might have said.

'Steve was right when he called you a manipulative piece of shite. I can't think of a better way of –'

'It sounds like she's speaking in tongues,' Dr Grady grumbled. He turned away from Jo, silently ordering a priest to return her gag and remove her from beneath the altar. As soon as he had gestured for Melissa to take her place, the two priestesses laid her in the centre of the pentagram.

Once again, he pretended to warm the blade, allowing it to glide near to the candle's flame but never actually be touched by it.

Staring up at him, Melissa thought he was putting too much into the charade and prolonging her torment far more than he had made Jo suffer. She could understand why the brunette had looked so apprehensive because, from the floor, it did look as though he was genuinely heating the dagger. A part of her was struck by the worry that, this time, he might be meaning to make her suffer an ordeal by the flame. The idea unsettled a pit of nervous snakes that writhed in her stomach. She stared fearfully up at him, suddenly aware that her body was drenched with sweat. When he finally guided the blade towards her, she struggled to remain motionless.

'Don't even think about moving,' Dr Grady warned her. 'You wouldn't want me to make a mistake while I'm holding this, would you?'

Horrified by the threat of violence, Melissa remained rigid as he moved the dagger nearer to her breast. She could see he was trying to press the flat side against her nipple and wished that the bud hadn't stiffened with anticipation. It was the last thought she had before he flattened the cold silver against her flesh.

It was almost an anticlimax to find the dagger hadn't been heated but Melissa still found there were waves of pleasure to be had from her relief. For an instant she had been able to imagine the anguish of having a red-hot blade pressing into her nipple. The prospect left her sweltering in ice-cold sweat.

'This one didn't even flinch when the hot blade touched her,' Dr Grady told Dinah. 'There's a chance that this one also might be the witch that you're looking for.' He pulled the gag away from Melissa's mouth and glared solemnly. 'Am I right?' he asked. 'Are you a witch?'

Knowing that he didn't want her to say yes, not sure what the proper answer should be anyway, Melissa lowered her gaze.

Dr Grady placed his fingers beneath her jaw and tilted her head back until their eyes met. 'I asked a question and I demand an answer,' he growled. 'Are you a witch?'

She shook her head and released a small sob. 'No,' she whispered. 'I'm not a witch.'

'So, it's neither of them?' Steve growled. He had returned from the furthest corner of the church and was talking to Dinah, but his tone was loud enough for everyone to hear him. 'You brought him here just so he could tell us it was neither of them. What a waste of time.'

'It could still be either of them,' Dr Grady said. 'There are other tests to perform yet.'

Melissa was chilled by the idea that there was more to come but she didn't get the chance to make her feelings known. One of the priests pushed the ball gag into her mouth while another began to lead her out of the pentagram. Jo was dragged past her, taken back to the five-pointed star's centre, and Dr Grady retrieved his cane from his carpetbag.

'One of you is a witch,' he declared. There was an undercurrent of anger in his tone and it grew sharper with each blow he delivered. The crisp whistle of the cane, the swift snap of its impact against Jo's flesh, all sounded more severe than they had before. 'One of you is a witch, and you're going to tell me which one of you it is.'

Jo thrashed against her restraints, clearly pained by her suffering. Her backside was a crisscross of pulsing red lines and Melissa was torn between envy and pity.

As she bent double, her cleft was exposed and it was obvious that her suffering had inspired arousal. Her hole looked wet, excited and open.

Dr Grady delivered six brisk slices, then commanded that Jo be led away and replaced by Melissa.

She didn't wait for the priests to force her to bend double, assuming the position in readiness for him. Although she didn't want to be subjected to the pain and humiliation, she knew that a part of her needed it. She was already in the demeaning position of being naked beneath the scrutiny of strangers but, while her mind was insisting that this was wrong, Dr Grady's punishment seemed darkly desirable. A part of her wanted to feel the blazing sting across her buttocks and she knew she wouldn't feel properly satisfied until the punishment had taken her beyond the brink of orgasm.

The caning was over all too quickly.

When the first strike landed she was overcome by the belief that she had been wrong. The pain was too severe to be enjoyable and whatever part of her mind had decided she wanted it was seriously misguided. That belief held less sway when the second blow landed and waves of bubbling heat began to melt the flesh between her legs. The warmth grew stronger with the third and fourth blows and she was close to euphoria when the fifth struck.

Dr Grady paused and Melissa could hear that his breath was laboured with exertion. She tried to picture him standing behind her, wondering whether he was testing his aim or building the strength to make the final slice of the cane a truly punishing one. The idea was enough to make her pussy muscles clench and her knees tremble with the threat of impending orgasm.

Mercilessly, Dr Grady flung the cane against her.

Melissa heard its crisp bark as the impact scorched her backside. The blow didn't provide the release she needed but it came disturbingly close. Her pussy lips tingled with excitement and she knew that one more strike would be enough to push her body through the barrier of her climax. She briefly considered begging Dr Grady for another three strikes, then stopped herself. It wasn't that she feared the humiliation that such a request would bring – she felt beyond concern about such trivia – but she knew she would be unable to speak with the ball gag filling her mouth.

'What are you going to do now?' Dinah asked.

Melissa was taken out of the pentagram and Jo was led back to its centre.

'He's got no idea what he's going to do now,' Steve grumbled loudly. 'Can't you see that he doesn't have any real plan here? Can't you see that he's just doing this for the sadistic pleasure that he gets out of it. He's not doing this for our benefit.'

Dinah was already telling him to be quiet when Dr Grady turned around. His face was livid and he looked set to hurl his cane at the horned one. 'I won't stay here and tolerate that pagan's insults,' he told Dinah. 'If you want me to stay, then you'll get him to be quiet.'

'Please, Steve,' Dinah insisted. 'If not for me, then for the sake of the coven.'

'I don't trust him,' Steve replied. He got no further, stopped by something in Dinah's pleading expression. With a wave of resignation he nodded and stepped back.

'How are you testing them?' Dinah asked.

Dr Grady glared at her. 'Am I hearing your mistrust as well now?'

'Not at all,' she said stiffly. 'I just thought it might pacify Steve's doubts if you explained what it is that you're doing.'

Dr Grady looked as though he was considering this, then nodded. 'There are traditional ways of testing a witch,' he began didactically. 'My ancestors used several sly methods, all of them involving pain, but most of them proving tragically fatal. I don't propose to use anything that might prove fatal, but that's the only concession I'm going to make. I personally guarantee that every device I use will inflict nothing less than the utmost physical suffering.'

'Why is pain so important?' Steve demanded.

Dr Grady glared at him and didn't answer the question until Dinah had repeated it.

'Tell us,' she said quietly. 'Why is pain so important?'

'A true witch can tolerate any degree of suffering,' Dr Grady explained. 'One of these women is a pretender and she will eventually break and confess that she has no purpose in being here. The other will endure her suffering without complaint.'

'But they've both complained so far,' Dinah observed. 'Surely –'

'Did you call me here to cast aspersions on my methods? Or did you call me here to get results?'

The question silenced her and Dinah stepped back to Steve's side.

'Is this how you intend to behave when you reach the inner city?' Dr Grady sneered. 'I doubt there are many urban pagans who will be so tolerant of your constant questions.'

Seeming satisfied with his put-down, he fumbled through his bag and retrieved two small plastic clips. Melissa thought they looked like miniature pliers and she wondered how he intended using them. She didn't have long to mull over the question because Dr Grady looked intent on working swiftly. He took the dagger from the altar and cut the twine that bound

Jo's ankles. Issuing abrupt commands, he got a priest and a priestess to hold her feet in place, encouraging them to spread her legs wide apart.

A sick excitement stole through Melissa as she watched. She knew what Jo was suffering – the pain, the humiliation and the excitement – and she secretly envied the woman for being the first to endure Dr Grady's malevolent mistreatment. But her arousal came from more than that. The knowledge that she would be suffering the same indignity filled her with dark trepidation.

'We'll test you with the cross,' Dr Grady said quietly.

His words seemed to defy his actions because, instead of reaching for the crucifix that poked out of his bag, he took hold of one of the clips. He struggled to prise the jaws apart and Melissa could see that his efforts were hampered by the clip's strong bite. It seemed like a torturous implement to be applied to any part of the body but, when Dr Grady clamped it against Jo's cleft, it looked sickeningly inhumane.

The brunette howled. If she hadn't been restricted by the ball gag her cries would have shrieked loudly around the church. In spite of that, she still managed to do an impressive job of making her discomfort known. She writhed against her restrained hands and tried kicking her legs free. But it was all a useless show of defiance. It seemed even more futile when she repeated her ineffectual protest after Dr Grady had fastened the second clip between her legs.

'There,' he said, pointing to the priests. 'Keep her legs apart, and hold those in place for me.'

They acted quickly on his instruction. Dr Grady seemed confident in their obedience as he turned to his bag and retrieved his crucifix. He held it awkwardly, reminding Melissa of the vampire hunters she had seen in old horror films. He brandished the cross warily towards the coven and seemed to strike a semi-majestic pose. She might have thought he was trying to ward off the evil that he saw in them, but a glimpse at the back of the crucifix made her think otherwise. The light was poor throughout the church but, because she wasn't with the rest of the coven, Melissa could see there was something painted on the back of the cross. She squinted to try to make out what she was looking at but couldn't make out anything more than a gelatinous smear. For some reason that she couldn't fathom – possibly the pungent, minty smell that struck her nostrils and her knowledge of Dr Grady's plans were unfolding – Melissa guessed the crucifix had been daubed with liniment or vapour rub.

'The test of the cross,' Dr Grady proclaimed. He held up the crucifix and then pushed it down against Jo's bare breast.

She struggled beneath the indignity, and her muffled cries whispered past the edge of her gag.

'This one doesn't like it,' he grinned.

As he spoke he rubbed the crucifix back and forth over her orb. Melissa could see the line of red flesh he was leaving and she wondered whether he going to use that mark as proof that his test was working.

'This one doesn't like it at all,' he said again. He raised the crucifix briefly, only to thrust it against Jo's other nipple. He was clearly using more force this time because the brunette tried to roll away. The priests encouraged her to lie flat but it was a struggle that neither of them would have managed alone.

A movement at the back of the church caught Melissa's eye. She didn't think the rest of the coven had noticed, but a newcomer was entering the nave. Keeping to the shadows, a slender redhead crept silently closer. She was clearly transfixed by the events she had stumbled into but had enough sense not to draw attention to herself. Melissa watched her for a moment, then decided that her concentration ought to be devoted to the more pressing concern of what Dr Grady was doing.

'I think this one might be the witch that you're looking for,' Dr Grady told the coven. 'Should I give her the final test?'

He didn't wait for a reply. Instead, he pushed the back of the crucifix hard between Jo's legs. The miniature clamps were spreading her pussy open and Melissa knew that the liniment would be burning the sensitive lips of the woman's sex. She could imagine the torment involved and empathised with every one of Jo's frustrated cries.

'Is it her?' Dinah asked eagerly.

Steve was standing beside her and his expression-less goat's-head mask seemed to be asking the same question.

'Is it her?' Dinah repeated. 'Is she the one?'

Dr Grady rubbed the cross briskly against Jo's cleft. Melissa thought the pressure would have been severe without the vapour rub but she imagined that the searing agony had to be unbearable. Jo was still howling with the pain when he tore the ball gag from her mouth and bawled the question into her face.

'Are you the one?' he demanded. 'Are you a witch?'

'Why are you doing this to me?'

'Are you a witch?' he screamed.

'No more than you are,' Jo returned. She looked set to say something else but Dr Grady was already shoving the gag back into her mouth. He motioned for the priests to take her away and replace her with Melissa.

'If she's the one, why isn't she admitting to it?' Steve asked.

'How am I supposed to know?' Dr Grady sneered. 'Isn't it bad enough that I know the workings of your coven without understanding the psychology of its warped participants?'

Without allowing Steve a chance to respond he turned back to Melissa and glowered down at her. As he had with Jo, he cut the twine that bound her ankles, then motioned for the priests to hold her legs apart.

The clips weren't as bad as she had expected. She had seen the way their bite pressed into Jo's pussy lips but it wasn't the punishing thrill she had been hoping for. There was an exciting moment of frisson when Dr Grady tugged her labia into their jaws but, aside from that, their pressure was little more than a firm, innocuous hold. Even when the priests tugged her open, pulling her sex wide apart and exposing her gaping wetness, Melissa was more aware of the psychological discomfort rather than any physical pain. She was beginning to suspect that the same lack of satisfaction might hold true when Dr Grady scoured her with the crucifix, and she braced herself for the disappointment.

'The test of the cross,' he said dramatically.

The coven pressed closer as he pushed the crucifix against Melissa's breast.

The liniment burned her nipple, leaving a red-hot agony in its wake.

'This is impossible,' Dr Grady complained. His voice sounded overly pained, as though he was forcing the emotion to be there. 'They're both responding like witches.'

Pushing the cross to her other breast, he rubbed more firmly.

It was only a subtle friction, and Melissa doubted if it would be noticed by any of those watching. Even if they did discern any movement, she knew it would simply look as if Dr Grady was trying to hold the cross still against her writhing body. And, while it was only a subtle friction, the effect against her breast felt as though she was being branded by a heated poker. The crucifix was dragged back and forth over her teat and she bucked and thrashed as the eddies of painful pleasure washed through her. Tears of pure joy were streaming from her eyes and the onset of orgasm started to tremble in her loins.

'I think you're going to be disappointed, Dinah,' Dr Grady said quietly. 'I don't think either of these is going to give up her secret.'

Dinah and Steve cursed.

Melissa barely heard either of them because Dr Grady chose that moment to push the crucifix against her sex. The torment at her breasts had been uncomfortable but that was like the tickle of a feather compared with the burning pain that scorched her pussy. The liniment rubbed brusquely against her flesh, prickling and scratching with a coarseness that left her panting. As soon as he placed the crucifix against her hole, Melissa felt sore and tender. The instant he began to move his hand back and forth, the whole experience became too much.

Melissa began to appreciate why Jo had been screaming because, much as she wanted to suffer the extremes of everything that was going on, this torture was proving to be more than she could cope with. She rolled her head from side to side, silently imploring him to show some leniency.

He caught her eye and his cruel smile widened. Seeming to read her need for release, he pressed the cross against her clitoris and rubbed it more briskly.

'Are you the witch?' he bawled, pulling the gag from her mouth.

Melissa was caught in the throes of something that seemed like agony and might have been orgasm. To find her body in such a confused delirium was almost as exciting as the extremes that had taken her to that point.

Dr Grady caught her face in one hand and held it still as he glared at her. 'Answer me!' he demanded. 'Are you the witch?'

She sniffed back a tear and allowed his face to swim into focus. She was torn by the idea of saying that she was the witch, but she knew there would be repercussions if she did that. 'No,' she decided eventually. 'No. I'm not the witch.'

He pushed the gag back into her mouth and snapped his fingers for her to be taken away.

'How much longer are you going to carry this on?' Dinah asked.

'I can do this for as long as is necessary.'

'How much longer do you think these two can cope with it?'

'The pretender will break eventually,' Dr Grady said confidently.

He returned to his carpetbag and rummaged through its contents. Melissa could see that he was trying to decide which implement to use next and she was almost disappointed when he retrieved only his cane. He had used so much imagination with his previous punishments that a part of her had been looking forward to something crueller. It was shocking to find her thoughts so lecherous and depraved but, now that she had discovered there were such pleasures to be had, Melissa was looking forward to every new experience.

Dr Grady sliced three swift swipes across Jo's buttocks. The blows were delivered with more force

227

than he had used before but Jo didn't respond to them this time. She accepted her punishment like a woman who was broken and defeated.

'Tell me you're a witch,' Dr Grady demanded.

He tugged the ball gag from her face and punctuated the question with a whistling blow. The cane struck her buttocks and Jo arched her back as the pain coursed through her.

'Answer me,' he insisted. 'Tell me you're a witch.'

'Go to hell,' Jo growled.

With a snap of his fingers, Dr Grady called for Melissa to be brought into the pentagram. He tugged the ball gag from her mouth and threw it into his carpetbag. Once he had positioned the two women so they were bent over, he alternated his caning from one backside to the other.

'Are you looking for a witch?'

They all turned to face the voice. Melissa saw Dr Grady's frown deepening as though this wasn't a factor he had allowed for in his plans. No one else seemed to have noticed the expression because all eyes were looking at the redhead.

'Are you looking for a witch?' she shouted. 'Is that what you're doing?'

'Salvation,' Jo muttered.

'And what do you know about this?' Dr Grady demanded. 'What do you know about our inquisition?'

'I know that you've got your witch there,' the redhead said. She pointed a single, accusatory finger at Jo and her smile turned into a triumphant leer. 'That's your witch,' she proclaimed. 'And I think that it's time you dealt with her properly.'

Ten

'That's right,' Jo agreed.

The words surprised her even as she said them but she could see that it was exactly the right thing to say. She supposed that panic and confusion had stopped her from seeing the obvious way of escaping this punishment but, now that Sam had given her the means to try this ruse, Jo was determined to take advantage of it. She pulled herself out of Dr Grady's reach and stood up defiantly to face him.

'You're right and you've finally forced the truth out of me,' she declared. 'I am the witch you're looking for.'

Dr Grady glared at her but Jo was beyond being intimidated by him.

His eyes narrowed to angry slits as he spoke. 'She lies.' He fixed her with a warning finger and implored the coven with a wild, desperate expression. 'She isn't really the witch. She's not a witch at all.'

'She is a witch,' Sam called from the nave. 'I know her and I tell you she is.'

Jo reached for the lapel of Dr Grady's jacket and pulled him close. Forcing her voice to a guttural whisper, she said, 'I know what you did tonight.'

He looked ready to brush her hand aside but Jo held him firmly.

'I know what you did tonight with her,' she said nodding at Melissa. 'And I know what you did with her sister. Do you want me to start telling these people here all about it? Or would you rather I distributed the tapes?'

'Tapes?' A flush of guilt turned his features pallid. 'What tapes? What are you talking about?'

'I'm talking about the CCTV tapes that came from the camera I've had in your house,' Jo replied evenly. 'The ones that recorded what happened in your study this evening. Those are the tapes I'm talking about.'

His flushed features blanched. 'You've had a camera in my house?' Jo grinned into his mounting panic. 'Why have you done it?' Dr Grady hissed. 'What do you want?'

'To be frank with you, I want quite a lot,' Jo told him. 'You're not going to like what I ask. You're going to argue about a lot of it. But, now that you know I've got tapes of you and Melissa and her sister, you're going to do everything I ask.'

He looked set to argue but Jo didn't allow him the chance.

'The first thing you can do is back me up when I say I'm a witch.' In a louder voice, raising her tone so that it carried over to the coven, she said, 'I am a witch, aren't I?'

His features looked menacing. 'I think you might well be,' he agreed.

'See!' Sam cried. 'She *is* a witch. Didn't I tell you? She's a witch. She's a witch! Let's burn her.'

Jo glared at her partner but the expression was missed in the gloom of the candlelit church. Pushing Dr Grady to one side, unsteady on her aching legs, Jo staggered towards Dinah. 'If I'm the witch that your coven is looking for, that means I'm in control now, doesn't it?'

'The coven will always follow their leader,' Dinah replied.

Jo nodded and turned to Steve. If there was going to be any opposition to her plans she knew that he would be the one to make it. Knowing that she had to appear confident in her control, she spoke to him with a voice that was strict with authority. 'You heard what Dinah said. You take your orders from me now. Is that clear?'

Reluctantly, after giving Dinah a cursory glance, Steve nodded. 'I suppose that's clear.' His sullen tone told Jo that, regardless of how clear it was, it wasn't a situation that he liked.

'I want you to take the coven back to the stone circle. I want you to take them and prepare them for the night's final ritual.'

'And which ritual might that be?' he asked gruffly.

It wasn't a question Jo had been anticipating but she could see that everyone expected her to have an answer. The priests and priestesses were studying her hopefully and both Steve and Dinah looked as though they needed her answer before they would move.

'Go on,' Steve urged. His tone said that he knew she was bluffing and it sounded as if he was trying to taunt her into saying the wrong thing. 'Go on. Which ritual are we supposed to prepare for?'

Before Jo could answer, or jeopardise her situation with a show of ignorance, Verity was standing by her side. 'It will be the ritual of the black flame,' she said quietly. Smiling somewhere between Dinah and Jo, she filled her voice with conviction and said, 'If we use the ritual of the black flame, the candle will show us the way.'

Satisfied, Jo nodded. The answer seemed to be all the reply that was needed to dismiss the coven, because Steve and Verity began to lead them out of the church.

Jo stepped over to Sam, unmindful of the way that the redhead was glaring at her. 'A witch?' she asked, trying not to smile. 'You called me a witch?'

'It's not the first name that I wanted to call you,' Sam growled. '"Duplicitous cow" would have been my first choice. "Conniving bitch" would have been my second. Todd told me what you were up to. You're a control freak. Do you know that?'

Jo rolled her eyes. 'We can't discuss this now,' she began. 'It isn't the time or the place.'

'Of course it isn't,' Sam agreed. Her scowl darkened as she studied Jo's nudity. Sarcastically she said, 'There's no time to discuss anything while you're working to your interpretation of the no-fraternisation rule.' She graced Jo's bare body with a scathing glance and said, 'I can't believe you skived off the surveillance assignment to go partying with these weirdos.'

'I think you're misinterpreting the facts,' Jo started. She stopped when she saw Sam's scowl deepen. It was clear that nothing she said would convince Sam that she was mistaken and Jo couldn't see the point in having a confrontation. She glanced briefly in Dr Grady's direction and asked, 'Did you record him doing anything else after I'd left?'

Sam nodded. 'He's quite a naughty little lay preacher. I'd bet the pair of you could learn a lot from one another. He could teach you how to whip a backside properly, and you could teach him how to be deceitful.'

Sensing that they were on the brink of another argument, Jo decided it was time to close the conversation. 'We've definitely caught him in an embarrassing situation?'

'Todd said it would be embarrassing for a lay preacher to be filmed having his dick sucked by the uni student that he's just spanked,' Sam told her. 'Are you happy taking my word on that, or do you want to personally debrief Todd for confirmation? You've been wanting to debrief Todd since he joined us, haven't you?'

Not rising to the bait, Jo simply said, 'Lend me your mobile.'

Sam reached into her jeans and handed over the phone.

Jo asked Melissa for her father's home number and then punched it into the keypad. Not looking at Sam, trying wilfully to concentrate on anything other than the disapproval of her partner, Jo said, 'I want you to take Melissa back to her sister and then get them both home.'

'And what are you doing?'

'I've got other things to do here. Then, I think I've got to go out to the stone circle.'

'That doesn't surprise me,' Sam sneered. 'And it doesn't surprise me that you want me out of the way.'

Jo tried to interrupt but Sam seemed determined to make her point.

'I'll do as you've asked,' Sam agreed with sudden vehemence. 'I'll take Melissa and Jasmin back home. But mark my words: it'll be the last thing I ever do for the Flowers & Valentine Detective Agency. It'll be the last thing ever.'

Jo pursed her lips and said nothing.

Seeming frustrated that her threat hadn't evoked more of a response, Sam snorted angrily. She marched past Jo, dragged Melissa from the pentagram, and then took her out of the church.

'You make quite a commanding leader,' Dinah observed. 'I think the coven will be in good hands with you at their head.'

Jo ignored her. She fixed Dr Grady with her fiercest glare and said, 'Are you going to tell your ex-wife what you've been up to?'

'I don't do the bidding of heathens,' he said firmly.

'Maybe you didn't use to,' Jo said. 'But I think things are going to change.' She held out Sam's telephone. 'From what I understand, you need to phone their father before Melissa and Jasmin will be allowed home.'

'That's right,' he agreed. His smile turned nasty as he added, 'So your colleague is wasting her time trying to take them back there, isn't she?'

Jo shrugged, still holding out the phone. 'Sam might be wasting her time, but she's used to that. And I think you're going to decide to phone him, rather than let me make the call. Did I tell you that Sam's taking them back home in my surveillance van? That's the van that contains those tapes I've recorded of you, in your study this evening.'

A flurry of arguments crossed his face but Jo could see each one being squashed before he got a chance to voice it. He snatched the phone from her hand and pressed the green button to make the call. 'I'll do this,' he growled. 'And then I think you'd better return those tapes to me before I lay a blackmail charge against you.'

'What do the tapes show him doing?' Dinah asked.

As Dr Grady spoke into the phone, Jo turned to Dinah. 'He's been caught in a compromising situation,' she began. She had no idea what the tapes showed and, while she suspected her guesses might be right, she didn't want to say anything that could make Dr Grady think she was bluffing. She struggled to remember something salient from the events she had caught before leaving the surveillance van but nothing came to mind. She could recall so few details that she didn't dare say anything that might give away her ignorance. Thinking back to Sam's glib comment, and hoping there was some truth in it, she said, 'He had Melissa and her sister in his study. He's had them both doing his bidding and a part of that involved spanking and fellatio.'

Dinah nodded. There was no surprise or puzzlement on her face as Jo delivered the details. The only emotion she showed was growing anger. 'I should have suspected as much,' she grunted. 'I should have known that's what he was up to.'

'He's been very clever,' Jo concluded. She hoped that she sounded like someone who knew what they were talking about because she felt as though she was way out of her depth. She hadn't *seen* Dr Grady doing anything and the little that Sam had told her would prove useless if he asked her for any facts. All she had were a handful of suspicions and the hope that Dr Grady would be reluctant to have his indiscretions described out loud. Trying to steer the topic away from her ignorance, she said, 'He's put an awful lot of planning into this evening and you have to give him credit for that.'

'A lot of planning?' Dinah frowned. 'What sort of planning?'

'He knew you'd all be in this church,' Jo explained. 'He knew you'd be looking for a new leader. And he knew it would throw your plans into confusion if he sent Jasmin and Melissa up here.'

'Why on earth would he do that?'

Jo stared at her, wondering why Dinah couldn't see the obvious. 'He did it to be sure he was rid of you. He did it so, as soon as you were gone, your coven would have to disband.'

Dinah's mouth fell open into a surprised 'O'.

'You're right,' Dr Grady said angrily. 'And it would have all gone like clockwork if you hadn't shown up.' He had finished his call and pushed the phone angrily back towards Jo. 'If you hadn't shown up, these heathens would have decided that neither of those girls was a fit leader and the coven would have had to disband.'

Dinah stopped Jo from taking the phone and fixed her ex-husband with a frown. 'I think you'd best call Principal Dean,' she told him.

'Call Tom?' He stared at her scornfully. 'At this time of the morning?'

'If you've gone to the trouble of planning so much I don't doubt you organised the expulsion of Jasmin and Melissa,' Dinah growled. 'You can phone him now. I don't think Tom will mind receiving a call at this time of the morning. Not if he wants to avoid being involved in the scandal you've made.'

For an instant the couple were locked in a silent, angry exchange. Dr Grady looked loath to obey Dinah's instruction but Jo could see that he had no other option. With a frustrated growl he relented and began to tap the number into the phone. 'How much more do you think I'm going to do for you two bitches?' he hissed. 'How much more do you think you can get away with?'

Dinah walked over to the carpetbag and began to rummage through the contents. 'I think we're going to get away with an awful lot more,' she smiled. 'And I don't think you're going to enjoy a single moment of it.'

Seeing the woman's menacing grin, Jo guessed they were on the same wavelength. They waited patiently, listening as Dr Grady apologised for the late hour of his call, and urgently impressed the importance of reinstating Jasmin and Melissa. When he had finished, Jo took the phone from him and placed it safely on the altar. It sat neatly between the black candle and one of the wicker poppets.

'You wanted to know how much more we would want from you,' Dinah reminded him. She tugged a whip from the bag and studied it slyly. It was a short crop, topped with a dozen slender, leather tendrils. Seeming to decide it wasn't the implement she wanted, Dinah tossed it to Jo before finding a second whip. It was longer than the first and the ends were broad, thick straps that looked painfully heavy. Her grin turned evil as she tightened her fist around its handle. 'You wanted to know how much more we would want? The first thing I want is to see you down on your knees, praying for my forgiveness.'

'You'll never see that,' he growled. 'Never.'

Jo shook her head. 'Considering the tapes we have, I don't think that's the right answer.'

'Get down on your knees,' Dinah insisted. She raised the whip and took a step closer to him. 'Get down on your knees now.'

Slowly, glaring at them both with an expression of impotent venom, Dr Grady lowered himself to his knees.

Dinah grabbed the back of his head and dragged his face until his nose was nuzzled in the curls of her pubic mound. Brandishing the whip above him, she hissed, 'This is your first instruction, darling. And you'd be wise to obey it. I want you to lick me.'

He tried to struggle but it was a weak and hopeless attempt at escape. Dinah's grip was firm and she held him in place until he darted a tongue against her sex.

'You'd better lick me well,' Dinah warned him. 'The shit you made me put up with this evening really hurt, and I don't just mean when you whipped my backside. Your pious speech about being beyond the temptation of my charms . . .'

Her voice trailed off and Jo watched Dinah shiver with a spasm of obvious pleasure. Greedy to enjoy that experience, fired by her own welling excitement, Jo snatched Dr Grady's head from Dinah's pussy and pulled him towards her own.

'You haven't just hurt her this evening,' she said thickly. 'You've hurt me as well. Before you start pleasuring Dinah, I think I deserve a kiss better.'

He hesitated with his mouth only inches from her cleft. The warmth of each exhalation warmed the tops of her thighs and Jo knew he was trying to think of an argument that would allow him to resist. Not giving him the chance, tugging on his hair until she was sure he was on the verge of squealing, Jo bucked her hips closer to his face. 'Kiss it better,' she demanded. 'And kiss it now.'

Dr Grady placed his lips against her mound and pecked dryly at her sex.

Jo tightened her hold on his hair and shook him fiercely. 'Kiss it properly,' she warned. 'You're in no position for defiance.'

His hesitation lingered for a moment longer and then he gave in. A tentative tongue stroked her pussy lips and the warm, wet pressure of his mouth melted her sex.

Surprised by her own responsiveness, Jo groaned. The torment of her testing had left her feeling sore and used but the punishment had also fuelled her libido. She didn't doubt the lay preacher's tonguing would make her forget her suffering and that thought was driven home when he licked the centre of her need. A spasm of excitement flourished between her legs.

Dinah placed a hand on Jo's arm. 'I think he should start apologising before he does much more of that.'

It wasn't what Jo wanted Dr Grady to do, but she supposed Dinah had a point. Reluctantly, she guided his face away from her sex and allowed the blonde to take control of his head.

'You heard what I said,' Dinah growled down at him. 'Because of you a lot of people have endured a lot of suffering this evening. I want to hear your apology.'

Dr Grady wiped the back of his hand against his mouth, as though he was trying to wash away an unpalatable taste. 'Apologise?' he snorted. 'Apologise to harlots and witches? I don't think so.'

An expression of outrage crossed Dinah's features. She looked set to start using the whip on him before Jo broke in. Sure that she knew what was needed, governed by the unarguable dictates of her arousal, Jo snatched Dr Grady's head from Dinah's grip and repositioned herself. She bent over and thrust her buttocks towards his face. 'If you can't apologise, you can use your tongue for something more productive.'

He struggled to pull his head away but Jo was well practised at holding subordinates where they needed to be. She had done it so often with Sam that the dominating position had become second nature. His resistance began to subside when it finally became clear that Jo wasn't going to relinquish her hold.

'You hurt me tonight,' she reminded him. 'And you haven't properly *begun* to make up for it yet.'

'And what are you expecting me to do?' he sneered.

Jo glanced over her shoulder and frowned down at him. 'I'm expecting you to kiss my arse,' she said flatly. 'I'm expecting you to kiss my arse and, if you know what's good for you, you're going to do it.'

She didn't allow him the chance for further argument. Instead, she pulled his face towards her buttocks and thrust herself back on to him. There was a brief resistance and he tried jerking his head back, but Jo's hold on him was unrelenting. She kept her grip tight in his hair and waited until his tongue nuzzled her puckered muscle.

The eruption of pleasure was instantaneous.

His tongue squirmed into her orifice, stretching the tiny ring of her anus and plundering her forbidden depths. She writhed against him, chasing a deeper penetration with the certainty that it would rid her body of the last vestiges of pain she had been forced to endure.

She closed her eyes but, instead of being enveloped in a world of darkness, she found that her vision was tainted with a misty red haze. The colour made her think of Sam's Titian locks and, as soon as the image of her partner was in her mind, Jo was struck by a pang of guilt. She had wronged Sam over the past couple of weeks and she was unhappy that it was taking the tongue of someone like Dr Grady to help her see that fact.

Remembering Sam's parting words, suddenly fearful that their relationship might really be over, Jo toyed with the idea of leaving Dr Grady and Dinah and going off to sort out her personal life. There was a thrill to be enjoyed from Dr Grady's subjugation, but Jo thought it would have been more satisfying if she could have experienced the pleasure with Sam. However, there were other factors to consider and, in addition to resolving the current case, there was also the yearned-for orgasm that she was chasing. She knew that a woman with more integrity might have left anyway but Dr Grady seemed surprisingly skilled at anilingus and, because he had dominated her so cruelly, Jo was loath to stop revelling in the control that she had over him.

'This isn't getting us any closer to hearing his apology,' Dinah grumbled.

Jo shrugged, beyond caring about his apology. Her interest in that aspect of the case was negligible and nowhere near as important as her need to climax. She writhed against him, encouraging his tongue to wriggle further inside. She was vaguely aware of Dinah reinvestigating Dr Grady's carpetbag, but that was happening on the edge of her vision and seemed like nothing more than an unnecessary distraction.

'I demanded an apology,' Dinah said loudly. 'And, if I don't get it soon, I'm going to start getting angry.'

Jo didn't allow Dr Grady to respond, pulling him hard against her backside so his tongue could get deeper. She was close to orgasm and not even the note of ire in Dinah's voice was going to distract her from that goal. She silently repeated that assurance as she savoured his wet intrusion and braced herself for the impending release.

The slash of a whip broke her concentration. Jo glanced back over her shoulder and saw that Dinah was making use of the cat-o'-nine-tails that she had found. The blonde striped Dr Grady's arse, forcing him to buck forward and thrust his tongue deeper in Jo's hole.

'Ask for my forgiveness,' Dinah demanded.

Jo kept Dr Grady's face tight between her buttocks, not giving him the opportunity to reply. She thought about telling Dinah to wait her turn, and point out that there would be plenty of time for each of them to punish the lay preacher, but one glance at the woman's thunderous face told Jo that the argument wouldn't be well received. Dinah was raising the whip and flexing her biceps as she prepared to land another blow. Her determined frown said that nothing was going to sway her from this course of action. Glancing down at Dr Grady, Jo was surprised to see that Dinah had half stripped him in readiness for this punishment. His pants had been pulled down to his bended knees and his bare buttocks were

241

exposed to the empty church. His pale flesh was peppered with pulsing red weals where the cat's first blow had caught him.

Dinah hurled the whip down for a second time, forcing Dr Grady to groan. 'Ask for my forgiveness,' she repeated. 'I want to hear that now.'

Reluctantly, Jo allowed Dr Grady the necessary freedom to speak.

'I'm sorry,' he grunted. His cheeks were a vicious crimson and his eyes glowered with antagonism. 'There. I've said it for you. Is that what you wanted to hear? I've said that I'm sorry.'

Dinah raised the whip. 'Confess your sins and seek repentance,' she growled. She aimed the cat and Jo could see she was going to wield it with uncompromising force. Briefly, she considered telling Dinah to go easy, and thought about mentioning that it was possible to inflict too much pain. Then, remembering the misery that Dr Grady had made her suffer, Jo decided to let Dinah do as she wished. The blow struck him with the deafening report of a gunshot.

'You sanctimonious bitch,' he howled. He spat the words between laboured breaths. 'I thought your religion was based on beliefs of forgiveness and understanding. I thought that the head of a coven would frown on physical punishment.'

'You're right,' Dinah agreed. 'The religion of Wicca doesn't condone physical suffering. And you're right when you say that the head of a coven would never condone it. But you seem to forget: you've made me relinquish my position as mother goddess.' She hurled the cat at him again and scored another resounding smack.

As Dr Grady growled his way through a string of expletives, Dinah tossed the whip to the floor and went back to his carpetbag.

'I'm no longer the leader of the coven,' she told him, retrieving a fresh whip from the bag. 'And that means that I'm not governed by any rules that say I have to be forgiving or understanding.' Admiring the knotted tips of the new cat, she smiled tightly and then aimed another shot. 'The only thing I need to be is a pissed-off ex-wife with a grudge and a chance for revenge.'

Jo sympathised with Dr Grady's suffering but the emotion wasn't so much that she felt compelled to intervene. After the punishment he had made her endure, and the physical and mental torment that he had inflicted on Melissa and Jasmin, she thought it was only fitting justice that he experience a taste of what he had meted out. She pulled his face back towards her buttocks and tugged his hair until he returned his tongue to her anus. Her pleasure was made more satisfying when she heard Dinah inflict a swift succession of viciously loud blows.

'Look at you,' Dinah purred.

Jo glanced over her shoulder and saw that Dinah was down on her knees, by Dr Grady's side.

With one hand underneath him, she stroked the thickness of his rigid shaft. 'Earlier on you told me that you were beyond the heathen magic of my charms,' Dinah giggled. 'It certainly doesn't look that way now.'

He pulled his face away from Jo and glared at Dinah. 'You pagan harlot,' he gasped. 'You foul, depraved –'

Dinah tugged sharply on his shaft, silencing his diatribe. In a seductive tone she whispered, 'I wonder how you became aroused like this. You insisted that you were beyond the effects of my charms. And this excitement hasn't been brought about by having the chance to punish a defenceless young woman,' she continued. 'So where did this erection spring from?' As she spoke, she stroked her hand back and forth along his shaft. His length twitched and stiffened until it was full and thick and hard. 'You don't suppose that this means you have an unexplored appetite for pain, do you?'

His cheeks turned a flustered purple. 'You'll pay for this,' he told her. 'As God is my witness, you'll pay for this.'

Dinah smiled sweetly for him. 'Perhaps I will,' she agreed. But, then again, perhaps my marriage to you was payment enough.' She gave his shaft a brisk tug, then stood up and tossed the whip to Jo. 'You can punish him now,' she decided. 'I want his tongue inside me.'

Jo thought about refusing, pointing out that her own needs hadn't been satisfied and that she was now leader of the coven. But there was something in the gleam of Dinah's smile that said the woman wouldn't tolerate insurrection. In spite of the fact that Dinah had been used and manipulated, and in spite of the fact that she had given up her position as head of the witches, the glint in her eyes said that she was still very much in control.

Catching the whip in midair, Jo pushed Dr Grady away from herself and watched as Dinah forced the lay preacher's face between her legs. He began to nuzzle without any prompting and Jo wondered how much of his complaints and refusals had been made because he thought that was what they expected. From the greedy way that he devoured Dinah's sex, it was obvious that his need to do her bidding was stronger than he was admitting.

As she landed the cat against his arse cheeks, Jo wasn't surprised to see his shaft stiffen. She caught him with a second blow, marvelling at the way the pain seemed to increase his excitement.

'Don't go lightly,' Dinah barked. Her voice was thick with arousal and the warmth of growing passion. 'After the way he's treated us this evening, he doesn't deserve any leniency.'

'I have no intentions of going lightly,' Jo said, throwing a scouring shot across his buttocks. 'No intentions at all.'

She was struck by a pang of remorse, sure that she should have been doing this for Sam, rather than an undeserving specimen like Dr Grady. Again, the idea that she had wronged her partner inspired another bubble of guilt and she tried to exorcise the sensation by whipping harder.

The cat bit sharply, making him release a garbled cry. Most of the sound was lost as he pushed his face closer into Dinah's wetness, but there was enough anguish to make Jo know that she had hurt him.

Yet still that did little to make her feel as though she was doing the right thing. Much as Dr Grady deserved to be thrashed – and she had to admit that it had been a while since she had met anyone so deserving of this brand of suffering – Jo still wished she was enjoying the experience with Sam.

'Now, you'll suck here,' Dinah demanded.

Jo blinked herself from her reverie and watched the blonde guide Dr Grady's face towards her side.

The lay preacher tried to protest, shaking his head and repeating the word 'no', but Dinah didn't give him the opportunity to resist. She forced his face beneath her breast and made him suck on her third nipple.

The pleasure overtook her instantaneously. Her eyelids fluttered as though she was in the throes of extreme euphoria and she clutched his head tighter to herself. Her fingernails clawed like talons against the back of his head and she stumbled away from him, as though she was trying to escape a joy that was too powerful to accept.

Watching from behind, Jo saw that Dr Grady's erection looked painfully thick. His scrotum was a tight, preclimactic sac and his need to climax was obvious, even from a distance. Jo raised the whip slowly, unconsciously tensing the muscles in her arms as she took aim. She shot the cat against him and the knotted tendrils landed with a crackle. They scorched his arse cheeks and punched at his balls and anus.

Dr Grady howled. As he gave voice to the cry, his shaft twitched and spurted underneath him.

Laughing cruelly, Dinah released him. Her elated smile showed that she was still enjoying the aftermath of her own joy. After blinking down at the lay preacher, she shook her head in a theatrical gesture of disappointment. 'Look what you've done,' she said, pointing at his spattered seed.

The rivulet of white spend puddled on the dusty floor beneath him and some had even splashed beyond the chalk-drawn lines.

In a tone of mock horror, Dinah said, 'You've soiled our sacred pentagram. How horribly sacrilegious.'

He glared up at her, his cheeks flushed with impotent fury. 'You base and heathen –'

'Don't bother insulting me,' Dinah broke in. 'Just lower your face to the floor and then lick it up.'

A scowl of revulsion twisted his lips and he shook his head. 'You can't even think that I'd do –'

'Lick it up,' she insisted. 'Or we'll make you go through this again and again.'

It was clear that, in spite of her threat, he was still trying to find a way to refuse. However, something in the determination of Dinah's gaze seemed to convince him that there would be no point in continuing his defiance. With obvious distaste, he lowered his face and began to lap the semen from the floor.

Dinah didn't bother watching him. Instead, she walked over to Jo and took the cat-o'-nine-tails from her hand. 'I can't say it's been the best night of my life,' she said sadly. 'But I must thank you for all the help you've given me. My only regret is that you had to suffer under that bastard.' She cast a disparaging sneer in Dr Grady's direction.

He seemed aware that she was talking about him because he looked up from the floor. A string of his ejaculation dangled from his chin, and his mouth looked white and greasy. If he could have seen his reflection, Jo imagined the lay preacher would have believed his humiliation to be complete. Seeing the cowed glimmer in the back of his eyes, she suspected that he was deliberately trying not to think about the image he presented.

'You can whip me all you like,' he gasped desperately. 'And you can humiliate me from now until Judgement Day. But none of it's going to change a thing, is it? You'll still be leaving the village by the end of the week and,' he added, nodding at Jo, 'I doubt the coven will last two minutes under her control.'

Dinah's face showed her dismay. She looked ready to use the whip she was holding when Jo stopped her.

'I have a confession to make,' Jo said. She widened her smile so that it incorporated Dr Grady. Speaking loudly, trying to emphasise the importance of her revelation, she said, 'I'm not really the witch you were looking for.'

'That changes nothing,' Dr Grady proclaimed. 'In fact, that makes it even better. You can both whip me all you like but it won't change a thing. I've defeated you, Dinah. You're leaving the village and your

247

coven is without a leader. Those godless heathens will disband and I'll have absolute control of the village's moral standing.'

'That's like putting the rat in charge of the cheese parlour,' Jo whispered. She considered trying to retrieve the whip from Dinah, wanting to find some way of staunching Dr Grady's smug triumph. Before she could snatch the cat-o'-nine-tails, Dinah was stepping away from her and towering over the lay preacher. 'You sent the coven to the stone circle?' she asked Jo.

Jo nodded.

'And they're preparing to perform the ritual of the black flame?'

Not sure what they were doing, and only vaguely remembering that Verity had said something about a black flame, Jo nodded more doubtfully this time.

The answer seemed to satisfy Dinah because a glow of radiance transformed her features. She stared down at Dr Grady and used her toe to point out a droplet of his seed that he had failed to lap up from the floor. While he grudgingly lowered himself to lick it away, she retrieved her cowl from one of the pews and wrapped it around her shoulders.

'Your planning has been well thought out, darling,' she told him. 'And I'm impressed by the way you've managed to manipulate so many people to do your bidding. But I don't think things are going to work out exactly the way you expected. In fact, I'm *sure* they're not going to work out the way that you expected.'

A worried frown crossed his brow. 'What are you talking about?'

Dinah's grin blossomed. 'You wanted to know what else I wanted from you before I was done? There's only one more thing, and you can go back home and do that now.'

'What is it now?' Dr Grady demanded. 'What else do you think I'm going to do for you?'

Jo grinned when Dinah told him.

Epilogue

'... the candle will show us the way ... the candle will show us the way ...'

This time, Verity didn't scream when she saw the horned one. Towering seven foot tall, his yellow eyes still gleaming in the candlelight, he was to her no longer the truly terrifying spectacle he had been. He was only Steve, consort to the mother goddess, whoever she might now turn out to be. In the few short hours since she had become a neophyte, and more worldly in her understanding of the coven, Verity could now see that there was no reason to fear him. In fact, as she stared up at his imposing figure, she began to wonder whether there was even any reason to believe in him.

Once again, her fellow witches had tied her to the corners of the pentagram and she lay there secure, naked and vulnerable. Her hands and wrists were bound, spreading her open and ready for the horned one. But Verity no longer felt exposed or embarrassed by her position. Even when the remainder of the coven danced past, still chanting that the candle would show them the way, Verity was unaffected by their voyeuristic interest.

The only feeling she was aware of was a growing burden of disappointment.

As a probationer, she had never allowed her conviction in the magic to waver, but now her doubts were beginning to set in. She had believed that the combined strength of Beltane, and the ritual of the black flame, would find the coven a new leader, but it didn't seem as though any of that had happened. And, after all that she had seen and done this evening, Verity was no longer sure that a new leader was what the coven needed. The idea of worshipping beneath a different mother goddess from Dinah seemed as wrong as all of those horrible things that Dr Grady had done to Melissa and Jo.

'. . . the candle will show us the way . . . the candle will show us the way . . .'

She released an exasperated sigh as she listened to the chant, wondering how the priests and priestesses could still pay lip service to that misguided belief. The candle hadn't shown them the way. The candle had only taken them to a church where they had found unworthy impostors. As she lay in the pentagram and reflected on the disappointment of this Beltane, Verity grew more convinced that neither Jo nor Melissa could take Dinah's place as the coven's mother goddess.

'It's time for the ceremony to begin,' Steve said gruffly. He held a long, black candle in one hand, and a taper in the other. Placing the light to the wick, he paused until the flame had caught and the candle was burning brightly. His jaw was set solemnly beneath his mask. 'Neophyte!' he called. 'Are you ready?'

Verity didn't feel ready but she knew that the ritual wouldn't wait until she was in the mood. Nodding for him, not caring that the gesture pulled her hair, she whispered, 'Yes.'

He cast a frown and Verity could see that her meek reply was insufficient. Trying to inject her voice with an enthusiasm that she didn't feel, she spoke more loudly and gave her answer to the night, 'Yes, horned one,' she declared. 'Yes, I'm ready.'

He stepped over her, placing a foot on either side of her body. His cloak was pulled back over his shoulders, but even the sight of his glorious nudity wasn't enough to draw her out of herself.

Earlier in the evening the idea of having Steve had charged her with a furious arousal. Now, although her anticipation remained strong enough to make her pussy muscles squirm hungrily, she realised her need for the experience was no longer the demanding urge that it had been. The realisation that the night hadn't turned out to be a success filled her with sadness and that emotion seemed perversely wrong for her sacrificial position in the centre of the pentagram. Trying to shake off her doubts, trying to believe that even at this late hour there was still time for the candle to show them the way, Verity urged herself to push the negative thoughts out of her mind.

'We have to begin this ritual with a reminder of the rule of three,' the horned one proclaimed.

It wasn't an aspect of the ceremony that Verity had forgotten and she clenched her bound hands into fists as she braced herself for the impending discomfort. Dinah's introduction to the rule of three had been a revelation in dark pleasure but, instead of remembering the joy that she had received, Verity could only think that it wouldn't be the same experience without the true mother goddess there. She doubted that the horned one alone would be able to inspire her with the same thrill and her growing reservations increased her belief that everything had gone wrong.

Steve lowered himself over her.

The dark curls of his scrotum tickled between her breasts and his erection hovered close to her bare chest. Her sex muscles began to tingle more greedily and she idly toyed with the idea of giving herself over to the arousal. Quickly, before she could submit to that licentious thought, Verity checked herself. Admittedly, there was a satisfying sexual pleasure to be had from the coven's rituals. But Verity knew that if she just gave herself over to that hedonistic thrill she would be missing the most vital part of the magic. If she concentrated only on the sexual aspect of what they were doing, she knew the experience would be hollow and only physically satisfying. A part of her was already beginning to fear that all of the coven's problems this evening were the result of her surrendering to those craven indulgences during the first ceremony and she was determined not to make that same mistake twice. Focusing intently on the spell, she quashed her thoughts of sexual excitement and willed herself to believe that this time the magic would work.

'. . . the candle will show us the way . . . the candle will show us the way . . .'

'The rule of three,' Steve said loudly. He held the black candle above her breasts. Its long flame grew taller in the night. 'A single moment's pain in return for three times the pleasure. Are you ready for that reward?'

'Yes,' Verity whispered. 'Yes, I'm ready.'

Her reply was barely spoken before he tilted the length of wax and allowed it to spill against her. There was a moment when Verity thought that her memory of the pain had become exaggerated since the night's first ritual. She had remembered the discomfort as being severe and unbearable but this dribble seemed to do little more than warm her breast. And then her nipple was seared by the molten wax.

Verity sucked air. She writhed against her bondage as the spasm of pain almost crippled her. She was still struggling with the discomfort when Steve reached for her breast and began to toy with the rigid cap of wax that coated her.

'A single moment's pain, in return for three times the pleasure,' he repeated.

He plucked the hardened wax away and placed his mouth over her teat. His tongue was a silky friction and his saliva a cooling balm. A delicious ripple soared from her chest, filling her with a rush of excitement and need. As he gently sucked, then teased, the sensitive end of her breast with his teeth, he whispered, 'A single moment's pain, in return for three times the pleasure.'

She wanted to relax and wallow in all the enjoyment that he could administer but she was convinced that it would be wrong. Wilfully, Verity stopped herself from revelling in the indulgence and tried to concentrate on the ceremony.

However, the more she thought about what they were doing, the more certain she became that the coven had made a mistake. To be honest with herself – and she supposed that her position as a neophyte in the centre of the sacred pentagram made it imperative that she be honest – Verity believed that she was the one who had made the mistake. Reflecting on all that had happened since the night began, she saw that the entire evening was a catalogue of all the misguided choices she had made. She had briefly believed that Melissa was the chosen one, but Steve had proved her wrong by showing what the blonde would allow herself to accept while in the centre of a sacred pentagram. Also, before being told to leave the church and return to the stone circle, she had entertained the idea that Jo might be the coven's new leader. Yet now, remembering the woman's flippant attitude to their beliefs, Verity was wondering whether that was another error of judgement. She began to reason that, if she had been wrong about those two facts, perhaps she had been wrong in her suggestion that they should look for their new leader in the abandoned church. She was even beginning to think that they might all have been mistaken in their belief that it was time for Dinah to relinquish her command of the coven.

Even as the second stream of wax spattered against her, her thoughts were more involved with the wrong choices she might have made rather than the painful pleasure that she was receiving.

Steve sucked her breast, biting more forcefully and shocking her with a bewildering joy. Verity groaned beneath him but she couldn't convince herself that the sound was purely inspired by what he was doing. To her own ears, the noise sounded like a wail of regret. She half watched as he moved lower down her body and then raised the candle for a third and final time. His smile glinted from beneath his mask as he appraised her body with an honest lechery.

'A single moment's pain in return for three times the pleasure.'

Her sex was scalded by the flow of molten wax.

Verity struggled against her bondage as the pain rushed through her. Her suffering was briefly eased by the horned one's breath against her pussy lips. And then she realised her body was on the verge of climax. Quite where the build-up of pleasure had come from was a mystery that she couldn't understand. Her thoughts had been detached from everything he was doing, yet still she was caught in the throes of a serious need for orgasm. As his tongue began to chase the rivulets of wax away, she realised that the moment of release was only a whisper away.

In spite of her reservations, in spite of all the efforts she had put into remaining unaffected, she was prepared to give herself over to the climax. She was on the brink of allowing the pleasure to take her when a woman's voice broke through her thoughts.

'Prepare to welcome your new leader.'

Verity glanced into the darkness. She squinted into the night above her, wondering where the woman's voice had come from and why it sounded so right. Beyond the head of the horned one's mask, she could see a half-naked figure stepping towards her, but it was impossible to identify who it was, or why she seemed so familiar. Verity supposed that the evening had been filled with the sight of so many inviting feminine figures that she had reached a saturation point where each one was indistinguishable from the others. Her gaze focused on a pair of ripe, swollen breasts and she had time to notice that the nipples were cerise and stiff with arousal.

'. . . .the candle will show us the way . . . the candle will show us the way . . .'

The priests and priestesses renewed their chant with a welling excitement that made Verity feel sure that she was missing something. She tried to raise her head and see what was happening but, with her hair secured at the peak of the pentagram, the task was impossible.

'A coven without a leader is like a candle without a flame,' the woman proclaimed. 'This candle is no longer without a flame. This coven is no longer without a leader. Neophyte! Prepare to pay homage to your new leader.'

Not able to see who it was, Verity was aware only of one thing. The horned one had the candle clutched to his chest and its long yellow flame was blinding her. As the new leader stepped into the pentagram, the flame flickered and then burned in a solid black light. Its surreal brilliance lasted only for a faltering moment, little more than a couple of seconds, but it bathed them all with its eerie dark glow. That instant's inexplicable phenomenon convinced Verity that she was now in the presence of the true mother goddess.

'The candle has shown us the way,' she whispered. 'The candle has shown us the way.'

Pushing the horned one aside, the mother goddess stood over Verity's body and lowered herself down. She performed the action with an athletic grace that seemed natural for someone with such a perfect, feminine figure. Her naked thighs eclipsed the night and the split of her sex hovered over Verity's face. The blonde curls around her labia were sticky with wetness but Verity recognised the pussy lips in the same moment that she identified the woman's voice.

'Dinah,' she gasped. Verity was unable to hide the adoration from her voice. 'It's you. You're our leader.'

'Did you ever doubt that?' Dinah smiled. Affectionately, she stroked a tear of joy from the corner of Verity's eye. 'Did you ever doubt that for a moment?'

Returning her smile, unable to stop a fresh tear from replacing the one that the mother goddess had removed, Verity continued to grin adoringly up at the woman. She was still smiling broadly when Dinah repositioned herself and pushed her cleft over Verity's face. The mother goddess continued to lower her body until the weight of her labia pressed firmly over Verity's mouth.

Not wanting to resist the unspoken command, anxious to involve herself in every aspect of the ceremony now that she knew it had all worked out as it should, Verity began to lap at Dinah's musky scent.

She allowed her tongue to slip against the delicate folds of flesh, savouring the intimate flavour and relishing the experience. From a distance she heard Steve's puzzled voice but, even though he was asking the same questions that had formed inside her own mind, Verity was busy concentrating on the task of welcoming the coven's new leader and couldn't be bothered paying proper attention to the exchange.

'You're resuming leadership of the coven?' Steve whispered.

'You have no problems with that, do you?' Dinah replied.

He laughed at the absurdity of the suggestion. 'No problems at all. But what about your transfer? How are you going to lead the coven if you have to take a new position at a health centre two hundred miles from here?'

'The position at the health centre is going to be filled by *one* of the village's Dr Gradys,' Dinah explained. 'But it won't be me.'

She moved back, taking her sex briefly out of Verity's reach.

Longing to continue, Verity struggled to reach her but her bondage made the task impossible. She glanced briefly at the new faces gathered around her and saw that Jo was standing behind Dinah. The two women were smiling fondly at each other, as though they had reached an understanding that bordered on friendship. The observation was only a passing one and it was virtually gone by the time Dinah returned her pussy lips to Verity's mouth. It suddenly struck her that all her doubts had been misplaced and there had never been any reason for her faith to waver. From the first moment, during the night's first ritual, the candle had shown them the way. Its magic had taken them to where they needed to be to secure the leadership of the coven's rightful head and Verity saw she had been right in her assertion that they would find their leader in the abandoned church. The magic had worked, she thought happily, and the candle *had* shown them the way.

'Jo was kind enough to help make my ex-husband see how much benefit he could give to the health centre of an inner-city development zone,' Dinah told Steve. Her voice came from a million miles away, muffled by distance, the weight of her thighs and Verity's own lack of interest.

'Considering the amount of magic Jo's worked this evening,' Dinah continued, 'she really could have been my replacement.'

'You've done a good job,' Steve told Jo. 'You've done a really good job.'

Jo seemed uncomfortable with the compliment. 'I might have been able to do it more quickly if you'd revealed yourself as my client earlier on.'

'Client?' Dinah asked.

Verity could feel the word trembling through the woman's body. She tried urging her tongue deeper and was rewarded by the mother goddess's gratified shiver.

'What do you mean by "client"?'

'Steve asked me to keep an eye on your ex-husband,' Jo told her. 'Of course, because he's spent the entire night wearing that mask, I didn't realise Steve was my client until fairly late on this evening. But I think he should be happy about the way that you and I have used the tapes he wanted recording.'

Verity paused for a moment, wondering whether she was going to hear anger or upset in Dinah's reply. She could sense that the mother goddess had stiffened but she didn't know whether that was in response to sexual pleasure, concentration or growing annoyance. Even as a probationer she had thought it was difficult

259

to judge Dinah's mood swings and reactions. Now, as a neophyte, she realised she was still in no position to guess how the coven's leader was likely to respond.

'You did a good job for us,' Dinah told Jo. 'I think I speak for the entire coven when I say that we owe you a debt of gratitude. How can we thank you?'

'Pay your invoice within fourteen days,' Jo said quickly. 'That's all the thanks I need.'

Verity stroked her tongue along the length of Dinah's sex. The pulsing nub of the mother goddess's clitoris throbbed against her upper lip and she briefly toyed with the idea of teasing it between her teeth. She knew that her sacrificial position in the pentagram made her inferior but that didn't stop her from thinking that they were all overlooking the importance of the ceremony. It seemed wrong that the mysticism of the ritual was being spoiled by the distraction of their conversation and she wanted to remind Dinah where her priorities should be focused. Before she had a chance to nibble on the pulsing bud, Dinah sat back on her haunches, stealing the treat of her sex away from Verity's reach.

'Surely there must be something personal we can do for you?' Dinah asked Jo.

Turning to look at the brunette, Verity saw that Jo looked briefly sad. The light from the candles deepened her frown lines and temporarily spoiled her striking beauty.

'I doubt that even your spells would be strong enough to work the magic that I need,' Jo said quietly. 'But thanks for the offer.'

'Does this concern that red-haired girl?' Dinah asked. 'The one who appeared in the church and called you a witch?'

'Her name's Sam.' Jo grinned. 'And yes. Like most of the things in my life that make me unhappy, this does concern her.'

Dinah glanced behind Jo and her smile briefly widened. 'Sam's coming this way now,' she observed. 'Maybe you ought to go and discuss your problems with her?'

Not hiding her surprise, Jo turned to Sam.

The moonlight glinted against the lenses of the redhead's spectacles, making her expression unreadable. There was a nervous lilt to her smile but beyond that it was impossible to say what she might be thinking.

Verity didn't get the chance to see anything further because Dinah chose that moment to cover her view. The warmth of the mother goddess's sopping cleft was returned to Verity's mouth and she was allowed to use her tongue as she wanted to. From a distance, above the chanting of the priests and priestesses and beyond the growing pulse of her excitement, she could hear the murmur of a conversation.

'Does the Flowers & Valentine Detective Agency still exist?' Jo asked softly.

'I suppose that's what I came up here to find out,' Sam replied. 'You were trying to set me up with Todd. And you were going to use that as a reason to punish me, weren't you?'

'You would have enjoyed it,' Jo pointed out. 'And, while we're on the subject of punishment, I think you deserve disciplining for trying to get me burned at the stake.'

Their voices were growing smaller and Verity guessed they were walking off into the darkness.

'That was a bit naughty of me,' Sam agreed. 'Are you going to make me suffer worse than I've ever suffered before because of that?'

Jo was silent for a moment and Verity thought the couple had moved out of earshot. When she heard Jo's eventual reply, she realised the woman had only been considering her response.

'No,' Jo told Sam. 'I don't think that your trying to get me burned at the stake merits your suffering worse than ever before. You'll have to try harder than that. You'll have to try much harder.'

There was a longer silence and this time Verity really did think the couple had gone for good. The priests and priestesses continued to chant, their voices promising to drown out any reply that she might detect.

'In that case,' Sam said suddenly.

Verity strained to hear what she was saying.

'Before you decide how I'm meant to suffer,' Sam continued, 'perhaps I should tell you what's happened to all the tapes of Dr Grady and Jasmin.'

There was a cheerfulness in the redhead's voice that said their argument had finally been reconciled.

Lying in the centre of the pentagram, blissfully tonguing at the mother goddess's sacred hole, Verity realised that, even for Jo and Sam, the ritual of the black flame had worked, just as it had for all of the coven. Convinced that she had been wrong for harbouring any doubts, she could see that, for each and every one of them, the candle had shown them the way.

NEXUS BACKLIST

This information is correct at time of printing. For up-to-date information, please visit our website at www.nexus-books.co.uk

All books are priced at £5.99 unless another price is given.

Nexus books with a contemporary setting

ACCIDENTS WILL HAPPEN	Lucy Golden ISBN 0 352 33596 3	☐
ANGEL	Lindsay Gordon ISBN 0 352 33590 4	☐
THE BLACK MASQUE	Lisette Ashton ISBN 0 352 33372 3	☐
THE BLACK WIDOW	Lisette Ashton ISBN 0 352 33338 3	☐
THE BOND	Lindsay Gordon ISBN 0 352 33480 0	☐
BROUGHT TO HEEL	Arabella Knight ISBN 0 352 33508 4	☐
CANDY IN CAPTIVITY	Arabella Knight ISBN 0 352 33495 9	☐
CAPTIVES OF THE PRIVATE HOUSE	Esme Ombreux ISBN 0 352 33619 6	☐
DANCE OF SUBMISSION	Lisette Ashton ISBN 0 352 33450 9	☐
DARK DELIGHTS	Maria del Rey ISBN 0 352 33276 X	☐
DARK DESIRES	Maria del Rey ISBN 0 352 33072 4	☐
DISCIPLES OF SHAME	Stephanie Calvin ISBN 0 352 33343 X	☐
DISCIPLINE OF THE PRIVATE HOUSE	Esme Ombreux ISBN 0 352 33459 2	☐

NYMPHS OF DIONYSUS £4.99	Susan Tinoff ISBN 0 352 33150 X	☐
THE SLAVE OF LIDIR	Aran Ashe ISBN 0 352 33504 1	☐
TIGER, TIGER	Aishling Morgan ISBN 0 352 33455 X	☐
THE WARRIOR QUEEN	Kendal Grahame ISBN 0 352 33294 8	☐

Edwardian, Victorian and older erotica

BEATRICE	Anonymous ISBN 0 352 31326 9	☐
CONFESSION OF AN ENGLISH SLAVE	Yolanda Celbridge ISBN 0 352 33433 9	☐
DEVON CREAM	Aishling Morgan ISBN 0 352 33488 6	☐
THE GOVERNESS AT ST AGATHA'S	Yolanda Celbridge ISBN 0 352 32986 6	☐
PURITY	Aishling Morgan ISBN 0 352 33510 6	☐
THE TRAINING OF AN ENGLISH GENTLEMAN	Yolanda Celbridge ISBN 0 352 33348 0	☐

Samplers and collections

NEW EROTICA 4	Various ISBN 0 352 33290 5	☐
NEW EROTICA 5	Various ISBN 0 352 33540 8	☐
EROTICON 1	Various ISBN 0 352 33593 9	☐
EROTICON 2	Various ISBN 0 352 33594 7	☐
EROTICON 3	Various ISBN 0 352 33597 1	☐
EROTICON 4	Various ISBN 0 352 33602 1	☐

Nexus Classics

A new imprint dedicated to putting the finest works of erotic fiction back in print.

------ ✂ ---------------------------------

Please send me the books I have ticked above.

Name   ....

Address   ....

....

....

.... Post code ....

Send to: Cash Sales, Nexus Books, Thames Wharf Studios, Rainville Road, London W6 9HA

US customers: for prices and details of how to order books for delivery by mail, call 1-800-805-1083.

Please enclose a cheque or postal order, made payable to **Nexus Books Ltd**, to the value of the books you have ordered plus postage and packing costs as follows:
    UK and BFPO – £1.00 for the first book, 50p for each subsequent book.
    Overseas (including Republic of Ireland) – £2.00 for the first book, £1.00 for each subsequent book.

If you would prefer to pay by VISA, ACCESS/MASTER-CARD, AMEX, DINERS CLUB or SWITCH, please write your card number and expiry date here:

....

Please allow up to 28 days for delivery.

Signature   ....

------ ✂ ---------------------------------